AB⟨ ⟩ıHORS

Saoirse Cussane

Saoirse is the author's pseudonym. *Manhunting in Manhattan* is her first novel, co-written in collaboration with Amy Killingbeck. In her other life, she is a certified life and sexual well being coach and focuses her practice on helping women (re)connect to and enhance their sexual wants, needs, and desires. She advocates for sex-positivity and embracing pleasure. She identifies as a nomad and shares her living time between London, France, and NYC.

Amy Killingbeck

Amy is a ghostwriter and copywriter born and bred in the north-west of England. *Manhunting in Manhattan* is the first novel she has co-written – a journey that began as a ghostwriting project but became so much more than that – unravelling important conversations and creating a long-lasting friendship. Amy currently lives in a small Lancashire village with her husband, dog, and two cats.

MANHUNTING
IN
MANHATTAN

SAOIRSE CUSSANE
with
Amy Killingbeck

Troubador Publishing Ltd
Unit E2 Airfield Business Park,
Harrison Road, Market Harborough,
Leicestershire LE16 7UL
Tel: 0116 279 2299
Email: books@troubador.co.uk
Web: www.troubador.co.uk

ISBN 978 1 8051 4312 3

British Library Cataloguing in Publication Data.
A catalogue record for this book is available from the British Library.

Printed and bound in Great Britain by 4edge Limited
Typeset in 11pt Minion Pro by Troubador Publishing Ltd, Leicester, UK

For my beautifully spirited daughters, E and L

'I have too many fantasies to be a housewife…
I guess I am a fantasy'.
Marilyn Monroe

Dear Reader,

Welcome!

This novel relates the story of Lilith, inspired by my own journey – a story of deep emotions, sexual exploration, and self-affirmation. As I was going through this transformation, I had an urge to capture and share my experience to help empower other women and got the idea to write a book, building on the journals and notes I took at the time.

In 2022, I met Amy Killingbeck, an amazing woman and talented copywriter, who helped me shape and write this book, which was born out of our incredible collaboration. Although it is inspired by my story, I didn't want it to be all about me. So I chose to write it as a fiction and under a pen name – Saoirse Cussane. Saoirse means freedom in Irish and Cussane is an ancient Celtic name, which is part of my own heritage.

The book touches, in a fun and candid way, on many topics related to female (and male) sexuality, pleasure and other topics that are still taboo – my hope is that it helps create a space for conversations and connections. Ultimately, this is what life is all about, no matter where, when, or how… or who with :)

Enjoy and please tell a friend.

Saoirse

One

Lilith knocked her alarm clock to the floor as she scrambled to shut it off and drag herself out of bed.

'Fuck,' she exclaimed out loud. 'Yet another thing that's broken.'

The numbers were now obscured and flashing on and off as if she were at an underground rave, partying until the early hours. Only she wasn't. Because she was here. And she couldn't be further away from the electrifying lights of a hardcore clubbing atmosphere. Come to think of it, neither could this alarm clock as the flashing soon faded until all that was left was a smudged blob of orange in place of the numbers that had reminded her that time does, in fact, go on regardless of whether you want it to or not.

Lilith dropped back down onto the bed with her feet still on the plush grey carpet beneath her, whilst letting the top half of her body be caressed by the white Egyptian cotton sheets – the main reason she struggled to get out of bed in the first place. She allowed her eyes to close for just a second before saying out loud, 'Five, four, three, two, one,' (a tool she'd picked up from a self-help book) and pushing herself back up onto her feet and swiftly out of the room.

The house was particularly dark today and its walls a little colder than the day before. The low winter sun peeked through the square windows as Lilith stood briefly at the kitchen sink to fill the kettle with water and watch the snow skim the leaves of the big old oak tree towering over the house, before gently falling to the ground.

She might not be in England but drinking a cup of tea felt like the perfect way to start a snowy, upstate New York Saturday. Sitting down at the kitchen table, she clasped both hands around her mug to heat her hands and inhaled deeply before asking Alexa to play some upbeat music to kickstart the day. 'Fake it until you make it' was top of the agenda today...

She drank her tea quickly so as not to be staring at the same view for too long and unenthusiastically skipped up the stairs to get dressed. The kitchen cupboards were bordering on empty, so it was time to do the dreaded grocery shop – her least favourite part of the week. As she pulled on her jeans (the type that hugged her bum and made her feel like she could take on the world), she heard the girls giggling in one of the bedrooms. Sometimes she forgot about the responsibility she had to keep them fed, watered, loved, and looked after. Ella was thirteen and Hannah, eleven – both so mature for their respective ages, but still her babies, and it often pained her to see them grow up so fast and watch the years melt away.

Popping her head around the door, Lilith asked them what they wanted to eat today and whether they wanted to come with her to 'choose their weapons', or chill at home in a parent-free household. Of course, they chose the latter, so Lilith headed downstairs and zipped up her coat before closing the door and locking it from the outside.

'Fuck,' Lilith exclaimed out loud for the second time this morning, as she realised it was even colder outside than it looked – which was pretty good going considering she already knew it was snowing. These winters in New York were something else. Why couldn't they have chosen to live somewhere warmer? Somewhere life could be a little more easy-going. Somewhere with cocktails on tap served by hot, topless waiters in short shorts...

Lilith giggled to herself before snapping herself back into reality and sliding into the driver's seat of the black Range Rover she loathed so much but that would actually heat up pretty quickly with all its mod cons she hadn't chosen. As soon as she turned the engine on and placed her hands on the wheel, she could already feel the heat spreading and, for once, she was grateful for it.

Before she reversed out of the drive, she pulled down her sunglasses and checked herself out in the rear-view mirror. Tucking her long red locks behind her ears, she admired her blemish-free face and thanked the universe for a decent night's sleep. She didn't usually wear much make-up because she'd been blessed with the genes of a baby with barely a wrinkle in sight (or so she'd been told) but she carefully applied some colour to her lips in case she bumped into anyone interesting at the grocery store.

Her piercing green eyes stared back at her, hiding a world of secrets and desires, and she gave herself a cheeky wink before sliding her sunnies back onto her face and pulling away from the house.

The grocery store was busy today. Of course it was, it was a Saturday. And every busybody housewife, people-pleasing mother, and downtrodden spouse was in there. The house was just *one* of the places Lilith despised… the grocery store a close second. It was precisely the life Lilith aspired not to have. But yet here she was, pushing a trolley, picking up avocados to smash, and trying to choose appropriate sandwich fillers the girls wouldn't turn their noses up at for the following week at school.

Was this it? Was this what everyone works for? Was this the life that everyone—

'Oops, sorry about that – are you okay?'

Lilith looked up after falling into an intense daydream to see that she'd bumped her trolley into the guy in front of her. And yet he was apologising to her, with a cheeky glint in his eye as though he'd stepped into her path on purpose so he could strike up a conversation. He wasn't bad-looking, she supposed, although when he'd flashed her a smile, she realised his teeth had definitely seen better days. Plus, he was much older than her. Weathered, you could say. And very likely one of her neighbours who had a wife of thirty-plus years, some sneering adult children who lived off his credit card, and a three-legged dog he tended to as if he had birthed it himself. No, it definitely wasn't him but the image alone was enough to put her off, so she made her apologies for the 'bump' and quickly veered her trolley out of the way and down the next aisle.

Aha, the booze aisle – how serendipitous. Lilith scoured the shelves for her favourite gin and breathed a sigh of relief as she spotted it just in arm's reach. She was a slender five-foot-seven, but the top racks still had her on her tiptoes, and that's where all the best products were. She picked up two bottles of St. George Botanivore Gin (just to be safe) before walking up and down every aisle twice to find some bay leaves to garnish, as well as tonics of course. *She wasn't quite ready for the hard stuff.*

By now the trolley was fairly full and, as always, she was sure she had missed something important, but she didn't care enough to double-check what that might be. The sooner she was back in the fresh air, the better – even though it was Baltic outside.

She took one last look around the store before marching over to the checkout to endure some painful, mindless chit-chat with the cashier, then headed out to the car where she heaved five heavy shopping bags into the trunk and collapsed into the front seat.

What could she do that was fun today?

Lilith placed her hands on the steering wheel and slowly spun out of the car park back onto the road to home. *Well, to the place she called home but that felt like the furthest thing from it.*

New trees of the same size lined the streets, equally spaced from each other so that you could be in the exact same spot whether you stood at the top, middle, or bottom end of the road, and every house had a white picket fence – the type you dreamt about and drew as a child – to go with the perfectly symmetrical detached house and nuclear family.

That's what this life was all about. 'The American Dream'. 'The Perfect Family'. 'The Dream Life'. Only it wasn't quite like that at all. Not one little bit. Even if you did manage to choose a place called 'Little Haven' to set up home. *Little maybe, but Haven, definitely not…*

As Lilith turned onto the street she lived on – Chester Drive – she felt a sharp pain shoot across her chest and her breathing intensified. Anxiety had been rearing its ugly head more and more lately but today it hit different. It was crippling. Debilitating.

She didn't know how she managed to make it in one piece to the driveway, but, somehow, she did, before stumbling into the hallway and plonking her bum on the first step of the stairway.

'You alright, Mum?'

Ella bounced past her on the stairs to see the front door wide open and gave a concerned look.

'I'm fine, sweetie, just tired and a little light-headed. I might go up to bed to rest it off, but the car needs unloading.'

And with that, Lilith managed to proceed slowly but purposefully up the stairs to her bedroom where she could scream into her pillow and shout all the expletives under the sun without consequences.

Two

Three months earlier

Dear Diary,

Christ, how old am I?! I'll tell you how old I am… nearly bloody forty, and I'm writing to my diary as if I'm twelve years old. But here we are. If my life's about to be over, I might as well document it in this crumpled-up pink notepad I found at the bottom of my daughter's old school bag.

I've just moved to New York. But not the New York with the bustling nightlife, towering skyline, and endless city lights… nope, over an hour away in a sleepy, upper-class 'village' by the water – only you can't really access the water unless your property is there. And this house is most certainly not.

I loved my job back in London but because I have to wait for my visa to come through, I can't work yet. So, I'm basically doing fuck all, until I can start contributing to society again.

Fuckkkk. I want to liberate myself from everything. I feel so trapped; I can't breathe properly. It's like every day of my existence I'm slowly suffocating to the point I'm going to die. A bit OTT maybe but you get the picture.

I've spent the past thirty-nine years of my life pleasing everyone around me; being the good girl, the good daughter, the good wife, the good mum, the good friend, the good colleague... And I can't do this anymore. I'm halfway through my fucking life and I've lost all momentum. It's like I've gone backwards instead of forwards. I love my girls, but I've always wanted more than just being a 'mum' or a 'wife'. If I did it again, I don't know if I would even get married or have children. There's this constant expectation and pressure on women to become mothers – and to be fulfilled by it. And whilst I don't mind expending my energy for others, I just wish I could be using it for something I've actually chosen to do for myself...

Who am I? Deep down, who am I really? OMG, am I having a midlife crisis? What the fuck is wrong with me?

I always thought midlife crises were a mental construct for other people. But is this what it feels like? Do people become so aware of the relative shortness of their lives that they freak out and act like maniacs? I'm not there yet but I don't know what I'm about to do next.

I've been very aware of my own mortality from a young age. You know that anxiety that comes from deep within, the kind that makes you skip a breath 'cos you're on the verge of the void, touching the limits of your humanity? Yeah, that's me. I'm emotionally intense and always have been. I'm terrified of dying before my time. Before I've done all the things I want to. And yet here I am at the halfway point, suddenly feeling like I haven't done close to what I want to.

I've changed. I've definitely changed. I resent all men (well, most of them!). For not having to endure heavy periods, for not experiencing body-morphing pregnancies (and the joys of throwing up anywhere, including at the supermarket, and any time – definitively not just 'morning' sickness), for not almost dying during childbirth, for not leaving work early enough in the evening because that's not part of their company's culture, for their ability to drive their careers without challenging the gender pay gap… We keep hearing it's changing. But is it really? Some men are definitely on board. But how long before we reach proper equality? And not just in the Western world but everywhere…? I'm feeling a deep anger on behalf of all the women who are trapped. Trapped and lonely. I'm screaming internally (and often into my pillow) on a daily basis to get out of this rut and routine, to say what I really think, and to be who I really am. But quite frankly, I don't even know who I am and what my needs are anymore.

The one thing I'm sure about is that living in a wealthy NYC suburb is most certainly not where I want to be. This is not what I want to be doing. This is not MY life.

At what point did I forget about myself? I moved from living with my parents, to studying at university, to getting into a job, to being married, to having children… No time ever just for me. Was I so scared to live alone? Did I not trust myself enough to think that I could be okay on my own and that I didn't need someone else to make me happy?

And yet here I am now, still living out the same old story. Feeling like that girl from twenty years ago – afraid to be alone. Fucking *terrified* to be alone.

Then there's the fact that approaching forty makes me feel old. I don't want to be old. I don't want my body to age. It's scary to become an older woman in a society where youth prevails at any cost and where ageing is not welcome. Especially if you are no longer able to have kids. You become invisible and disappear into the limbo of menopause land. I want to go back in time and relive my youth with my twenty-year-old self, free of aches and pains – and free of the day-to-day stresses that life gives you when you reach this age.

Speaking of body, I've just stopped taking my pill. Twenty bloody years I've endured it (excuse the pun!). And now, I'm starting to feel different. Is this what happens when you stop taking it? When you no longer have synthetic hormones pumping into your body daily? A massive surge in your libido?! I thought it was supposed to have the opposite effect. Why aren't we told about it? I need to properly research this. Fuckkk, I feel so down and horny at the same time. I want to have sex. A lot of it. Good sex. All the time. With many different people. Possibly sometimes at the same time. What the fuck is happening?

Three

The alarm on Lilith's phone started vibrating under her head, quietly at first, as another day dawned in Little Haven. She stirred slightly, before rolling over and pulling the duvet tightly over her face.

It was 7 a.m. and still dark outside, but there was no snowfall this time. Just thick, grey cloud cover, the glint of hard ice on the ground, and below-freezing temperatures. Certainly not a day to jump out of bed full of vigour and energy – which is precisely why Lilith stayed put. Until, of course, the alarm switched from vibration to an annoying, monotonous tune she had set the night before to force her from her pit and into the world again.

Lilith groaned out loud before scrambling around under her pillow trying to find the 'off button' on her phone. It was somehow easier with the now very much broken alarm clock, which kindly shut off as soon as you threw it on the floor. Instead, she had to first locate her phone, which kept sliding away and threatening to fall down the back of the headboard as she snatched for it, before then having to press down her sweaty fingerprint or enter her password to turn the damn thing off.

Lilith heard pots clanging in the kitchen – another cue to pull back the duvet and face the day ahead. And so, she reluctantly emerged from her safety net before throwing on the clothes she'd worn the day before and dragging a brush through her hair. When you had no job and you didn't see anyone of interest in the surrounding area, Lilith realised there was little point spending hours in the morning beautifying herself if no one was going to see the benefit.

It hadn't started on the right foot. Moving here.

It had been sold as the dream – a move to New York City. Bright lights, late nights, the city that never sleeps… In contrast, they'd ended up in the village that *always* sleeps. A big, sprawling house with a white picket fence, close to the girls' school and just a train ride away from the city. In reality, the train station was an excruciating thirty-five-minute walk, with trains only departing once an hour, on the hour. A haven for some maybe, but definitely not for Lilith.

The darkness had hit the moment they stepped foot in the house. It didn't matter if the sun was shining brightly outside, the house remained dark inside and miserable. Not least because of the giant tree lurking above the house, blocking any signs of sunlight, which would cut in two and destroy the house in a big storm. *Which wouldn't necessarily be a bad thing as long as no one was in the house at the time…*

The living space spread across three floors, with a ginormous generator taking up half of the basement, ready for when the inevitable snowstorms hit. Lilith refused to go down there unless it was an absolute necessity. (She could always sublet it for low-budget horror movies – the perfect set-up for gruesome crime scenes.)

The one good thing about the footprint of the house was that there were four bedrooms, with one on the ground-floor level at the furthest possible point away from Lilith's room on the first floor. She had moved to her own bedroom just two weeks after they set up this new life. Initially, temporarily. And then permanently. At least she could enjoy the luxury of sleeping without someone else in the bed. She'd never starfished so much in her life and wound up with cramps from stretching out too much.

How on earth did it come to this?

If she'd been asked whether it was a good marriage, she would have probably said yes. But since they had moved to NYC (only they weren't in the city, more like dead suburbia), she had started to feel different. Different and resentful. Different because all she could think about all day (and night) was sex. Resentful of men in general and of herself from being away from her beloved London – from the life she'd built there and the friends she'd made, and the career she had started to forge for herself. In its place sat a restrictive visa that didn't allow her to work for months. God, how much she wanted to get back to the work she loved instead of having to play desperate housemum. She didn't have a clue what to do with this new version of herself. *Fucking joy.*

Lilith made herself a bowl of cereal. And her morning thoughts got interrupted.

'Is your sister not up yet?' Lilith asked Hannah as she poured them both a glass of orange juice.

'Yeah, she just said she's not hungry.'

Lilith rolled her eyes and grabbed some snacks from the cupboard to sneak into her daughter's bag for when she inevitably would get hungry in a couple hours' time.

Ten minutes later, the clan had assembled, and Lilith waved them out of the door before shutting it firmly behind them and staring at the blank white walls of the house. There were no pictures up yet, which could be argued as being part of the 'minimalist design', but really it was because it didn't feel like home. And it never would.

The sun had started to make an appearance now – perhaps the perfect morning for a run? *There was nothing else to do.* Lilith two-stepped up the stairs, finding some renewed energy for the day, and pulled on her thermal leggings, thick socks, hat, and reflective gear. You could never be too careful of the twenty-kilometre-per-hour drivers – they could blindly reverse into you at any given moment.

As she stepped outside, she popped in her AirPods and took a second to take in the deathly silence. There were no cars on the road (the men had all gone to work) and the majority of the women were stuck inside just like her, but probably enjoying the peace much more than she was. It was like stepping back in time to when traditional gender roles were still very much the norm – and that wasn't a norm she was comfortable with.

Then there were the women that actually left the house to abstain from their cleaning and housekeeping duties to socialise with other women just like them. The golf clubs, the sailing clubs, the ladies who lunch – the exclusive groups you could only be a part of if you were 'one of them'. Not that Lilith wanted to be a part of any of that shit. But it definitely added to the complete, utter loneliness.

The houses on her street and the streets that followed were very much the same. It was like being part of *The Truman Show* – big, symmetrical houses and perfectly placed trees. It didn't look real. It was almost as though you could imagine everyone inside the houses looking precisely the same too. An illusion. Only, sadly for Lilith, it wasn't an illusion. It was very much real and this was the life she had to deal with for now.

The life where she couldn't even run along the fucking beach because it's all private, except for a small patch reserved as the 'Dog's beach' for the local dogs with Gucci collars to shit on. *Seriously.* And even though that was the case, as it was the only spot with direct access to the water, this is where Lilith always ended up when she ventured out of the house. Dog shit and all.

Luckily, today, it either hadn't been frequented or all the poop had been picked up (although definitely not advisable to chance taking your shoes off). The clouds were clearing, and the sun glistened on the water ahead. A bench was perfectly positioned close to the shoreline, calling to be sat on, even though Lilith was only ten minutes into her run.

This was her spot. The place she came to breathe it all out and imagine a different life. A life where she wasn't living in the shittest (literally) village in North America. A life where she woke up and longed to get out of bed instead of wrapping herself up and struggling to face the world. A life where she satisfied her freshly reborn (and untapped) libido and had amazing sex every single day.

Yep, this was the dreamer's bench.

But before she got too comfy, two yappy chihuahuas came trotting over with, you've guessed it, their sparkly pink Gucci collars shimmering under the sunlight. Today was not the day when Lilith fancied watching a dog do its business (neither was any other day for that matter) and so she quickly peeled herself up from the bench, politely smiled over at the owner, who was typically engrossed in her phone, and began running again.

This time she ran with aimless direction, relying on her recently found dance music Spotify playlist to keep her going when all she wanted to do was slump to the ground and be transported somewhere much more invigorating than here.

Instead, she made it to the 'high street' and surprisingly found that one of the two coffee shops was open. The opening hours here were nothing short of erratic. Almost everything was closed on Mondays and Tuesdays. Then, even when things were open later in the week, the opening times would differ from day to day. But it was the closing times that were more of a problem.

Lilith had coined a 'lemon test' (because that's how much time she had on her hands). If you couldn't buy a lemon from anywhere after 8 p.m., it probably wasn't worth living there. She'd discovered this during week one when she'd 'nipped out' to buy some lemons for her gin and tonics. It was 8.30 p.m., and the streets were scarce. Out of the three places she could have remotely located any, they were all closed – and two hadn't been open all day. Bloody Little Haven.

But today, at least, a café was open, so Lilith slowed down her pace, ran her fingers through her hair, and pushed open the door. The lady behind the counter glanced over briefly before returning to chatting to a similar-aged woman sat next to her with a buggy and restless child in tow. They were clearly friends, and probably attended the same mummy classes or other exclusive club.

There was an empty bar stool at the window facing away from everyone else in the coffee shop. Lilith pulled up a pew, so she didn't have to pretend to be unfazed by the lack of social contact.

'Why the fuck have I come in here?' Lilith thought to herself as she picked up the menu and ordered an espresso so she could leave just as quickly as she'd come in.

The loneliness was stifling. She felt it at home but coming out into the 'community' was even worse. She didn't belong here. And everyone knew it.

Running home, Lilith felt a tear trickle down her cheek. She rarely cried but today called for it. She was completely and utterly trapped. Trapped in this village, trapped in the house, trapped in this set-up, and trapped in her own mind.

She opened the door of the big blue house to silence, taking herself off to bed and closing the curtains tightly. As she lay there, she remembered the diary entry she'd written three months before and hadn't picked up since. She'd thought it stupid to be writing to nobody and pouring out her deepest, darkest thoughts and desires. But right now, she had no one else to talk to.

Four

Dear Diary,
   I'm back.

It's not even fucking lunchtime yet and I'm back in this house in my bed, tucked up as if I'm ready to go to sleep for the night. It's cold outside but it's light. Yet here I am stuck in the dark, gloomy dungeon, basically giving myself a life sentence.

I'm so fucking fed up with living here. It's been over three months now and every day has been a battle. A battle to get out of bed in the morning, a battle to keep up appearances and pretend everything's okay, and a battle to try to create some kind of liveable life in this shithole. I'm done with the battle. I'm putting down my sword and accepting my defeat.

I can't keep up with the mums at school who spend their lives attending PTA meetings and baking cakes for all the random school events I never know are happening. I can't keep up with the women who live on our street, packing their husband's lunches and waving them merrily off to work whilst they mop, scrub and clean, and barely break a sweat as they fold away the endless piles of laundry. And I definitely can't keep up with the ladies who lunch with the most expensive bottle of champagne and play croquet on the lawn (although I could definitely keep up with that level of drinking each day).

This place was not designed for me. Or, I was not designed for it. And it's not helped that I've been feeling my body changing over the past few months. It's been unsettling and mind-blowing at the same time, and I don't know whether I'm coming or going.

I stopped taking my pill when I first moved here. My latest supply had almost run out and I couldn't be bothered with the rigmarole of getting a new prescription. *How do you even go about renewing a prescription in this country?* I can't believe I've spent the last twenty years on that thing, and now I want my body back. (Plus, seeing as I'm not having sex anymore, what's the point of putting my body through hell for no return?)

Anyway, it's definitely the best thing I've ever done because, like I mentioned the last time I wrote here, my libido is through the roof! I've never felt anything like it. I feel like I'm eighteen years old again. Except even when I was eighteen, I didn't feel like this either. I never used to understand people who said they had a real urge for sex, but now I'm waking up every day like a new woman – exploring my body like I never have done before…

I started reading up on the effects of the pill after my last diary entry – and it explains A LOT. The fact that I've always felt kind of indifferent to sex. That it's not been high up on my priority list. To not find myself being remotely sexually attracted to anyone for the last twenty years.

Apparently the pill influences basically everything related to love and sex, and women who stick to their natural cycle, without taking the pill, seem to enjoy way better sex – and choose different types of partners. *Go figure.*

The thing is, I never thought of myself as particularly sexual. Until now. So now it's got me wondering if this new self is actually the 'real' me? Have I been missing this all this time? What would my life have been like without the pill? Would it have been more than the three men I've been with so far? How many more encounters? How many more men? (Or women even?) And, most importantly, how many more orgasms?

I remember how terrified I was to have sex for the first time. Everything we were taught in school was geared towards protecting yourself from pregnancy and diseases. Why were we not ever taught about the exploration, intimacy, pleasure, fun, and dare I say, joys of sex? It was only ever just about the fucking risks and red flags – no wonder I held off until I turned eighteen.

When I eventually managed to have some sex, it was pretty shit (like for most people, I've heard). But because I didn't know anything else, I thought this was how it was supposed to feel every time. Of course, it got a bit better with practice, but I've never ever focused on making myself feel good. Each time I thought it was only all about what the guys 'wanted', what turns *them* on, and what I could do to make them feel good. No wonder I don't know what I want. I've never had a chance to discover it. And I suppose I've never really *wanted* to discover it. It's always been something I felt I could almost live without. I don't even own a bloody vibrator!

So here I am, turning forty next week, without really any positive experiences relating to sex, but all I want to do is fuck everything with a pulse (okay, maybe too extreme) and to satisfy my true desires. I want to know myself more deeply. I want to know what I like and dislike. I want to experiment, to explore, to find out what turns me on and what turns other people on. Even writing this turns me on.

Okay, so obviously I need to go and buy myself a vibrator as my birthday present to myself. Not from Little Haven – could you imagine?! I mean, there definitely isn't a shop that caters to that kind of stuff – there'd be uproar from the local 'do-gooders'. Nope, I'll have to take myself off to the city. A girl's trip, just for me. Something I'd usually revel in but not as much now it's in the name of my fortieth bloody birthday. Ugh, can't I just stop time so I can acclimatise to my impending fate? I'm absolutely dreading it.

Five

It was Friday. The day before Lilith's birthday. The final day in her thirties before her life was about to change drastically overnight – or so it felt. It was a funny thing to attach such a feeling to a number – to an age. But given the year Lilith had had, it signified so much more. She thought by now she'd have all her shit together, that she'd be settled, content, and fulfilled, that she'd have achieved a lot of the things that she wanted to achieve and be at a place in her life where she felt at peace. But if she was being completely honest with herself (and she was finally being honest with herself for the first time in her life), she felt the exact opposite.

How she truly felt was confused. Overwhelmed. Scared. Worried. Lonely. But also, curious. And she was about to put that curiosity to the test because today was the day she'd put aside for her 'me day'. To buy a special, sexy present for herself. An item she'd never even looked at, yet alone used.

She'd originally started scouring the internet for 'the best vibrators 2017' but then she got concerned the girls might be able to get into her laptop and access her search history, so she'd quickly deleted all trace from her web browser and shut her laptop tightly as if they were right behind her. She was alone, of course, but she'd convinced herself that an in-person trip would be much better anyway – no need to hide from the postman. So, a solo trip to the city it was, with a list of possible X-rated stores to try, in order of sexiest-sounding name. A foolproof plan, surely.

She arrived at the first shop feeling like a deer in headlights, worried that she looked like one too, as she tried to act casual, pushing open the door that was actually a pull. Pink Pussycat Boutique was the name of the store – and only now had Lilith realised what the name obviously alluded to. It looked cute (and pink) but one glance at the women behind the counter and Lilith had turned back around again and scuttled onto the street. They were stunning. Much younger than her – and clearly a lot more experienced. Today was not the day to be confronting even more of her insecurities than she already was. She wanted today to be about feeling empowered, not embarrassed. And so, she hedged her bets on the next option. SHAG. Straight to the point, definitely less 'girly', and somewhere you couldn't get confused with somewhere else.

Lilith went to pull the door open this time, only to find it was indeed a 'push', so almost fell inside as she put her hands on the door. There were a few people wandering around. A beautiful couple, probably mid-thirties, covered from head to toe in tattoos (not that Lilith could see that much but she could see their ankles, arms, and necks, and they were all inked). And an older woman – older than

Lilith – holding up some corsets to herself and admiring them in the mirror.

'I like the red one,' Lilith said as she walked past.

'Oh, you think? It's not too much?'

'Never too much,' Lilith responded with a smile as she spotted the toy section in the far right-hand corner of the store and made a beeline.

There was no one else in this area of the shop, which was either a blessing in disguise, or a curse – because she had no idea what she was doing or what she was looking for. In her head, she'd imagined there'd be just one type of vibrator, possibly with a choice of colours, and that would be the hardest part of her decision before she went to the till. In reality, there was so much more to choose from. SO much more.

There were some tiny things called bullets that actually looked like they could belong in a shotgun, there were some large contraptions called wands that definitely didn't look like the sort of wands magicians would use, and there were some wonky-looking things with two protruding parts that looked like they could cause a lot of damage if not used correctly. Lilith stood there for a while, examining all the different packets and turning things upside down to try to figure out where they went before she felt a presence behind her.

'Can I help you with anything?'

Lilith swung round, dropping one of the bullets on the floor.

'Oh shit, sorry,' she said as she scrambled to put it back on the shelf before facing the person that had caused her face to start heating up.

The voice belonged to a youngish camp guy, who, judging by his name badge, obviously worked there.

'I can leave you to it if you want, you just looked like you could use some help... or recommendations?'

Lilith's cheeks were still flushed bright red, but she definitely wanted a recommendation, so she decided to amuse him.

'A recommendation would be good. Which one of these things do I want? Just for me?'

'Well, as you can probably tell, I don't have a vagina, but my girlfriends have told me that they can't live without their wands,' shop guy responded. 'They're actually great for play all round, but if you want a fail-safe option that's guaranteed to get your good spot, that's what I'd go for.'

Lilith nodded, impressed at his clear and insightful knowledge – whilst also being impressed at her own ability to allow him to recommend something for her without running away or dropping something else. The redness had almost disappeared from her cheeks as she thanked him and followed him to the till.

'Fortieth birthday present to self – complete,' Lilith said to herself in her head triumphantly. And she couldn't wait to make use of it.

Six

It was the morning of her long-anticipated birthday and Lilith was already downstairs in the kitchen, twirling her spoon round in a bowl of cornflakes that she'd been struggling to eat for the past half hour. The likelihood of her eating any more was now 100/1 seeing as the milk had well and truly soaked into each flake and they were soggier than a pair of socks submerged in a river, and probably tasted just as bad. *Yum.* She'd been awake since 4 a.m., longing for the day to be over already, but the clock had only just ticked past 7 a.m., so there were a lot of hours to get through before she could rest her head on her pillow again and open her eyes to a new decade.

The house was silent as Lilith contemplated being forty today – so far from what she'd imagined. Her phone buzzed a couple of times as messages came through from friends back in London wishing her a 'Happy Birthday' and a great day – complete with party popper emojis. They had no idea what her life was really like and how she was feeling. In a way, it was easier to pretend – especially to people so far away who she didn't see face to face. Yep, it was easier to type a message back saying, 'Thanks so much! My friend is taking me for a birthday dinner tonight – can't wait!' The feigned enthusiasm they would never uncover unless they caught her off guard on a FaceTime call and, even then, she was slowly perfecting the art of fake smiling.

In reality, this 'friend' was her neighbour who lived a few doors down. They'd initially met at the school gates before realising they lived on the same road, walking home after drop-off and chatting the entire way. She was different to Lilith – for starters, she loved her suburban life – but Lilith liked her. They just didn't know each other that well yet.

Speaking of the devil, Lilith's phone buzzed again as a message came through from Elena.

'Happy BIG birthday, Lilith! Can't wait for later. I'll pick you up in a cab to the train station at 5.30pm ready for our 7pm booking. Cocktail attire! x'

Lilith felt herself do a deep inhale as she closed her eyes for a second and internally sighed. How had she ended up here? Still, it sounded better than nursing a bottle of wine to herself and crying on the floor as she wept over the current status of her life. Her eyes quickly opened again as the girls came swooping into the kitchen, gushing over her, and wishing her the happiest of birthdays. This was what made it all worth it. They loved her and they showed it, and that felt good considering she'd had such a hard time forming strong bonds with them after they were born. She'd struggled for months after each birth with severe postnatal depression, which she'd not been able to confide in anyone about because it wasn't 'the norm'. The societal expectation that everyone should be parents and be happy about it. That you should get married, have two point four children, and live happily ever after…

'Are you looking forward to your dinner tonight?' Hannah asked Lilith as she massaged her shoulders and jumped on the spot in giddiness as she waited for her mum to open her birthday present from her and her older sister.

Ella looked less enthusiastic but that was likely because now she'd hit her teenage years, she wasn't a morning person. Lilith could relate. She wasn't an anything person right now.

'Yes, can't wait, although I'll miss you both,' Lilith replied.

Her au pair, Sophia, was staying until Lilith got back later – 'as long as she needed', even though Lilith had insisted she wouldn't be back late. She'd already checked the trains home and the 9 p.m. one was looking particularly appealing – dinner, drink, then home to bed.

That was the one thing Lilith hadn't been willing to compromise on with the move here – hiring an au pair. Yes, she might not be working right now but she would be (and she couldn't wait to get back to work so she could socialise with other like-minded adults and have a purpose again). Plus, she wasn't the kind of mum who did the school runs every day and sat to do homework with them each night. Sometimes she did if it was a topic she was interested in, but the curriculum at this school was a little too top-tier. It was the most 'prestigious school this side of the city' the real estate agent had said.

The real estate agent had said a lot of things, but they all seemed so irrelevant now that they were living here and nothing could make up for the fact that it was a pretty shitty place to live unless you owned a property on the water and had a shitload of money to throw at everything in the area to keep you entertained. The house would be going back up for sale soon now that it had lost its purpose as the family home and Lilith was already armed with the rehearsed speech they'd been given when buying the place.

'Mummmm! Open your present!'

Lilith snapped herself out of it again and blinked her eyes in anticipation to see what the girls were so excited to give her. The garish pink wrapping paper was wrapped neatly around a smallish oval type of box, tied up with silver ribbon. If nothing else, the effort into the wrapping was present enough and Lilith felt herself genuinely smile for the first time in what felt like a long time. She undid the ribbon and paper carefully, so both could be used again, and revealed the gift underneath… Her eyes lit up in shock. A Ray-Ban case with some uber sexy sunglasses inside with classy black frames.

'Girls!! How have you afforded this?!'

'We've been saving,' Ella replied with a small shrug.

'Well, you shouldn't have,' Lilith responded. 'But I love them, thank you so much.'

And with that, she pulled them both in for cuddles, despite Ella's protests, and gave them each a big kiss on the head. She was going to enjoy rocking these new sunnies every day. She'd just need to plan a few more trips to the city to enjoy them.

The day went by quickly even though Lilith procrastinated from doing the household chores (it was her birthday after all) and she found herself wondering how it had got to 4 p.m. already, especially seeing as the girls had gone shopping for the day and she was on her own. She'd been invited of course, but she'd lied and said she'd arranged a Skype call with her London friends before they headed to work. Really, she just wanted to mope by herself and kick off the fake smile for a while.

She also hadn't remotely decided what she was going to wear tonight, despite the prearranged dress code (perhaps a shopping trip would have helped), but she figured there would be a little black dress hanging somewhere in her wardrobe that would be desperate for a night out – more than could be said for Lilith right now. She usually loved travelling to the city but the pressure of it being her birthday meant she was feeling less than enthused.

Heading upstairs to her bedroom, Lilith remembered about the gift she'd bought herself the day before. The elusive wand. If ever there was a time to road-test it, the time was now. She had the house to herself, an hour until she needed to get in the shower and start getting ready, *and* it was her birthday. She took off her jeans and hoodie and sidled into bed, pulling her knickers down, as if she was getting in with a hunky new lover (she wished!) and turned on the wand.

'Ooh!' Lilith was glad she was home alone right now as the vibrations were stronger than she'd thought. Maybe a little *too* strong. She moved it up and down and round and round, moving her body into different positions, but something just wasn't quite hitting the mark. In fact, she'd turned it up to the highest pressure it would go and as well as almost making her fall off the bed, it was now just outright hurting and making her feel numb – and not in a good way.

'Shit,' Lilith exclaimed out loud. She had not intended on turning her vagina into what felt like a giant orange. So much for 'self-love'…

She face-planted into her pillow and turned the wand off, feeling frustrated and sore. Not quite the birthday treat she'd imagined. After a few moments of lying still and letting her breathing return to normal, Lilith forced herself out of bed and into the shower, spending longer than usual letting the warm water cover her body and wash away the last few months' events. The one good thing about this house was the water pressure.

'Make mental note to entice any future buyers with that snippet of information.' Lilith giggled to herself.

Once she'd finished lathering herself all over and rinsing it all away – and likely using up any water the street had left – Lilith stepped out of the shower and pulled a towel around her body as she moved towards her wardrobe to pick out the first black dress she saw, along with a black jacket to match. She'd probably be freezing later on but she didn't fancy carting a large coat out with her – plus she was relying on the wine to warm her up.

Sitting at her dressing table, Lilith applied her make-up carefully as she looked at herself more closely in the mirror. She was tired. And not just from being awake since the early hours. She took one last look at herself (and at her yet-to-be-tamed dildo lying lifeless on her bed) before picking up her bag, sliding on her new sunnies, and heading down the stairs to be seen off by the girls, who'd just got home, and Sophia, who'd just arrived at the doorstep.

'Have fun,' they chimed in unison as she closed the door behind her and jumped into the cab with Elena.

***

The restaurant was exactly as Lilith had imagined. A smartly dressed doorman on the door ready to open the door for her, and marble floor that looked like it had been polished by hand to get it sparkling the way it was. She almost needed to put her shades back on. Lilith waited for Elena to give their booking details, but instead she felt her hand grab hers and guide her towards the lift.

'Where are we going?!' Lilith asked, confused and intrigued at the same time.

'There's a covered rooftop bar at the top – let's go for a drink there first,' Elena replied, pulling her into the lift and grinning widely.

Lilith was sure she was up to something but a drink on the rooftop (even a covered one) sounded fun – and completely unexpected.

As the lift doors opened, Lilith was greeted with an aquarium of multicoloured fish in the lobby area, a member of staff to take coats to the cloakroom (although Lilith kept her jacket on for now), and then, out of the corner of her eye, an array of silver, white, and pink balloons making a balloon arch into the bar area, which had been blocked off for what looked like a party...

'SURPRISE!!!'

Numerous heads with glasses in hands appeared from nowhere and started making their way towards her. Lilith looked at Elena, who was beaming and pushing her forward, and realised that this was for her.

'What the...'

'I couldn't let you not celebrate your birthday in style, could I?' Elena replied. 'I'll introduce you to the people you don't know – I invited some of the mums from the school gates but they've obviously brought their husbands, and there's some neighbours here that live down our street, and then some people I know from the gym, oh, and the local coffee shop owner!'

Lilith was struggling to take it all in. Clearly a lot of effort had gone into this. A pretty waitress with blonde hair and red lipstick was walking around with a plate of canapés on a silver platter, serving all the unknown guests, and there were decorations everywhere. Her gut instinct was to turn back around and go home – she hated surprises – but she could see what Elena had tried to do and it was really kind. If not completely and utterly overwhelming, and well out of her comfort zone.

The first group who came to wish her happy birthday were women she recognised from the school gates but hadn't minded herself to talk to very much. Mainly because at least one of them was on the PTA. She soon found out their names were Coral, Tina, and Helen, and it was PTA Coral who gave Lilith an over-exuberant hug and birthday greeting, before the other women followed suit. Lilith awkwardly hugged them back, thanking them for coming, before gratefully accepting a glass of champagne from a waiter who was circling around with a drinks tray. The women had come with their husbands, who were huddled on the other side of the room, clearly talking sports as they had their phones out watching a game, and clinking beer bottles together. That looked more like Lilith's vibe right now and she wasn't even into sports...

Lilith forced herself to smile as she knocked back half the glass of her champagne in one large gulp, noticing a fleeting look and eyebrow raise being exchanged by the three women. Talk quickly turned to home life as the canapés came past, and Lilith found herself shovelling them down and finishing the rest of her champagne as she nodded along and listened to them talking about their husbands that were rarely around and the various clubs the women were a part of to fill up their days. Coral leaned towards her, about to ask her what clubs she had joined, so Lilith quickly seized her moment to excuse herself to go to the bathroom.

She immediately shut herself into the furthest toilet cubicle away in the women's bathroom and leaned against the door for a moment, kicking off her shoes and finding some mints at the bottom of her bag to munch on. It was sad that she was finding this a more enjoyable way to spend her time right now, but she needed some space to gather her thoughts, whack a fake smile back on her face, and prepare herself for more mindless chatter with people that she had simply *nothing* in common with.

She always wondered how people did it. 'Fit in'. Maybe it was easy pretending to be something that you weren't. Lilith had been doing it for a long time. But she'd never been enticed by the housewife role. Nor the doting mother role either – despite how much she loved her girls. She was never going to be a member of the PTA, or bake cakes for the school bake sale, or sit in the country club in all white clothes and a fancy hat. Where were the women that rode motorcycles for fun and got tattoos on their bum? Maybe that was a step too far, but that was more the type of vibe she was looking for. Something a bit more taboo. Adventurous. Exciting…

Lilith slowly pulled down her tights and started running her fingers up and down her thighs, pausing briefly, before circling her clit – softly and slowly at first, before getting harder and faster as she grabbed onto the door behind her and lost all her inhibitions, sinking to the floor as she released all tension from the day. Well *that* was definitely taboo. And not what she had planned when she first came to the bathroom.

The main toilet door swung open and Lilith heard the chatter of two undistinguishable women as they tottered into the cubicles next to her.

'Shit,' Lilith thought to herself as she scrambled to put her shoes back on and straightened herself up, flushed the toilet, and headed back out to the party.

She spotted Elena chatting to her next-door neighbours whose names had escaped her, as well as some other slightly familiar faces that she was sure she'd seen around the village, perhaps at the school gates or the dog park. That's where she'd head over to next. Plus, hopefully Elena would help with the (re)introductions, so she didn't have to pretend to know who they were and what their names were. She was terrible with names, especially if she didn't really care for they were.

The tray of champagne came past her again, so she

picked up two glasses, downed one, put the empty glass back on the tray, and strode over to where Elena was standing, slowly sipping from the glass she still had in her other hand.

'Lilith, there you are!' Elena reached out her arm to pull her into the group. 'You've met Ian and Kathy, right? Our lovely neighbours.'

Lilith smiled and nodded enthusiastically as she gave them each a kiss on the cheek and thanked them for coming. The booze was already going to her head, so she had to briefly steady herself on Elena's arm to stop herself from toppling over. She remembered she'd barely eaten anything all day, save for the few cornflakes before they'd become a pile of mush. Where were those canapés again?

Lilith engaged a little in the small talk she so hated, after introducing herself (apparently for the second time) to Louisa and John, who she hadn't, in fact, met at the school gates, but who owned the local delicatessen, as well as a number of other businesses in the area. 'Good people to know,' Lilith thought to herself.

A plate of fresh canapés made their way over to the group as Lilith disengaged and grabbed as many as she could fit into her hands. The waitress who was serving them giggled.

'I haven't eaten all day,' Lilith whispered to her. 'And it's my birthday!'

The waitress wished her a happy birthday and said she'd be back with another plate soon and would come to her first, for which Lilith almost kissed her but instead she quietly excused herself to buy another drink from the bar.

Lilith pulled up a stool at the bar as she watched

everyone around her chatting away and enjoying themselves. She still didn't have a clue who the majority of them were, but she supposed they'd at least know who she was now – not that that was necessarily a good thing either.

'What can I get you?'

Lilith swung back around to meet eyes with a very sexy-looking barman. He was probably no older than twenty-five but something about him said that he'd experienced a lot.

'Let's do a shot of tequila,' she said seductively. 'Maybe two.'

The barman slowly smiled at her as he reached for the bottle of tequila and started pouring it into four shot glasses in front of them.

'It's my birthday,' Lilith continued. 'And I don't know half the fucking people here.'

'Well, in that case, these are on me,' sexy barman replied.

Lilith smiled at him as they took the shots together, sucking their respective slice of lemons at the same time and locking eyes with cheeky grins.

'Fuck, that was strong!' Lilith exclaimed as her eyes started to water.

The barman laughed and handed her a napkin to dab at her eyes to stop her mascara from running, their fingers briefly touching as Lilith took it from him and giggled.

'I should probably head to my people,' Lilith joked. 'But I'll be back for more later!'

'I hope so,' he responded with a little wink.

Luckily for Lilith, most of the night passed quickly

without her having to speak aimlessly to too many more people or equally sit in a corner waiting for the night to be over. Most of it was spent either at the bar, flirting with her new barman friend (who had given her his number… she couldn't quite believe it…), or on the dance floor dancing in her own little world as if no one was watching her. They all were, she was sure, but it was her birthday, so who gave a damn?

Last orders were announced at the bar and Lilith looked down at her empty glass as she felt the floor wobble beneath her. It definitely wasn't the floor that was wobbling. She almost toppled into the 'sports husbands', who hadn't moved from their spot all night, but managed to ground herself before she did, only slightly brushing against one of their arms as she stood up tall, trying to act less drunk than she was.

'You okay, birthday girl?' the one whom she brushed arms with said, putting his arm around her to keep her steady.

'Ah, almost fell for you, didn't I?' she said cheekily, before stroking his arm and clinking her glass with his.

She was about to engage in conversation with them but suddenly noticed Coral, Tina, and Helen making their way into the group with their coats on.

'Everything okay over here?' Coral said as she squeezed in between Lilith to escort her husband away. 'It's time for us to go home now.'

'Of course,' Lilith replied. 'Thanks for coming.'

She went to clink her glass with Coral's but realised Coral had nothing in her hand to clink, so she instead did an awkward wave goodbye, and twirled back onto the dance floor.

Slowly but surely, everyone started to say their goodbyes and leave the party as the bar closed and the lights came back on again. Some of them were heading out to continue the night until the early hours, whilst others were rushing back for the babysitter. Suddenly, all Lilith wanted to do was go back home, drink a pint (or ten) of water, and go to sleep. Elena, however, was definitely staying out for the night as she spun her around on the dance floor and begged her to stay out.

'I need to get back for Sophia,' Lilith replied. 'But thank you for arranging this for me. It was amazing.'

'Next time?!' Elena asked, with her pinky finger outstretched.

Lilith giggled, linking her pinky finger with hers. 'Yes, next time. I promise!'

And with that, Lilith picked up her jacket that was drooped over one of the bar stools, blew her sexy barman a kiss goodbye, and headed outside into the brisk Arctic December air to flag a cab back for the long journey home.

Seven

One week later

How the hell do you date in your forties? And how do you date again after twenty years of monogamy?!

I'll tell you how… There are many, many apps. Dating apps, I mean. The new marketplace of the twenty-first century – where demand and supply match but rarely meet expectations. Gone are the days of meeting someone in a bar or passing someone in the street and having an 'instant connection'. There's no dating for dummies book – no manual to figure it all out and find the perfect match. Instead, I'm sitting on my ass at home, spending quite a substantial amount of time figuring out how these various 'dating' apps work… if you can call them that.

There are the soft ones where you're promised you'll find your soulmate (I'm clearly the wrong target), the less romantic ones (inspired by the gay community) for non-exclusive people, but where hearts still get broken, and then, there are the ones that put you in control of who you match with. It's a fucking minefield – literally.

Still, I'm in a better position than I was a few months ago – and I'm sure I'm about to be in a few more interesting ones if I stay on these apps…

My work visa just came through, which means I can *finally* work again. I've picked up the freelance contract that I had in London, which allows me to work virtually, from anywhere, and in any time zone, so it's ideal for my current situation. I'd still like to be working from an office and have the buzz of co-workers but, for now, this will definitely do. I'm excited to get myself to cool coffee places in the city, to be surrounded by people on the train 'going to work', to be one of them, and to feel like I have a purpose again… Even if I have no idea what I'm doing with my life right now.

OMG. My phone just pinged. 'You have a new match'.

I literally dropped my phone out of my hand in equal measures of excitement and nervousness. My first match ever! He's called Evan. Beautiful blue eyes and enigmatic smile. Latino and Jewish – a rare combination, I'm told. My type of guy. (Do I even have a type?!) Direct, flirty, smart, witty, intriguing, good sense of humour. We've been chatting for hours whilst I've been cooped up in my bedroom with the curtains closed. Luckily, it's a Sunday.

I've actually been laughing out loud – a lot of 'LOLs'. That's the only acronym I know (for now). We've arranged to meet on Tuesday in the city. Holy shit, I'm nervous. My first date in twenty years. Could he be the one? I might be over-fantasising slightly. Surely, he is going to be the answer to all my problems. I can feel it. He likes maps of the world. I do too. We have so much in common already, right?

Okay, I'm losing my mind a bit. Breathe, Lilith, take it slow. I can't help but let my mind wander all over the place. I have so many questions. I wish I could talk to someone about it. Are there such things as sex coaches? Like a safe pair of ears (and hands hehe) who could give you some tips on how to navigate this new madness? There must be so many women lost like me out there... but I digress...

What will he be like in person? How will I be in person? What's it going to be like kissing another person? Touching someone else? Sleeping with someone else? Will I even want to rip his clothes off or will I want to run a million miles and suppress my desires? What should I even wear? And, most importantly, how the hell am I going to concentrate until Tuesday?!

Eight

Lilith sat in a coffee shop on East Twenty-Ninth Street, tapping her fingers on her laptop but not actually typing anything. She'd been like this all day. Scrolling aimlessly through her emails, feeling disconnected on her work calls, and nipping to the toilet every hour to release her nerves.

She must have drunk around ten cups of coffee; she was so jittery. At least that had meant she could stay here all day without being pushed out. She always had a cup in her hand. It felt amazing to be in the city for a purpose this time. She was finally working – and in the evening, she'd be dating! A true New Yorker.

As soon as 6 p.m. hit, Lilith folded her laptop away, and headed to the toilets with her 'day bag'. She'd slipped in a slinky underwear set and dark blue dress (both came as safe recommendations from her online research on what to wear on a first date). Shit, it was actually happening. She'd been preparing for this moment for the past seventy-two hours but now it was here, she felt like she needed more time. For what, she wasn't sure – to breathe maybe? To feel like she was ready?

They were meeting at a jazz bar round the corner. His suggestion. A place Lilith had never been before, but it exuded sexy vibes. He was waiting for her at the door, his (very blue) eyes glimmering as he slowly took her coat, brushing his hands against her neck and shoulders, before pecking her gently on the cheek. Lilith got shivers.

They sat down at a table in the corner and ordered drinks. The conversation flowed effortlessly. It was fun and light-hearted. Maybe this was what she'd been craving – simply the company of a man. No deep, meaningful chats, just surface-level fun – which was actually what Lilith needed. But it was about to get a lot deeper soon…

'Wanna get out of here?' Evan whispered into her ear, before sitting back and waiting for her to respond.

'Wow, that was quick,' Lilith thought to herself in her head, but before she could stop herself, she felt the excitement within her rise and replied out loud, 'Let's go!'

It was actually happening. She wanted him to touch her so badly. And she could tell he wanted to touch her too. What. A. Thrill.

They headed back to his flat, picking up the pace to a run, as they giggled avoiding scaffoldings (which he didn't like. Not the easiest task in NYC – they were everywhere you looked). No PDA either. Evan identified as a millennial. And come to think of it, so did Lilith, even though she was technically a lot older (not in spirit, of course), and not that he seemed to mind. He seemed intrigued by her age, her experience, and her outlook on life.

As soon as the flat door shut behind them, they

kissed, deeply. Holy shit, this was what Lilith had been unconsciously waiting for all these years.

She threw him against the wall and kissed him some more, biting his lip whilst feeling a complete sense of euphoria. She had an intense urge to get fucked by him. Fast and furious. No need to chat anymore. No need to see the rest of his apartment. And enough with the cute Latino accent.

They were highly compatible. It felt so good when he pushed her back against the wall and entered her. She felt whole again. This is what she'd been missing, and fuck had she been missing a lot. Within minutes, she exploded all over him and they fell to a heap on the floor, giggling like teenagers.

No time for hanging around, though. Lilith left his apartment with one more parting deep kiss, before catching the last train, even though she was desperate for more. She felt like she was growing wings overnight as she headed home and flopped onto her bed with the biggest smile on her face. The wings of desire…

Now *that* was a night to remember.

***

Lilith was up early the next morning to get a train to DC for work, still with wings on. She'd read that there'd been an explosion (a different kind) near Evan's office so took the opportunity to message him and book in another encounter together a few nights later. She was sure everyone on the train could tell she was getting turned on as she shifted herself around in her seat to try to get comfortable and stop herself from throbbing. She wasn't sure how she was going to concentrate these next few days before she saw him again. She wanted him now. Again and again and again.

A few painful days of work later, exchanging tempting messages back and forth, she'd made it. She was back in the city again, going straight to his flat (no need to make it a date, they knew exactly what they were here for).

She approached his door and had to double-check she was at the right place. The door was bright red with a gold knocker on it – something she definitely hadn't noticed last time she was here. Come to think of it, she hadn't looked at anything in detail – it was all a blur. A big, sexy, erotic blur. She'd barely knocked on the door when Evan greeted her, swooping her inside quickly, presumably so none of his neighbours saw. His hair was flopped to one side and still wet, and he wore just a towel around his waist.

'You had a shower without me?' Lilith asked cheekily.

Before she could say anything else, Evan started taking her fast from behind. Another explosive encounter where neither lasted long as their bodies connected as one. They went again – this time Lilith murmuring to him that she loved him as he came inside her.

She was definitely confusing lust and love but she didn't know that just yet. Evan, however, had heard enough and jumped out of bed, pulling his clothes on abruptly, throwing Lilith's clothes towards her, and ushering her to get dressed.

'Shit.' Lilith thought to herself, 'What did I just say?'

'That's enough now, let's stop this,' Evan said exasperated. 'I don't want to fall in love.'

It was too intense for him. Of course it was. Lilith had fast-tracked things and it wasn't looking pretty. No more wings. She was devastated. Free falling. Heartbroken. A *slightly* excessive reaction for someone she'd only met twice in her life. She couldn't look him in the eyes as she said goodbye and let him close the door behind her, so she didn't have to look back.

An hour later, she was on the last train home again with her overnight bag that Evan hadn't noticed (thank God), and took her drama back to the suburbs.

As she approached the house she loathed so much, she felt tears start to fall down her face. The 'for sale' sign was swinging in the breeze – a stark reminder that barely anyone had been interested in taking the house off her hands so she could be free again.

'Pull yourself together, Lilith,' she said sternly to herself, praying that none of the nosey neighbours were looking out of their windows right now.

That's all she needed – being the focus of neighbourhood gossips who clearly had nothing else better to do. This isn't how she intended on spending her 'last night of freedom' before it was her turn to have the girls again the following day. She was supposed to have a wild night in the city and come back on the train tomorrow morning with rosy cheeks and a spring in her step. Still, she'd had a wild night, just not in the way she expected.

'Love?!' What was she thinking? She barely knew the guy! She had no idea what his last name was, what he did for a living, or what he liked to do for fun – other than fucking random forty-year-old women in his apartment.

The house was quiet, so she took her shoes off at the

door and tiptoed into the kitchen, before remembering that she was home alone tonight. Still, at least she could wallow in self-pity all night if she wanted to – quietly, of course. No need to wake up the neighbours or give the squirrels something to chirp about. She used the torch on her phone to guide her to the fridge as she realised she'd made it halfway across the room unscathed without switching on the light switch, and poured herself a large glass of white wine from an unopened bottle of Sauvignon Blanc. She had a vague feeling it was her last one and she'd need to refill tomorrow when she did the weekly shop.

'Ugh, don't remind me,' Lilith whispered out loud.

She hated doing that goddamn shop. At least it would be the last one of the year, seeing as the following week she'd be on a plane with her girls to France for the holidays. Not that she needed reminding of that either.

Lilith sank down into the sofa and threw back her glass of wine, before jumping up and grabbing another, pouring the wine to the brim of her glass. She figured the more she drank, the less she'd remember in the morning. Maybe she could forget Evan, forget what she said, and pretend that none of it ever happened. *Wishful thinking.*

After devouring the bottle, Lilith felt her eyes become heavy as she pulled over a blanket and fluffed up the cushions behind her head. She couldn't be bothered to move up to the bedroom, plus the low winter sun coming through the downstairs windows would wake her up early enough to get her shit together and be prepared for the week ahead.

***

The next morning Lilith was woken by a group of squirrels staring at her through the kitchen window.

'What the fuck?!' she screeched out loud as she almost fell off the sofa.

Maybe squirrels had a sixth sense for human despair. That would certainly explain why they seemed to thrive in the suburbs.

Lilith glanced at the watch on her wrist. It was 6.30 a.m. and she still felt slightly drunk. She'd only had a few hours' sleep and she felt like ass. And nope, she hadn't forgotten what had happened the night before either. Far from it.

She pulled out her phone from down the side of the sofa and opened up her dating apps, one by one. She'd had more matches overnight but no message from Evan. He'd been online too. Lilith scrolled for a few moments but couldn't help herself. She sent him a message apologising for last night, begging him to put it to one side and see her again. She couldn't let that be the last time, not the way things were left. Plus, she was desperate for him. For his touch, for him to be inside her again, for her to feel the way she felt when she was with him. Like she was on top of the world, a Sexual Goddess… with wings. Christ, she'd never felt like that before and she needed to feel like that again, pronto. Especially because she felt the furthest away from feeling or looking like a Sexual Goddess right now.

She'd fallen asleep in her clothes with a full face of make-up on that had partly worn off from her teary outburst, but still left her with panda eyes. She let out a loud groan, pulled herself up, wrapped the blanket around her and scooted off upstairs. Why she hadn't slept in her own bed last night, she didn't know.

She opened her bedroom door, quickly closing it behind her, and looked at the dishevelled face staring back at her in the mirror.

'Jesus, Lilith, you look like shite.'

It was times like these she was glad of the en-suite attached to her bedroom. At the time of buying the house, she hadn't seen the need for all these extra bathrooms. She preferred to live much more minimally, in smaller spaces. You know, like an apartment in the centre of the city, for example. But right now, she couldn't have been more glad of having a shower that she didn't have to wait for and share with two teenage girls and their unique approach to bathroom tidying.

As the water ran through her hair and all over her body, Lilith's mind raced back to the night before. Part of her wished she'd never gone but the rest of her just wanted to go back. Rewind the clock, erase herself from saying silly things like 'I love you', and enjoy the moment for what it was. Two people having great fucking sex.

Instead, she'd now have to spend the next week going over it again and again and again until it drove her crazy. No matter what, she wouldn't be seeing him, or any other guy for that matter, for the next week – and that sucked.

Living a 'double' life seemed so much fun until she had to immerse herself in the dual part of her life that involved her coming straight home from work and staying in the suburbs each night, as well as having the sole responsibility of the girls. Thank God for Sophia. But even thinking that made her feel uneasy too. She was so privileged, yet so lonely.

***

The next week ticked by slower than ever as Lilith immersed herself as much as she could into suburban life. She even planned a pizza and popcorn night with the girls one night, which was fun. Maybe not the fun she'd had the week before, but a different kind of fun that managed to warm her soul. By the end of the week, however, she was ready for her own week of adult fun. Only, she'd somehow forgotten that it was almost Christmas and she'd be getting on a plane to France the day after tomorrow.

Evan hadn't messaged since Lilith last did but all of sudden her phone pinged as she tried to drag herself away from the realisation that she wouldn't be having any more New York fun until the new year.

It was him.

He wanted to see her again. Turned out he couldn't stay away from her after all. But how bloody typical that he messaged her when she was about to head to France for the next two weeks. Still, maybe it would be fun to have the sexual tension rising. It would make for a more explosive meet once she was finally back in the city in January.

And with that, she started packing her suitcase.

Nine

Happy fucking Christmas to me.

It's Christmas Eve and I'm back in France for two weeks, hiding out in the loft. I've been allocated the small room in the attic – I guess this is where badly behaved (and separated) daughters end up. A subtle way of signalling disapproval of said behaviour. Everyone else is still downstairs and I've conveniently blamed the jet lag to retire. I always find Christmas exhausting anyway. And this year, my mind is in a different type of 'spirit'…

I keep sneaking myself away to see who's messaged me or matched with me on my beloved apps. There's something thrilling about being a million miles away – we can look but not touch. Although obviously, I'd much rather touch.

Me and Evan have been texting non-stop since I got here. He's gone to Israel for the holidays (much more exotic than here) and even sent me a drunken video last night mouthing that he misses me. Surely that's love, no? Must snap myself out of that. I don't know if it's because he's the first guy I've connected with and had mind-blowing sex with, or I literally don't know what love is. Probably both. Either way, I need to get that word right out of my mind or else Evan will never speak to me again.

Right now, I'm on Tinder, scrolling through my current matches. Can't limit myself to one person, right? Who knows what else/who else is out there waiting for me? I find myself giggling to myself as I ogle over all these gorgeous guys in my inbox. Who'd have thought I'd end up here, like this? Well, I definitely didn't expect to be in France alone this year. But I equally didn't expect to be spending the holidays swiping through sexy men on an app that had never frequented my phone before. I think I could definitely get used to this…

OMG. Hot guy alert!

I've matched with someone who's just come online. It's almost midnight. He's tall, slim, piercing eyes, focused. Focused on me soon, I hope? I don't ask why he's also online so late on Christmas Eve. He doesn't ask either. His name is Victor and he draws me in instantly. Even the name demands some kind of hot, authoritative presence despite him being much younger than I am.

We chat about life, love, and sex. He says we share the same vision. Maybe. But what I think we share is instant attraction. Even though I can't see him IRL (another acronym, yeah!), his energy is electric, and I can feel him pulsing through me. The talk gets dirtier and dirtier, and I feel like he's in the room with me. (That would be weird obviously, considering where I am right now and that he hasn't quite met the parents yet, but I still want to feel his touch in real life.)

The chatter downstairs turns into muffled background noise as I get transported to my happy place. We end up having virtual sex, climaxing as quietly as I can – something I've never done before, but something I'm definitely going to do again. I'm discovering untouched territories and bathing in new types of pleasures. My small attic room feels like a sauna right now. Not such a bad Christmas after all.

We talk a little longer before both of us feel like it's time to go to sleep, exchanging numbers because we say we want to stay in touch. Yeah, right, of course we are. He lives in Paris and asides from holidays, I'm in NYC. What are the chances? I don't intend to come to France much after this but who knows?

We sign off and I sit cross-legged on my (single) bed and put my phone to one side. I've been glued to it since we got here. Not being present or in the moment – well, I'm present on my phone to everyone who's on it but not here, in this house, with my family. My kids. I don't think they've noticed. They've been swept up in the cheer, the full house, the gifts, the music, all of that stuff. Meanwhile, all I've been swept up with is thinking about who I can talk to in order to switch off to my parallel dimension.

I've certainly succeeded tonight. I want to be back in NYC so badly. Or Paris. Or Israel. I'm not fussy. As long as I'm with someone who can make me feel things. Who can help me explore my body and tap into my desires. I can't believe I've been monogamous my entire life – expecting one person to fulfil all my sexual needs. That doesn't seem possible right now. And I still couldn't tell you what all my sexual needs actually are – I'm barely scratching the surface. It's exciting, it's liberating, and it's also confusing. I don't really know who I am. I feel like a fraud – pretending to everyone around me that I'm someone I'm not. Have I always been doing that or is this a new part of me? Either way, I need to make a promise for the coming year that I'll stay true to myself and step into this undiscovered part of my body and soul. To listen to what I really want and screw the rest. *Literally.*

Last month, I had very limited connections. Now I have the possibility of multiple. Whether they're the right ones, who knows – but I feel slightly less lonely. My apps make me feel alive again. Who knew? I've always poo-pooed technology. Now it's my lifesaver.

For now, though, I'm going to be present in the moment away from my phone and my dual life. Here's to the new year and what awaits!

Ten

2018, baby! Lilith was relieved to be back in NYC. The holiday period had been the longest two weeks of her life. Although, Christmas Day had surprisingly gone without a hitch apart from a few odd disapproving comments from her parents on her relationship status, which was nobody else's business, as far as she was concerned. They were clearly disappointed in her, but she doubted they would ever fully express that.

'Why couldn't you make it work?' they'd asked. As if it was a simple answer. As if staying was the harder thing. When, in reality, the hardest thing to do had been to leave. Still, it was her decision and she owned it.

The days that followed were long and slow. Nobody wanted to do anything other than slob around in PJs, watch TV, and eat party food. Lilith, however, was itching to do something – or rather, someone. She took herself out for runs most days even though it was often icy or snowy – but this just meant that no one else was out there, so she could be alone with her thoughts and find herself a little bench to scroll through Tinder or Bumble.

She and Evan talked every day, but he'd decided to extend his stay in Israel into January too. Who could blame him? NYC would be miserable, cold, and depressing at this time of year – though Lilith intended to make the most of having to stay indoors. After experiencing the ecstasy of giving way to her sexual desires, the gates were well and truly open and about to get flooded. In all senses of the word. Lilith was on the hunt. *Manhunting in Manhattan.*

***

Her next match claimed to be an actor waiting for his big breakthrough. Clearly nowhere near yet, considering he was willing to hang out with her, but she'd reserve judgement. All she wanted to experience was that same intensity she'd had with the last two guys so she could feel human again. It was freezing cold here and she needed warmth. In person.

They met at a sushi bar in the city, wrapped up in big coats, scarves, and hats, and took a while to de-layer before introducing themselves properly. He was good-looking but a little thin and Lilith wasn't sure if the chemistry was there. Definitely not enough to be popping sushi into each other's mouths like the couple next to them, so probably best to leave pretty quickly.

She brought him to her conveniently located (a two-minute walk away) Airbnb to try and recreate the same level of intimacy she had with Evan and erase her non-reciprocated feelings for him in the process. To find her next flame. Because, after all, she was quite the romantic, it seemed. Whilst she thought of it, maybe she could get a special membership from Airbnb for very regular, random usage. But hey, she digressed. Out of the bathroom and back to the matter at hand.

Lilith stripped off her clothes (he was already undressed – okay, he's keen!) and pushed him to the bed. He lay on his back whilst she fucked him on top, hard.

But it didn't flow. They couldn't get into a rhythm and at one point even bumped heads as he tried to kiss her when Lilith was just going to hold on to the headboard to give her more power. She had no desire for him or his rather lean body. He, however, came quickly and rolled over onto his side whilst Lilith got herself dressed and washed her face in the bathroom before seeing him out and flopping back onto the bed.

This wasn't the night she'd planned for herself. Hell, their encounter hadn't lasted much longer than ten minutes! This wasn't what she'd waited the last few weeks for. This wasn't the whole point of doing this – to feel no connection and, worse than that, to not come. Not even near. NYC was feeling colder than ever before. But at least she had a bed for the night.

***

The following week, another new match and another date in the city. This time with an American guy called Jason. They met for a mezze meal on the Lower East Side but neither of them could eat anything. Maybe going for food beforehand simply wasn't necessary anymore – although she was enjoying trying out all these new places she'd never been to before.

She quickly realised all he wanted to do was fuck her. It was her idea to meet here; she just hadn't thought that's what he was after considering his messages on Bumble were rather soft. It suited her well, though, so she definitely wasn't complaining…

They left the restaurant and layered up again as it was freezing outside. Lilith was tempted to grab his hand but she thought better of it and instead walked a half step behind him as he led her to his flat. Thankfully it was close by, although he'd failed to mention that he shared it with three other guys. They were sitting on the sofa with bottles of beer watching a game (Lilith had no idea what kind as she wasn't into sport), so she simply said 'Hi' and followed Jason into his bedroom.

She wondered what they thought about his arrangement with a woman fifteen years older than him. Maybe he did this all the time – they certainly didn't seem fazed. And she was surprised that neither was she.

Jason's room was exactly what she expected for a guy in his twenties – but at least it was clean. It only just fit his double bed with not much space for anything else and he'd clearly just washed his blue sheets as they smelt of fresh linen and were freshly creased from being tumbled out of the dryer. An effort she was grateful for.

Lilith jumped onto the bed with him and revealed a sexy new blue underwear set (to match his bed). She was having fun picking out all these lingerie outfits she'd never dared buy herself before. He looked pretty pleased at what she was wearing too. She'd never seen a dick so big and hard.

With that, she started to give him a blow job that she

hoped he would tell his flatmates about – he certainly looked happy with her efforts – and then he fucked her from behind on the bed. This time, she surprised herself and came just before him. A novelty, it would seem! A novelty she hoped she could repeat. She could almost feel herself getting attached. Not quite to the same level as with Evan, but enough to mention him to her new friend from school the next day at an anti-Trump rally.

Unfortunately for Lilith, Jason started ghosting her and didn't respond to any of her messages after their meet. Ghosting was an alien concept to her but probably something she should get used to. The reason his flatmates barely looked up when she arrived and then left was probably because he had a different woman every night, so there was no need for introductions as they'd never see her again.

Okay, onwards and upwards. Who was next?

Another American boy. Lilith was using the word boy for anyone in their twenties, plus this one had a completely hairless, smooth, and super-hot body. He also happened to live in Little Haven, which was a big surprise, so she'd have to be careful about the neighbours. Luckily, he lived on the other side of town, which she rarely frequented. Not that it really mattered. One of her newly made-up rules was to only hook up with people who didn't live near her. For now, anyway. He was a slight deviation from the rule but seeing as she was the rule-maker, she gave herself a free pass. Still, it would be safer to meet in NYC where he was working.

They met at the bar of a cinema downtown to check if they wanted to spend some deeper time together. Their whole (online) conversations up until this point had been about his obsession with fucking an older woman and Lilith was more than happy to comply. She hadn't realised this was such a thing – were younger men really attracted to older women? She was certainly starting to notice a pattern in her encounters and she liked it. It made her feel powerful, wanted, desired… A feeling she hadn't felt in a very long time, and a feeling she wanted to hold on to.

American boy was a bit nervous when they met but Lilith was attracted to him, and him to her, so they agreed to proceed. How formal. However, he did refuse to jump in a taxi with her back to the hotel she'd booked near Grand Central and instead took the subway separately. It seemed he was scared to be seen and judged by people. Lilith, on the other hand, didn't give a fuck. Didn't give a fuck about what people thought about her or what people thought of him. In fact, she simply didn't give a fuck about anything anymore. This was her life now and she was ready to own it. American boy, however, was not. He wanted the thrill but wasn't quite ready to fully step into it.

'Christ,' Lilith thought to herself as she sat in the taxi. 'I can't even remember his name.'

She scrolled furiously through Tinder to find his profile. How could she forget? He was called Evan. *Go figure.* She felt a tug at her heartstrings even though she'd promised herself to stop feeling so attached to anyone, especially not Evan number one. But she missed him. And she was pretty sure this experience wasn't going to be up to her standards. Still, she was here now – and she'd paid for the hotel room – maybe Evan number two would surprise her.

They rendezvoused at the hotel, Evan walking a few steps behind her as she located their room. These vibes really weren't it but Lilith was determined to make something of it. She locked the room behind them, closed the curtains, and put some music on whilst he sat on the end of the bed – she'd recently bought a pink boom box to help create the 'right atmosphere' and get her in the groove. *So far, it was working wonders.*

She closed her eyes and stripped slowly, caressing her skin and slowly moving her body in a way that felt good. Whatever she was doing was working as he sat closer to the edge of the bed and started wanking, with his eyes glued to her body. Lilith smiled as he came super quick and let out a loud moan. He seemed shocked by his reaction but beckoned her over so he could kiss her neck and play with her hair.

'This is more like it,' Lilith thought to herself.

They took things slowly and Lilith went down to her knees to blow him. Again, he came super quick and then dived under the bedcovers as he let out a big grin.

'That was amazing,' he said, before hopping out of bed and heading to the bathroom for a shower.

He emerged from the bathroom fully dressed and as though he'd put a comb through his hair. Lilith frowned. No reciprocation? He was clearly still in training!

She pushed him to the bed, with him thinking he was in for round three, and then stood over him ready to lecture him about her freshly acquired wisdom. She softened her tone (being too harsh with him wasn't going to get her anywhere) and told him exactly how it was.

'Listen. This is not how you do things. Women desire

to be pleasured. Especially older women like me. We want to be touched, teased, turned on, and satisfied. So no more of this one-way-street business, pulling up your trousers, and revelling in your own satisfaction… Unless, of course, you'd rather cut your sexual life short and live alone with a blow-up doll for the rest of your years.'

Lilith barely paused for breath but was pleased with her delivery.

Meanwhile Evan lay steadfast on the bed, staring at her in admiration – pretty much falling in love on the spot, nodding along enthusiastically whilst expressing that he wanted to meet again.

Lilith politely declined and shooed him out of the hotel room, with him almost begging for her to give him another chance. Like a lost puppy desperate to find a home.

Her evangelising mission was only just beginning, though, and she had no time for love.

In the meantime, it was still early and Lilith wasn't ready to head back to the house just yet, so she went back into the hotel room and jumped in the shower to wash away the evening's events. Not that she'd got too dirty in the process. Still, she'd imparted an important lesson and she could only hope that the next woman he was lucky enough to wind up in bed with would enjoy much better treatment.

She'd been thinking about the whole 'MILF' concept for a while now. And she was finding it wasn't just a concept. It was a real thing. There were even dating apps for it (and yes, she was on those too). A whole host of younger guys were attracted to more 'mature women'. In fact, every guy she'd slept with or conversed with so far was younger than her. By quite a stretch. Was it because older women were more experienced and knew what they wanted? Or was it nothing more than a fantasy or a bucket-list item to cross off the list?

Lilith was quite sure about what she wanted right now (simplicity at this stage in her life) but she definitely wouldn't call herself experienced – even though she was clearly a fast learner. She'd been with the same person for the last twenty years and married very young, so definitely not a lot of experience there. She'd been shielded from so much and kept herself playing small. Some life experience for sure, but not to the same extent people might be hoping for.

Well, that was soon to change anyway. It already was changing. And Lilith was ready for the ride.

Eleven

'**B**oom. Good to match. How are ya? I am French, 40, just moved to NYC. Looking for someone to show me around and have fun with. Interested?'

I do not even bother personalising my messages anymore. I just copy and paste this intro repeatedly. Over and over. On Tinder. On Bumble. On Tinder. On Bumble… Check. I'm in my element – and I'm in control. Any matches? Swipe. Swipe left, swipe right, swipe left, swipe right, swipe, swipe, swipe… Swipe first thing in the morning. Swipe last thing at night. Swipe through the night. Swipe on trains. Swipe at the supermarket. Swipe at work. Swipe at breakfast, lunch, and dinner. Swipe in the car. Swipe at bars. Swipe in the loos. Swipe everywhere. Swipe all the fucking time. Swipe, swipe, swipe…

January has notoriously been a slow and painful month, but not so much this year. I've almost longed for more days so I can keep on feeding my addiction. My longing for more men, more experiences, and more swiping. I've barely paused to take a breath. But for good reason…

I'm training in the art of industrious hooking up. Time-consuming but an excellent way to numb how I'm really feeling. And when it comes to hooking up, it turns out I'm a very good learner. But I know there are still so many things to learn. I want to swipe my life – start afresh. I want to fill that void. I've hit the age I thought I'd have my shit together and yet, instead, I'm suffocating. I keep going, for more and more. I'm insatiable. I've even upgraded my Tinder membership to gold. At some point, I've ended up with more than 4,500 matches. How that's even possible in the space of a few weeks, I don't know. But guess what? That's still not enough. What am I actually looking for? Fuck knows but a lot of fucking for sure.

I'm aware that these dating apps are completely taking hold of my life. I'm aware of it but I don't want to stop it. Much as I'm aware I sometimes have one too many gins, but I don't want to stop that either. It's the feeling of immediate gratification. Pour a glass of gin and tonic – instantly feel good. Swipe through my matches on Tinder – instantly feel good. I can wake up in the morning feeling like I'm longing to have sex that day, and by the end of the day I've succeeded because I've found so many willing participants on the app. It's easy. And it's fulfilling. Or is it? Whatever it is, I know I'm addicted. And it's an addiction I don't want to stop.

My estimated success rates? Let me share the stats. I've worked out that about thirty per cent of my likes match me back. I then start the scrutinous selection process. Using my beautifully crafted intro, I launch into lyrical dialogues. Any dick pic sender is either immediately kicked out or I make sure that they get one in return, instantly (of a random dick pic – not mine, to be clear). I find it amusing – most of them don't. Not my problem. I don't do after-sales.

Often, the chat goes nowhere. Sometimes, it does. Sometimes, there seems to be a spark. Even the smallest, I'll take it. I'm longing for connection. Which means we move on to the next stage: meeting in person for real-life assessment. Don't be fooled – the sales cycle can be either extremely slow (often resulting in nothing at all) or extremely fast. From morning to evening in one day. I work fast. I love the pace. I thrive on it.

I meet about ten per cent of the thirty per cent of my matches. When you have 4,000 matches, that's a lot of dick pics. A lot of chats and drinks. And a fairly good amount of fucking. I'm never scared. I know personal safety can be a potential issue when you're meeting strangers in person. I always tell someone where I am and who I'm meeting and where. Usually my friend, Elena, who arranged the elusive surprise fortieth birthday party for me. She won't gossip, though. She's the only one in the neighbourhood who knows. She's so different to me. She loves suburban life. Loves being a wife and mother. Loves everything that comes with it. Loves her house. Loves the village. I'm happy for her, and sometimes I wonder why she wants to be my friend. But we connect. We laugh. We talk. We look out for each other. And sometimes, I wonder if that's the type of connection I really need.

Anyway, back to the men. I always meet them at a bar first so that I'm meeting them in public for the first time to check them out. Obviously I'm checking them out in other ways, too, but I can usually tell if something's 'off' about them. Then we go to a hotel room or their place. Never to mine, obviously. I wouldn't have a stranger there and, quite frankly, it's way too far from the city. Nope, the hotel room or their place puts me in control. I get to leave whenever I want. I never stay the night. At least, not for most of them. A few exceptions to the rule, of course. When I do leave, though, I'm alone. I feel elated and sad. I have this great big opportunity to start over, to pursue the things I really want to pursue, to feel the things I really want to feel, and to just be who I want to be. And yet, I feel extremely lonely and alone (apparently, these are two different concepts). I miss my life in London. I miss my friends. I miss my family. I miss being in love and being loved.

So for now, I'm keeping swiping. I'm opening myself up to new experiences (in every sense of the word). I'm taking off my 'good girl crown' and delving into the woman who's been hiding under it for so long. Because I don't even know if I fully know her yet either.

Twelve

February started in a way that Lilith wanted to forget. It was her 'week off' or her week on, more like, but it was her time away from the kids (the week they were staying at their dad's, like every other week), doing what she wanted. And that's exactly what she was doing. It had started with a couple of drinks at Elena's house. Where Lilith now wished it had ended – but as with anything, hindsight is a wonderful thing...

Lilith had put on a pair of skinny jeans and a slinky black top that made her feel ten years younger and grabbed a nice bottle of white wine she'd chilled the night before in the fridge. She'd also decided to wear a pair of strappy black heels that made her six-foot tall and feel on top of the world, despite the fact that she couldn't really walk in them and that it was still freezing outside. But hey, she looked good and she felt good – even if her feet might not feel the same way the next morning. Plus, Elena would be impressed at her efforts.

Elena was indeed impressed and was also wearing her finest skinny jeans, as well as a pair of gold, skyscraper heels that made Lilith's look like dolly shoes. The difference was Elena could actually pull them off and walk in them. She looked like a model. Damn, her husband was a lucky man – *and he knew it.*

Their house was slightly less oppressive than the infamous dark, blue house. For one, they didn't have a giant oak tree taking up the entire backyard, nor did they have an alternative co-parenting living arrangement across two houses. Everything was white, though, which Lilith had noticed was a high-class American thing. Everyone loved clean white lines and shiny surfaces. Everyone also had cleaners to keep it looking that way.

But somehow, Elena was different. She might have been a housewife, which Lilith usually loathed, but she was bubbly, fun, and witty – and she listened. She cared for Lilith and Lilith cared for her. And that was the one thing Lilith had been missing from her life these last few months.

One bottle of wine in and the ladies were ready to hit the town. They were getting the train to the city to continue the night and just managed to make it to the station as the train pulled in, otherwise they would have been freezing their asses off on the platform waiting an hour for the next one.

They'd snuck a can of pornstar martini each onto the train with them, so they were already quite tipsy once they reached Grand Central Station when Lilith suddenly slipped on the marble floor and landed full force onto her left shoulder.

'Shit, are you okay?'

Elena's immediate response had been to laugh as it

looked quite comical, but the look on Lilith's face said otherwise. She looked as though she were about to cry.

'Fuck,' Lilith responded as she tried and failed to get herself back on her feet.

The pain was immense but with help from Elena and a couple of unsuspecting commuters, she was back up on her feet and determined to continue the night they had planned.

'Are you sure you don't want to get checked out at the hospital?' Elena asked, concerned.

'No, I'm good. A few more drinks in me and I won't even feel it,' Lilith responded, before putting on her best fake smile and grabbing Elena's hand with her fully workable arm.

And with that, Lilith smoothed down her hair with her good hand, took a deep breath, and marched as confidently as possible to the closest bar so she could party the night away in Manhattan to numb the pain, downing shots and dancing on the dance floor as if no one was watching. They were, of course, approached by numerous guys but tonight wasn't the night. Lilith just wanted to drink herself into oblivion and savour the moment of being out in NYC, with her new best girlfriend, as if she was in her teens again. And that's exactly what she did.

Unfortunately, the next morning didn't look so pretty...

Lilith was thankfully in her own bed and woke up in absolute agony. Her shoulder felt like it was on fire and she could barely move. She had to call Elena to come and help her out of bed. The previous evening was rather blurry – all she could recall was the acute pain and the drinks that had caused her hangover to mask the pain. *What a mistake.*

Elena and Lilith decided it was best to go to the hospital, so they called her a cab and she spent the majority of the day waiting in the ER for someone to see her. The perfect time for a bit of scrolling and swiping, no? Even that couldn't distract her from the pain, though.

She was rudely interrupted from her endless swiping with the news that she would need an MRI scan – which, upon entering the tunnel, led to the first (and hopefully last) proper panic attack of Lilith's life. She was told to lie perfectly still, which made her feel as though she was lying in a coffin – unable to breathe and about to die. Or, more precisely, about to be buried. Alive. *How light and pleasant.* She instantly felt a huge wave of panic rising over her.

Was she going to stay trapped in this hell machine forever? With these loud beeping noises ordering her not to move? She started screaming – a kind of deep primal scary scream – and asked to be removed with immediate effect. This clearly did the trick. She was sweating heavily (mostly alcohol from her boozy night but something else, too. Fear, she thought).

The doctor looked at her with concern and asked whether there was a possibility that she might be claustrophobic. Not necessarily the way she would have liked to find out about it but it seemed to be the case. Her (not very good-looking) doctor then offered her an alternative scan, which had been designed for people with claustrophobia. *It would have been much better if she'd been offered that in the first place, but that was America for you.*

The diagnosis came back as a broken shoulder.

'Fuckkk.' Lilith didn't bother apologising to the doctor for her language.

This was the last thing she needed. She'd be in a sling for weeks and was unable to have an op because the bone needed to heal itself. That meant a lot of keeping it still and in place – a concept she'd need to get her head around considering the month she had planned. Still, at least she was given a giant jar of opioids to help it heal, so that could be fun.

Wrong. As soon as Lilith got home, she popped one back as the pain was so acute she could barely breathe. Cue feeling completely high, experiencing total euphoria, no longer feeling any physical or mental pain, and having the best night's sleep of her life. And that's exactly where the addiction would begin, so the jar was thrown reluctantly away the following morning.

This unfortunately meant that the sling alone would have to do – which further added to her constraints and isolation – but she swore to herself she wasn't going to allow her temporary impairment to impinge on her sexual encounters. Nope, she'd just have to get creative. And creativity was turning out to be her middle name.

Thirteen

What. A. Month. And it's not even over yet.

I've fucked my shoulder and it's taking a while to heal. I'm currently in a sling and have been for the last three weeks and I just want to scream into my pillow – only I can't lie on my front to do that. Which poses more issues than one…

For the first time in ages, I've been pining for a male as a permanent fixture in my home. Someone to care for me. To help me get dressed when I can't get a frigging jumper over my head. To cheer me up when I'm feeling sad and frustrated. To cook me dinner and pour me copious glasses of wine. To feed me. To touch me. To hold me. Argh. I'm all for embracing my role as a strong, independent woman 'who don't need no man', but, right now, I really do.

The week after my injury, after a few weeks of intense negotiations, I met up with Evan number one again (not that I needed to clarify which Evan it was). Nothing was going to stop me from fucking that hot guy again, although I was definitely verging on desperation to see him again.

What have I become? Literally begging to see a guy to the point where I'd essentially broken him down so much he couldn't say anything but 'yes', even though that's the opposite of what he probably wanted to say. Anyway, the moment he opened his flat door, I almost leapt on him – being mindful of my shoulder obviously, so it was a little awkward. I clearly took him by surprise because he barely caught me as I flung myself towards him with my good side and almost found myself on my ass on his hall floor. But that wasn't the only awkward moment…

I was so hot for him, we ended up trying an adventurous new sex position that clearly didn't work that well for single-armed people, and I learnt the hard way. I jumped off him whilst he was close to the point of coming and I began crying out in pain, almost convulsing on the floor as he looked on in utter disbelief. I only caught his eyes for a minute (I couldn't bear to look at him) and instead quickly threw on my knickers (I'd kept my dress on), picked myself up off the floor, and swiftly left his flat, leaving him lying on the bed naked – and unsatisfied. Needless to say, his Latino pride was severely hit by my French exit and he messaged me an hour later to call things off once and for all.

And just like that, I'd lost someone. Someone who'd taught me how to feel again. Someone I was excited to see messages from when I woke up each morning. Someone who made my tummy flip over and over again and had me wanting for more. Gone. Just like that. All because of my stupid fucking shoulder and my intense need to see him and fuck him when I wasn't ready, when my mind was completely in the wrong place and I didn't know how to control my limbs. The thought of never seeing him again made me feel sad and sick (I actually threw up when he messaged me to end things) and I felt like I'd rather deal with the pain in my shoulder for the rest of my life than deal with the emotions surrounding my swift dumping.

So, that led me to getting (even more) reckless. All I wanted (and still want to do) was to numb the pain. The pain of losing Evan, and the debilitating pain in my left shoulder.

I decided to focus on perfecting blow jobs and other techniques instead, which didn't involve the use of my shoulder. The game was to see how far I could push it (quite deep, thank you very much!). I decided I didn't want to waste my time with the 'meeting at a bar stage', going against one of my only rules to keep me safe, and instead booked a hotel room midtown offering a crazy night for anyone available right now. *Someone in my already matched contacts, though – a lady still has to have some standards.* First come, first served.

Evan number three got the prize. *Seriously, what the fuck is with this name?! If I never meet another Evan again, I'll be relieved.*

Anyway, back to that night… I lay seductively on the hotel room bed with another new set of lingerie – red this time – and waited impatiently for his arrival. (As seductively as you can lay with a sling on, anyway.) I was so ready. Ready to feel the touch of another man on my body and fill me up inside.

He, however, was not. Evan number three was a total mess as soon as I let him into the room and he started crying. His mum was ill and he just wanted some company tonight. (Was he for real?!) Turns out he was in fact for real, and I quickly realised I wouldn't be getting what I wanted if I let him stay. Who did he think I was? His therapist?! I did listen to him and allowed him to vent his upset before nicely letting him know that I was meeting someone else and that he needed to go.

Closing the door behind him feeling highly frustrated, I took a deep breath and started working through my shortlist (a girl's gotta do what a girl's gotta do!). There was a guy I'd never spoken to before in my match list and he messaged me to invite me over to his. I was beyond thankful to be able to leave the hotel room – which I'm never going to book again by the way (it's cursed with the crying guy now) – so I put a coat over my lingerie and jumped into a taxi.

Writing this now, I can see how desperate I really was that night, but I don't regret it. When a girl's got needs, she's got needs.

The apartment I ended up in was actually really nice. Much swisher than some of the other places I've found myself in. No roommates there either. I've no idea of said guy's name but my freshly acquired blow job skills seemed to be much appreciated, combined with the expert usage of my other hand (the one that wasn't in a sling). I left as quickly as I came. Speaking of which, I didn't come. By the way, that's been my biggest stress – can I still wank fully with my broken shoulder? Self-pleasure has become such an important part of me as I explore what makes me feel good.

Anyway, I've decided to take a few days off. With guys anyway. I'm currently sitting at JFK airport, waiting for my plane to Geneva for a work trip. That's the great thing about my work – travel is part of the job role, and it always comes at just the right time when I'm in need of getting away. I don't really fancy battling with the language barrier as well as my hurt shoulder, so that's why I've decided to mainly concentrate on work – with my trusty apps on the side, of course. A little sexy chat never hurt anyone… *Only galivanting around train stations with marble floors apparently.*

Luckily no marble floors here – I've got an aisle seat right at the very front so I can have a comfortable flight and I plan to dose myself up with sleeping tablets and wine. In moderation obviously, but enough to send me into a lovely snooze so that I wake up on the runway in Switzerland fully refreshed. See you on the other side!

Fourteen

February didn't get any better for Lilith – even though she couldn't have imagined it could get any worse. She'd felt fine at the airport but the moment she'd stepped onto the plane, anxiety hit like it had never hit before and she wound up having a severe panic attack on the flight to Geneva. Luckily, she'd brought all sorts of medical concoctions with her, so took Xanax for the first time in her life, which eventually settled her down, but this was not how she'd imagined things would be. The flight attendants were lovely and the lady next to her had continually checked in with her to make sure she was okay, but by this point she was just embarrassed and fighting back the tears.

The work trip thankfully went without a hitch and the days flew by as she attended conferences and worked late into the night, distracting herself from allowing herself to feel anything. She barely had time to even glance at her apps, let alone engage with anyone. It was good for her to be distracted and to actually be able to focus on something she cared about, but she was masking so many problems.

The night before she flew home, she made a commitment to herself that she'd book an appointment with a therapist to start her healing journey – in more ways than one. That was a start at least. They always said the first step of healing was awareness – and then action. At least that's what Lilith was telling herself. Healing definitely didn't involve a world without guys or sexual pleasure, though, so Lilith decided that she'd ping someone once her flight landed back at JFK (a flight she was able to get through without incident due to the copious amounts of Xanax she had dosed herself up on).

And that's precisely what she did – literally the moment the plane's wheels touched the runway. She barely looked at the guys she was matched with as she messaged the first one she scrolled down to. Did he have a name? Most likely, but she wasn't going to bother herself with finding out. Instead she told him to be ready for her at 1 a.m. outside his house – and by ready, she meant ready for action.

After hailing a cab at the airport, she asked the driver to take a detour to this guy's place – conveniently only around a ten-minute drive from her house – (again, breaking her rules but surely they didn't apply to late-night shifts?) and tipped him before he drove away. 'The guy' was leaning against his car (he lived with his parents, so a car-meet was much more preferable) and he was definitely ready.

Lilith loaded her giant purple suitcase with her one abled-arm into his trunk (always so practical) and ordered him to fuck her hard from behind inside his car – as hard as he could given her sling – and not to say a single word. Much easier that way. She wouldn't have to listen to his

American accent… Or hear him cry. He obeyed perfectly and Lilith jumped out of the car, feeling satisfied as she straightened herself up. She blew him a kiss goodbye before walking around the block with her suitcase, back on cloud nine again, ready to call another cab to take her home. She was fulfilled for now and that was all that mattered.

***

It was Lilith's week with the girls again, and for once she was grateful for this side of her dual life. She was still feeling some anxiety following her frightening panic attack on the plane to Geneva, and her shoulder was still causing her some bother and taking its time to heal. A rest from everything was what she needed – which was hilarious considering most other people wouldn't consider parenting a rest. She was lucky and privileged to have Sophia in her life, as well as the fact that both girls went to school and were already fiercely independent (much like their mother!).

Lilith was also taking this time to fit in a couple of much-needed appointments in between her freelance work – which was getting busier and requiring more of her attention than the previous months. Something else she was seriously grateful for after the first few months of not being able to work. She was, however, missing having in-person colleagues and a set workplace to go to every day. It was a long trip into the city to café-hop to different places and try to find the most comfortable spots (and consume a lot of coffees in the process!)

Back to the appointments. Lilith hadn't done anything for her health – both physical and mental – since she'd gotten here. Aside from breaking her shoulder, of course – but that wasn't exactly a positive health experience. She had yet to see a physician since she got here, so she knew it was time for a check-up. Plus, she'd also promised herself she'd find herself a therapist to tackle the emotional side of her life. Y'know, like ending her marriage after twenty years, living in a new country, and trying to fill the void by fucking half of New York City.

The family physician was just a fifteen-minute stroll from the house. That was her first port of call whilst she spent the evenings Googling different therapists to see if she could connect with any. So far, she hadn't found one who looked like they could deal with what she was going to discuss with them. They all looked too 'prudey'. That was definitely a problem with this part of America (it was different in the city). People didn't talk about sex, let alone have it.

Lilith had requested a female physician, yet when she turned up at the practice, there was apparently only one physician on duty. And he was male. Lilith rolled her eyes before sitting down in the waiting room, scanning the reading material on the table next to her. There were leaflets about family planning with a picture of a male and female and two laughing children; a leaflet about a local retirement home on the water, with pictures of elderly people playing chess and sitting in comfy armchairs; and there was a leaflet about eating your five a day, covered in all types of different fruit and vegetables.

'Jesus,' Lilith almost thought out loud. 'Where the fuck am I?'

Before she had time to gather her stuff and leave, her name was called into room number one to see Dr Laithwaite. His head poked round the door to check she could find the room okay – which was funny considering she only had the choice of two – but she stood up and awkwardly waved to show him she had seen him. He was tall and lanky, and noticeably old. His hair was almost completely white and thinning at the top and his hands were visibly wrinkly with big purple veins popping out as he went to shake Lilith's hand and beckoned her to sit down. This was not the appointment she had envisaged. But it was an appointment she needed all the same, so she removed her coat and sat herself down.

'So,' said the doctor. 'You're new to the area?'

'Yes, well, I moved here around five months ago now.'

'Doesn't look like you've had the best of luck so far?' Dr Laithwaite pointed to her shoulder, which was still supported by her sling.

Lilith forced a laugh. 'Yes, that wasn't my favourite moment. Turns out the floor at Grand Central Station is rather slippery.'

'Ah, you found your way into the big smoke. It's not as great as people say, hey? Much better here in the quiet with no slippery station floors.'

Lilith went to protest but she'd already realised there was no point. This man had clearly lived here his entire life and she was sitting with a shoulder injury from the very place he said wasn't all it was cracked up to be. So instead she smiled and changed the subject to what she was actually here for.

'I'm here for some sexual health tests.'

'Oh, okay.' He looked a little perplexed, which Lilith found amusing. 'Are you not married, no? I assumed you'd made the move with your husband.'

'No, I'm separated,' Lilith replied, trying to stop herself from getting exasperated.

'Okay then. So am I to assume you're sexually active?'

What a way to phrase that question, Lilith thought to herself. 'Yes, I am,' she replied proudly.

'And are you on birth control?'

Ugh, there it was. That age-old question.

'No, I've recently come off the pill,' she replied.

Lilith zoned out as she watched him retrieve some leaflets from his drawer about the coil. A leaflet she'd seen in many different formats throughout the years, but still pushed the same damn message. That the coil was the best form of contraception for a woman past a 'certain age'.

Lilith tried to make it look like she was vaguely listening so found herself nodding along in the right places and looking down at the leaflet when he opened it up to show her how the contraption worked. Essentially a foreign object inserted into your body to control you. At least that was Lilith's opinion of how it worked.

She found herself drifting off again as she thought about the total imbalance between men and women, sex and contraception. She was tempted to ask Dr Laithwaite how he'd feel about an unknown copper device being shoved up his arsehole or through his dick, but she thought better of it. She still needed to get those tests, which was why she was here in the first place. He was just veering completely off track like they all did when it came to discussing sexual health.

Lilith politely interrupted him to say that it wasn't for her right now but she'd consider it. Of course, she wouldn't really – now she was finally off hormonal birth control, she'd had the biggest libido surge she'd ever experienced and was discovering her needs for the first time in her life. And she wasn't about to stop that journey anytime soon.

Condoms remained the solution, although Lilith had been surprised that a few of her dates had pushed back, which was obviously a deal-breaker for her. It was either condoms or no action.

'I'd really like to be tested for all the regular STDs and HIV, please,' Lilith said firmly.

The doctor shrugged, put the leaflet away, then nodded his head and left the room to go and get the appropriate tests. Urine, swabs, and blood – how delightful! But totally necessary. Lilith would need to wait a few days for the results but she left the practice feeling empowered, despite the conversations. She'd stood her ground and got what she needed. Now, she just needed to work on what was going on in her head. And that was a whole other ball game.

It was only ten in the morning, so Lilith decided to get the train into the city. There was one due in the next fifteen minutes, so she'd be there by half past eleven, which gave her plenty of time to get some work done and keep researching for her perfect-match therapist. There also might be a little time for finding her other perfect match on her favourite apps – especially on the train ride. The view out of the window was pretty boring and lifeless until you got close to the city, so she needed some entertainment.

Ooh, a bit early for dick pics – Lilith swiftly deleted the messages and kept swiping until she found something more palatable. Some nice shiny abs would do.

She sent a few messages to some potential 'suitors' before putting her phone back in her bag and closing her eyes for a quick power nap. That doctor's trip and various tests had taken it out of her more than she'd thought.

The city was its usual vibrant and bustling self as Lilith stepped off the train and into Grand Central Station. She was wearing trainers today – much more suitable footwear for the accident-prone. Plus it meant she could go for a nice long walk at lunchtime – maybe around Central Park, or just aimlessly meander the streets and see what she stumbled upon. That was the beauty of New York. There was always somewhere you hadn't yet discovered. Much like her sexual self.

There was no need to rush back today either. Sophia was picking the girls up from school, so she'd just make sure she was home in time for dinner so she could hear about their day and let Sophia get home early. Perfect. Why did she need a therapist again? Ah yes, just the slight issue of feeling completely and utterly alone even when surrounded by a sea of people, and wanting more and more and it never being enough. Talking to someone could help… maybe? She'd give it a go, anyway. It couldn't hurt.

The rest of the day went by in a blur. She found a great little corner spot in a coffee shop midtown that enabled her to put her headphones in and be shut off from the world for a little while. People came and went but no one disturbed her and her cup stayed filled with coffee. She got ahead of her deadlines and even managed to shortlist a few suitable-looking therapists. Suitable in Lilith's eyes meant they wore clothes that weren't suits, their hair colour wasn't brown or blonde, and they had something in their personal profile different to 'I live upstate with my husband, kids and little cocker spaniel named Rover.' She needed someone with a bit of bite to them. Someone who wouldn't be afraid of talking about sex. Hookups. Fantasies. Emotions. Thoughts she was afraid to say out loud.

Before she knew it, it was time to pack up her things and catch the train back home in time for a hot meal with the girls. She was planning on cooking dinner but now she just fancied kicking off her shoes when she got in, ordering in pizza, and chilling on the sofa with a bowl of popcorn, watching a movie with Hannah and Ella. It's a shame she didn't feel like this most nights as her life would likely be much less dramatic. But that was precisely the point. She wasn't made to stay home every day. She was made to get out there and discover the world – and everyone in it.

The girls were already snuggled up on the sofa when Lilith got home, so she quickly checked in with Sophia before letting her leave to go back to her family, so she could spend time with her daughters. They seemed to have settled in quite well with their living arrangements – probably because they'd seen it coming for a long time. Lilith guessed it was obvious, but, still, she was amazed by their resilience and their generosity. What cool kids they were.

'Mummmm, are you sitting down with us?' Hannah called over.

Lilith quickly snapped herself back out of her thoughts, flashed her daughters a genuine smile, and jumped on the sofa in between them as they picked out a movie together. For now, this was all she needed.

Fifteen

You know you've reached a low point when you're sitting at an empty bar somewhere in Connecticut, drinking crap white wine in the middle of the afternoon with a shitty live band playing tired hits in the background. Yep, that was me today. And worse than that, I've been there on so many occasions, the bartender knows me by name, and even though he's not remotely my type, he's become more and more attractive each time I visit and throw back those glasses of wine.

So you can probably guess what happened today... And where it ended.

The lines got well and truly blurred and before I knew it, I was in a basement room (I know, what was I thinking? Sounds like something out of a murder film) with *Game of Thrones* playing loudly on a massive flat screen. The fucking was medieval too, let me tell you. No dragons or Prince Charming to save me on that one. It was pretty hardcore. We didn't speak to each other, just went straight in there, fast, from behind. He came quickly – and I did not. I felt let down. Definitely a poor reward for the risks I took.

I'm getting reckless. Going into situations I wouldn't normally put myself in. I say 'normally' but I'm not sure what my 'normal' is anymore. Do I need to be more careful? Maybe I just need to find a French lover instead. Someone more attuned with my needs. I also need to find myself a therapist, but I'm still hesitant to book a session with anyone. My shortlist remains a shortlist that I'm slowly picking apart.

It can only go upwards from here, right?

15 March 2018

So, I took my own advice from the last entry I wrote. No, I didn't book a therapy session. I went and found myself a French man. A French cook, in fact. Called Alisen. Definitely sounded more promising on paper – wondering what kind of recipes he could show me. Picturing scenes of him showing me how to make things with his hands and ending up with ingredients all over us as we clear the countertops and fuck on the kitchen worktop…

Anyway, we met at a bar. I've been trying to get back into my 'usual' safer routine, so that's a start at least. He'd cycled there to meet me – apparently he cycles everywhere. Not my personal choice of transport but each to their own. He looked super cute (no, he didn't arrive in his Lycra, thank God) and had a strong Southern French accent. Not sure about that part, although he at least sort of reminded me of home? Whether that was a good thing or bad thing, I didn't know at the time.

I booked a room at a 'pod' hotel. Supposedly modern capsules but it was more like a miniroom/cupboard – quite claustrophobic. Made mental note to myself to not book one of those again. Also felt thankful I no longer had my sling on and was gaining more movement in my left shoulder. The healing journey is long and slow – and it's been taking every part of me not to break down and cry each night from the pain and frustration of not being able to move it like I could before. But I'm getting there. And I'm proud of myself that I've done this on my own.

Anyway, back to my pod guest... He kept talking about food. Go figure, he's a cook – but still, it wasn't exactly a turn on. Just how me talking about my job that I'm super passionate about probably wouldn't have been a turn on for him either. I found myself fantasising about ways to shut him up. I offered to gag him and play with his ass – something I've never offered before. Unfortunately, I hadn't read my audience very well. He was more the alpha male type and looked pretty offended. Whoops. It's weird how so many younger men claim to be 'open-minded' but remain quite conventional when it comes to fucking.

He also misread my proposition of dominating him and instead opted for dominating me. He used his belt from his trousers to tie me up to the minicapsule – which conveniently had a hook (and didn't involve strain on my healing shoulder). I wondered if it had been designed like that on purpose and started revisiting my thoughts on never returning there again to keeping it as a backpocket option. I decided to play along. But he was very focused. Too diligent. Not my bag.

Fucking is a bit like cooking. You might have all the ingredients but if you're missing the chemistry...

26 March 2018

I'm bored at work. I don't know if it's my surroundings or lack of human interaction but I'm just not in the 'working zone' today. Not that I've been well focused at work for a while. I find it super hard to concentrate. I'm usually an avid reader at home, too, but the books on my bedside table haven't been opened for months. I think I piled them there when I first moved in, thinking I'd get through them in a matter of days, but I haven't read a single page. I feel like I'm developing an attention disorder. My mind seems only able to focus on one thing. SEX. And hot guys. More specifically, hot guys I want to fuck. I literally can't think about anything else. And I don't think I *want* to think about anything else.

My next match is an opera singer. I'm genuinely interested in finding out more about him and his job. Not like the cook. Does he sing when he comes? I wonder. Again we meet in a bar in midtown first, for all of five minutes, before we head off to the hotel I've booked round the corner. I don't need Dutch courage anymore. I know what I want and I know how to get it. Turns out, not only does he have the deepest voice, he's also an experienced guitarist – with magic fingers. We skip the bed and head straight for the bathroom. He's already turned on the shower and stepped into it fully naked as I'm still undressing. A guy who knows what he wants too. I like him.

I end up liking him even more when he shows me how to squirt FOR THE FIRST TIME IN MY ENTIRE LIFE. I don't think I ever would have discovered those mechanics of my body if it hadn't been for him. We decide to spare the bed and go on repeat in the bathroom. This experience has been a complete revelation. I had no idea my body was capable of ejaculating. Female ejaculation. How cool! I thought that was a sport purely reserved for men. It's only taken me forty years to find out. More research on this topic clearly required! What more awaits me?!

Sixteen

The loneliness of Lilith's double life in New York was catching up with her. It was Saturday night and her week with the girls. They'd just finished the Chinese takeaway that Lilith had ordered in and now Hannah and Ella had rushed off to their rooms to play a new game they'd been chatting about all day on the Xbox. At least they could fend for themselves, but this now meant that Lilith was stuck with her own thoughts for the rest of the night instead of distracting herself with mindless gossip or chick flicks. She could put a film on, of course, but the thought of watching something alone made her feel sad and disconnected.

It was true she felt more connected to some parts of herself than ever before, but she still had a lot of unanswered questions. She knew what was fulfilling her right now (kind of) but what about long term? Where did she see herself six months or a year from now? That part looked blurry. How long was she going to stay in this house, in this village, living a life that wasn't meant for her? How many guys would she fuck before she found 'the one'? Did she even want to find 'the one'? Monogamy didn't appeal in the same way it had before. The thought of settling down and finding herself stuck again made her feel sick. Maybe limbo was a better place to be. No commitment to anything.

She poured herself a glass of white wine (she had been stockpiling the bottles every time she did a food shop so she could be sure she never ran out) and curled up on the sofa. The 'for sale' sign outside was gathering dust – there hadn't been any interest for weeks, let alone any viewings. No scrolling tonight – she was too tired. And confused.

***

The weekend dragged like it always did when she was at 'home'. The girls had a much better social life than she did, so they had both been at friends' houses on the Sunday, and before Lilith knew it, it was Monday again and she was opening up her laptop in her bedroom, ready for a day of work.

She needed an office. With other humans around her. She struggled to focus wherever she was at the moment, but being in the suburbs made things ten times worse. The static view from the bedroom windows. Being on her own all day – with only squirrels for company. She fucking hated them and the way they stared at her through the windows, almost taunting her. She was going to buy a gun and shoot them. That, or end up shooting herself. Too extreme? Maybe, but she felt so depressed, void, and empty. That was the appeal of living in the US. Guns were accessible for times like these. That was also the problem. Did the suburbs send people mad and that's how you ended up with mass shooters? Lilith shuddered at the thought. Enough thoughts about guns. They were not her solution.

A co-working venue, however, would be, so she spent the rest of the day scoping out the best-looking locations in the city, ringing round to iron out the details, and settling on a rolling one-month contract at a WeWork near Grand Central. *She wasn't about to commit to anything permanent any time soon.*

She felt a huge sense of relief wash over her as soon as she made the first payment. She'd finally have somewhere to go. 'Team members' to talk to maybe. A water cooler to gather around to talk about the day's events. Feeling like she mattered to someone. At least professionally, if not personally too.

The next day, she put on her nicest jeans (a suit would be too much for this kind of venue, plus she wanted to appeal to the masses) and called a cab to the train station. As usual, she'd left it too late to walk, unless she wanted to hang around on the platform for close to an hour. For the first time in a long time, she felt important. She had somewhere to be. And she was going to see PEOPLE. People she could potentially interact with. She was so desperate to connect with anyone. Anyone who would listen to her or simply say 'Hello'. She almost tripped getting onto the train, she was that excited, but steadied herself before it was too late. No time for any more injuries.

The co-working venue was bustling when she got there, with only a couple of hot desks left available, so she chose the one in the middle with the most people around and started unpacking her laptop, notepad, and pens, smiling and saying 'Hello' to the people around her. Some even said 'Hello' back. What a novelty.

Uh-oh, hot guy sitting at the desk opposite. She noticed him the moment she sat down and tried her best to avert eye contact. 'First day at "work", Lilith, must stay focused,' she told herself in her head. 'No sex.'

He was young and gorgeous though – with a beautiful smile. She couldn't help but smile back at him when she looked up again. It was so hard not to listen to his work conversations. Especially because it sounded like they could actually be colleagues. She could tell he was listening to hers, too. Climate change. Just another thing that kept her awake at night.

'Sounds like we have similar jobs,' Lilith said as he finished a phone call and looked over to her.

Hot guy smiled and started asking questions about her work – and herself. Of course Lilith naturally obliged. He was twenty-nine, based in DC (damn), but visited New York on a regular basis (yeah).

'Can I take your email address?' he said as he put on his jacket to leave to head back to DC. They'd been talking on and off for hours; Lilith hadn't noticed the time.

'Sure.'

Lilith handed him her business card and lingered just a moment to feel his touch on her hand as he took it off her, before wishing him a safe trip back to DC.

She stayed behind at the co-working space (she had lots of work to catch up on), feeling even more depleted than before she'd got there, finding herself staying there late into the evening to put off going back home alone.

The next day, the same routine, although someone else was sitting opposite her at the hot desk this time. They smiled and said hello, but that was about the most in-person interaction she got that day. Her inbox, however, was a different story. Amidst her highlighted work emails was an email from 'Brad'. She recognised the organisation name straight away and knew it must be Mr Hot Hot Desk-Guy.

They exchanged emails all day about work, very much distracting Lilith from getting on with anything meaningful as she kept refreshing her inbox, and before the day ended, she decided to send this:

'Coming to DC for an important meeting next week. Will only be a couple of hours so I have some free time before I come back to the city. Fancy meeting for a drink?'

She waited with bated breath for a reply.

'Sure. Would love to hang out. I know a great place by the river. Will send you the details'.

Lilith's heart skipped a beat as she tried to go back to concentrating on work, but it was no use. She packed up her laptop for the day and took herself out for a drink at a bar she'd spotted next door. It was full of banker-type people and lots of older guys in suits huddled together, so Lilith squeezed in to get a seat at the bar. She ordered herself an old fashioned before having a quick scroll through her apps. One of the older guys from the huddle tapped her on the shoulder to offer to buy her a drink but she politely refused. It wasn't her vibe in here – or level of man. She downed her drink and reluctantly headed back home. The fun would begin next week.

***

Luckily for Lilith, the next week flew by. She'd booked a last-minute trip to Costa Rica with the girls for the following week, so she spent the week preparing and packing and working extra hours so she could enjoy both her time in DC and Central America. Before she knew it, she was on the train to DC, heart pumping, and excited to see Brad again. They'd been emailing every day – mostly about work – but last night they'd started to get to know each other a little better, away from the climate change talk. Not only was he highly intelligent, but he was also cute and funny.

Lilith spent half the day working at the WeWork venue in the city before meeting at the bar by the river – pretending she'd just got out of her meeting. She saw him from a mile off and he looked better than she'd remembered. Dark blonde hair, clearly worked out, and with a smile that could knock anyone off their feet. Lilith almost fell over her chair getting up to greet him.

They defaulted to chatting about work and then he asked her why she was here, clearly not buying her 'urgent business trip' excuse.

Lilith answered in the best way she knew how. Honestly.

'I fancy fucking you.'

His eyes met hers and he smiled like she hadn't seen him smile before. It was different. Mischievous. Sexy.

'I felt the same way from the minute we met in NYC. And I really admire your work.'

Lilith smiled back. It was always nice to be appreciated for what you do, but he had no idea yet.

They set out looking for a hotel room. Not something

he'd done before. Something Lilith was now well-versed at and happy to show him the ropes. They found one not far from the bar that looked fairly high-end but, because it was mid-week, had lower-end prices. Lilith grabbed his hand and marched up to the reception desk. It was obvious what they were there to do but both of them looked like smart, respectable people, so who cared?

They got into the lift to the third floor and as soon as the doors closed, Lilith edged closer and kissed him slowly on his neck, smiling as an abundance of goosebumps appeared on the top half of his body. She'd gone all out this time. She'd brought her boom box as per usual, as well as some toys to enhance the experience, plus her sexiest lingerie set to date. He was in for a fun afternoon. They both were.

Brad was very clear about what he wanted. His fantasy was to be tied up to the bed, blindfolded, fully naked, at the mercy of a beautiful, mature woman. Lilith could definitely deliver on that one. Finally a guy who was ready to be dominated.

She stopped herself from undressing just yet, and instead ordered him to. His body was as beautiful as his smile (as she'd expected when she'd first seen him earlier today). This trip to DC was definitely worth it already. Lilith felt giddy, so she took a deep breath and closed her eyes for just a second, before getting back in 'the zone' and tying him up to the bed with his belt.

He was on all fours like a tamed wild cat, completely exposed, and it turned her on so much. Clearly so was he. His dick was hard and erect, waiting for her to take control and have her way with him. He started moaning in anticipation.

'This will never not be hot,' Lilith thought to herself as she could feel herself getting more and more turned on by the second.

He couldn't see her, so she took her time, determined to give him a day to write home about.

She used her hands to stroke him, softly at first, and then harder. She applied pressure on his spine, moving further and further down until he started begging her to take him. Lilith decided to have a little fun with it so made him repeat his wishes. Over and over again. *Consent is essential – nothing should ever be forced.* He asked for the third time, more insistently this time, so Lilith applied some lube to her hands and started massaging his asshole. She had the right audience this time.

'I'm going to come,' he said with his wavering breath.

Lilith could tell he was on the very edge but she ordered him to hold. He did for a little while but she could see how hard it was for him to wait. She was pleasuring herself at the same time, getting hotter and hotter, before whipping out a tiny dildo to vibrate up his ass for the grand finale. He came so hard, she was worried he was going to pass out. Luckily he didn't. And she came hard too, still dressed and having barely touched herself. How powerful! The trust and chemistry would be something to beat and Lilith already couldn't wait to renew the experience.

As he pulled his clothes back on and kissed her goodbye at the door, he told her he was relocating to Texas the following week.

What the fuck? Lilith flopped back onto the bed – she might not be in tears this time, but her pussy definitely was.

Seventeen

One thing Lilith had learnt was to always have a backup plan. Multiple plans in fact. B, C, D, E, F… all the way up to Z. The whole alphabet. The void she was trying to fill was immense now. As soon as she started to envisage any time alone, her anxiety levels started to rise up inside of her and she could feel herself fighting off more panic attacks.

Her solution? She needed to keep working on her pipeline. Especially when the cool, sexy guys she seemed to connect with moved all the way to Austin, Texas. How unfair. So instead of moping on the train home from DC, Lilith started looking for her next victim. The train journey was just over three hours – plenty of time to get acquainted with someone else who might be able to fulfil her needs and, most importantly, fill the void that was eating away at her.

Gazing around the carriage, she spotted him across the aisle. Good-looking in this American way, strong jawline, short hair, late twenties… No idea what was about to come his way. With all the confidence from her most recent encounter, Lilith got up and sat down opposite him. *The train was quiet so there were plenty of places to sit but she wanted him to know she'd sat there just for him.* Feigning indifference though at first, she started pretending to work, immersing herself behind her laptop with her glasses on (staring at a blank screen), and occasionally pausing to stare out of the train window – although secretly staring at him in the reflection and hoping to meet his gaze.

The train was moving at a fast pace now – almost in time with the beat of Lilith's heart. She had less than two hours to execute her plan. A cheeky prolonged gaze up from her laptop and she did it. She caught his eye and smiled lightly. He responded with a timid smile, not quite directly looking at her. Still, he looked cute, so Lilith decided to start the conversation.

'Heading to the city for work?' she asked curiously.

'No, just come from a quick trip to DC for work. I'm a consultant. I live in NYC on the Upper East Side…'

Lilith was watching his lips move, unsure of what he was actually saying now. All she'd needed to hear was that he lived in the city. She was already imagining those lips all over her, kissing her from her neck downwards, circling her belly button with his tongue, slowly moving towards her clit and making her come.

She shuffled around in her seat, managing to vaguely respond to his 'work' questions but her mind was on autopilot. She really wouldn't mind a consulting session with him. Lilith brought herself back into the room, well, carriage, before realising she actually did need to do some work. Plus, it was good to make herself not as available.

'I'm so sorry, I have a deadline I have to get to, so I best get back to tapping away.'

Lilith slid her glasses back on and prolonged her eye contact with him to see his reaction. He clearly wanted to keep talking.

'Sure, no problem. Why don't we exchange numbers and meet for a drink sometime?'

She liked a guy with initiative.

'How about tonight?' Lilith replied, still horny from last night's session and not in the mood to delay any further, especially not whilst he was so keen.

She wasn't sure how he was going to compare. Not that he'd offered to have sex (yet).

'Just a drink,' she followed up – just in case it was too forward for this time of day.

'Sure, why not. I never do this but you seem cool...' Blah blah blah, she'd heard it all before, but, still, it was exactly what she wanted to hear.

'Let's meet back at the station in a few hours and find some place close by so I can get home later,' Lilith replied as she packed away her things and put her number into his phone.

She blew him a kiss goodbye as she shouted 'See you later' before scuttling down the platform and out of the station concourse towards her beloved WeWork venue. She still wanted to provide an air of mystery and leave him lingering for more. And she seemed to have done exactly that.

Six o'clock soon came round. They'd exchanged a few messages since then – with him named aptly as 'DC train guy' in her phone. Who needed to know names when you could spot their glistening green eyes in a crowded bar? He'd ordered them a round of drinks, which Lilith was thankful for. She was tired from travelling and working up to the last moment to reach her deadlines, so needed something, or someone, to perk her up. She was pretty sure she was about to get both.

One drink turned into another one, and then one more. Just enough for them both to be feeling quite tipsy – and touchy-feely. His hands had already made their way from her waist to her bum and she wasn't complaining about it.

'Wanna come back to mine?' he asked, his lips lingering just in front of hers.

'Thought you'd never ask,' Lilith replied seductively.

There was just one teeny, tiny, minor detail DC train guy seemed to have omitted. He lived with his parents. A fact he told Lilith as he put the key into the front door and let her into the hallway, taking off her coat and hanging it up on the hooks by the door, ladened with other beautiful coats that clearly belonged to his mother.

They weren't in but Lilith was now slightly nervous about a potential encounter – especially with a woman who was likely a similar age to her. The promise of imminent action, however, was too strong. And he was already pulling her over to the sofa and undressing himself. How could she resist?

Turns out, DC train guy hadn't quite organised this encounter too well as his religious parents clicked open the door just in time to find their son in the missionary position on the sofa with a mature woman, who was in fact older than his mother.

Lilith had never moved so fast in her life, throwing her clothes back on and whispering 'Sorry' as she squeezed past them to grab her coat and make a quick exit into the night.

She burst into a fit of giggles as she stopped at the end of the street, hugging a lamp post and catching her breath. Just another item to cross off her bucket list that she'd never planned on having in the first place. What a day!

***

A few days later, Lilith was presenting at a launch event for work. The room was full and bustling with people eager to hear her speak – that or they were keen for her to finish speaking so they could go on lunch break. Either way, Lilith was in her element. She loved being able to talk to large audiences about what made her passionate. Plus it was a great place to connect with people – non-sexually of course.

Lilith had four rules. She didn't fuck women (she didn't like the taste of pussies, so wasn't sure what appealed for men), she didn't fuck married men or men in exclusive relationships (not fair for the other person), she didn't fuck men her age (too many potential complications if they or, God forbid, she, fell in love), and she didn't fuck colleagues.

She was about to break a few…

There he was, directly in her line of sight in the middle of the room. Completely off her radar until right now. He wasn't particularly attractive but something about him oozed sexual confidence and naughtiness – and that was just the sense she got from the intense, locked eye contact. He kept staring at her and he knew she knew it. She could feel that he was exploring. His smile was predatory.

She was about to experience how it felt to be chased and preyed upon. *Dangerous territory.*

So, he definitely didn't break the first rule – he wasn't a woman. *Well, so he said.* But he broke all the rest. Married. In an open relationship apparently. Lilith's age. And although not a direct colleague, he was on her professional periphery. He'd beelined for her the moment she finished speaking and had barely left the stage, holding two drinks in his hand – one for him and one for her. He started whispering in her ear all the things he wanted to do to her. Things she hadn't even dared exploring before. Golden showers, fucking him up the ass, threesomes, foursomes, group sex, anal sex, sex in forbidden places, BDSM... looked like she'd found a master. And for once, she wasn't in charge. It made her think of *Fifty Shades of Grey*, except he was no Christian. And she definitely was no Anastasia. Nope. They'd be having their own NYC version. Three episodes.

Episode One: Hotel lunch break in his room (he was staying over for the event). A total mess of fingers, dick, tongues, clitoris, body fluids (not going golden, as much as he begged for it), but no kissing. There was absolutely zero chemistry.

Episode Two: Bar toilets. They walked in separately with Lilith sneaking into his cubicle. She was still wearing the tights and dress she'd been wearing earlier for her presentation, so he pulled her dress up and tights down ever so slightly before fingering her from behind. She came in a minute as he pulled her hair. The ecstasy.

Episode Three: The service lift. This last episode, however, is completely platonic.

There was something that made Lilith feel weary about his instability. He was like an enhanced version of her own addiction. He was as lonely as she was and yet two lonely souls with no chemistry don't result in bonding – more like, destruction.

She decided she was uncomfortable pursuing this any further. For once, she had boundaries and she was setting this one firmly in the ground by telling him no more. It felt so empowering to say that, and he took it well. Although he messaged her a few hours later to tell her what an incredible day he'd had.

Lilith was exhausted. She'd experienced so much in the space of a few hours and definitely some of those things she didn't want to experience again. It was like she'd never really been there at all today. Just a shadow of herself, going with the motions. She needed a break. And fast.

Eighteen

I've just pulled down my sunglasses as I sit on the comfiest sun lounger of all time (honestly, it's better than my king-size bed at home) to be greeted by a hot, young Costa Rican in all-white linen clothes, serving me a pina colada. I smiled and thanked him before watching him totter back to the bar – but nothing else, don't worry.

That was the most action I'll be getting over the next couple of weeks and, honestly, I'm glad of it. It was nice to look and not touch, and simply take in the view. Speaking of which, the scenery (besides the men) is incredible. Everyone in New York seems to holiday in Florida or the Caribbean, but Costa Rica is where the real beauty lies. It's rugged, natural, and super green. An earth lover's paradise. Plus, it's ideal for the girls. They've already made friends with the hotel owner's teenagers, so they're currently playing in the main pool whilst I'm making the most of the peace around the adult-only pool. I'm one of the only ones here so I've even picked up a book from the communal reception area and settled into a sun lounger half in the shade. I've been craving vitamin D, but my hair colour means I'm also more prone to catching the sun a little too much, so best to be careful.

Checking in on arrival wasn't quite as smooth as I'd expected it to be. I was greeted with a 'Mrs' and 'When shall we expect your husband?', which was bizarre given he definitely wasn't on the booking. My 'Mrs' title, however, was. That's the shitty thing before the divorce papers come through. You're still married. You still have that bloody title. You still have people thinking you've got a significant other at home and that you're a wife. I'm not a wife – and, quite honestly, I don't know if I ever was. I've made a mental note to change all my personal details to 'Ms' for now. Not that that sounds much better. That makes me sound widowed or old. Of which I am neither. 'Miss', however, makes me sound too young. Naive. Inexperienced. And I'm none of those things either.

I need to put more suncream on my back, but I can't be arsed to go to the other pool to ask the girls to do it, so I've covered myself up with my shawl instead. When I order another drink from the hot bar man, I'm tempted to ask him to pop some on for me – although I'm not sure I'd be able to keep my hands to myself, so maybe I should abstain on this occasion…

Anyway, before I let my mind wander into dangerous territory, this holiday is exactly what I've needed. Getting away from it all. Feeling the sunshine on my face. Dipping my toes in the pool. Maybe I should move here. This would be much better than my dual life in the city. Although the girls wouldn't be able to visit often unless they moved here too and that seems a little far-fetched, so best to snap out of that daydream for now. A long-term change of scenery would be good, though. I need to get out of that house. And the WeWork offices still aren't giving me what I've been looking for: deep, meaningful connections. Everyone's doing their own thing instead of working together. It's lonely as fuck.

Also I realise I still haven't whittled down my pickings to a suitable therapist, let alone booked a session with anyone. If I'm honest with myself, I don't feel ready. And I don't know exactly what support I need. Some therapists get a bad rep. And I've completely bought into it. I can't be bothered for them to sit there staring at me and repeatedly asking me, 'And how does that make you feel?'

'Fucking shit, Susan, that's how it makes me feel!'

So, instead, for now, this is my therapy. Sitting around the pool with my journal in Costa Rica. Not bad, hey?

My topic for today is distinguishing sex from romance. Being able to compartmentalise. The million-dollar question: can you keep lust and desire intact in a relationship? Or does it erode with time no matter what? Is it easier to have a few regular 'friends with benefits' and not bother with intimacy because it makes you feel vulnerable? Can one person ever answer all your needs? Of course not. So why are marriage and monogamy so ingrained in our human culture? I think it's because we fear the unknown. We desperately want security. We think we want reassurance – which then morphs into ownership. When we feel attraction, we're desperate to remove the obstacles to reach intimacy. But what we actually end up doing is trapping ourselves instead of releasing ourselves. That's what I feel I've been doing, anyway. I put myself into a box I didn't really want to be in. And slowly but surely I've been banging down the walls and allowing myself to step outside of that box.

I'll always remember one of my best friends from London giving me his approval stamp when he heard I was on all the dating apps. 'Finally you're about to explore what you really desire!' It sounded like it was coming out of Lucifer's mouth (the Netflix series, not the actual devil, although he is quite devilish himself).

And he's right. I'm finally exploring what I want. It's not pretty sometimes and I feel like I'm on the wildest ride of my life with no sign of slowing down. But I know I'm on the right path. It's not for everyone. And there's probably another way to do it. One that involves less precarious situations and a lot less lube. But I'm enjoying the journey. That one, anyway.

I'm less enjoying the feeling of being out of control of my living situation. Being on standby. I want to move to an apartment in the city. Expand my new identity, single status, and show off my new self to the whole world instead of just a select few who don't even know me or the journey I've been on. I know I just need to be a bit more patient but if I can't stand the fucking house, why would anyone else want to live there?

I wish I could extend the trip here even longer and stay lounging, with countless cocktails being delivered to my hand by sexy guys who have no care in the world other than making their guests happy. Speaking of which, it's definitely time for me to order another pina colada after my self-therapy journalling session. The barman here is getting hotter the more I look at him and it's fun to play the role of the single, older lady who has nothing else to do other than sip drinks and look pretty.

Nineteen

Fresh from her Central American trip and all the accumulated heat, Lilith was ready to start a new chapter. Even if it wasn't in the way she'd imagined. And just like that, finally the universe magically aligned.

One of the consultants at Lilith's work, named Jared, who was based in the US, but she'd never met, remotely messaged her to say he was coming to NYC. She was so excited to spend time with another human for a few days. Especially a work colleague.

The day he was coming to meet Lilith at her WeWork, she had gotten herself there early so she could get some work done first before heading out to Starbucks to get them both a coffee. She didn't even know if he drank it, but she'd drink both if he didn't – she could always use an extra energy boost.

They hit it off straight away (as colleagues, nothing more), sharing the same banter, working side by side, and both enjoying coffee (phew). Lilith even got more work done than usual. It was the perfect balance. And she finally felt inspired. But that wasn't all.

'Hey, I've got someone I'd really like you to meet,' Jared said to Lilith as they both started packing up their things.

'Yeah?' said Lilith, suddenly intrigued and wondering where the day was going to take her next.

'You're going to love her. Her office is literally just around the corner from here. You cool to head over?' Jared asked with a big smile that would be hard to refuse in any situation.

'Sure!' replied Lilith, even more intrigued that she'd be meeting a woman.

'I've got to head back to my hotel to get ready to go out for a business dinner tonight, but I'll drop you round and introduce you. Lorna is amazing – we've been friends for years, and I think you'll get on like a house on fire.'

He wasn't wrong.

Lilith walked into Lorna's office and felt instantly at home. They both worked in the same field, so she knew they'd have lots to talk about, but something about Lorna already felt more personal. She had long honey-blonde hair, big brown eyes, and a warm smile. She gave Jared a big hug as they exchanged a few back-and-forth quips and giggles before Jared blew them both a kiss goodbye and headed back down into the lift.

'He's great, isn't he?' said Lorna. 'It's so good to meet you, come sit down. Do you want a coffee?'

So many pleasantries all at once, Lilith didn't know where to start. She settled herself into the couch by the window, looking around at the New York skyline, and nodded yes for a coffee.

'It's so nice to start connecting with like-minded people,' Lilith said as she gazed out of the window.

'Still can't get over the skyline, huh?' Lorna smiled as she took a seat opposite.

'I just love being in the city. I'm over in Little Haven and it feels like a million miles away from here. Just not somewhere I feel inspired to be,' Lilith replied without looking up.

'Ugh, I feel you. I'm over on the west side and even though it's a little closer to the city, it's still not close enough.'

Lilith looked up and smiled over sympathetically. 'You married?'

Lorna's smile faded slightly. 'Yes,' she replied hesitantly.

'I feel like there's more to that story?' Lilith sat up straighter and gave her full attention.

'Ha, let's just say sometimes I like to forget I'm married,' replied Lorna. 'And I think he likes to forget sometimes too.'

'I've just come out of something like that,' Lilith said before she could stop herself 'Me and a million other women I'm sure.'

A younger woman with glasses and a flattering navy pencil skirt walked over with two coffees on a tray, along with some delicious-looking chocolate biscuits.

'Now that's what the doctor ordered,' Lorna said with a big smile appearing back on her face as she thanked her assistant and took the tray off her. 'Please help yourself,' she ushered Lilith as she took a biscuit and nearly devoured it in one bite.

Both women laughed.

Lilith hugged her coffee mug to her chest and felt herself internally sigh. A sigh of deep relief. She felt like she was meeting her guardian angel at last. The person she'd been looking for all this time. They stayed chatting for close to two hours, as the lights faded throughout the office and everyone went home.

It was just the two of them and she didn't know how, but in the middle of nowhere she started crying in front of someone who was essentially a stranger. But there was something about Lorna that made Lilith feel safe. She was kind and she listened and she understood.

Lilith realised she hadn't had much female presence around her in the past few months, except for the girls. And she was hardly going to turn to them for advice or break down in tears in front of them and tell them how much she hated her life. The truth was she didn't fully hate her life, but she hated certain aspects of it. Her days had revolved around a lot of progesterone and sex lately, and not much else.

'Why don't you come work from here for a while and use these offices as your base?'

Lilith wiped the tears from her face and looked up in disbelief.

'Are you sure?' she asked, not quite wanting to hear the answer in case she instantly changed her mind.

'Absolutely. You'll get loads more done here and there's so many great people in the office, including myself, who you can bounce ideas from,' Lorna replied, smiling.

'You've no idea how much this means to me,' Lilith replied as she stood up to give her new-found friend, and now apparent work colleague, a hug.

'I'll see you tomorrow, right?' Lorna said, as she returned the hug and squeezed Lilith's hands.

'Bright and early!' Lilith responded, almost skipping on her way out.

***

The next couple of weeks were a godsend. It was such a relief for Lilith to finally feel part of something. That she actually belonged somewhere and was making a life for herself. She might have only been a 'guest' at the office, but she was a very grateful guest for now. It even gave her courage for a little while to stop constantly checking her apps and looking for her next match. Instead, she found her days far more focused. She was able to concentrate for longer periods of time, surrounded by other people she didn't know yet but that at least worked in the same industry as her – and they seemed genuinely nice. She'd often meet Lorna for lunch, putting their world of work to rights, not yet sharing anything too personal.

Post-work evenings, however, were still just as lonely as they'd always been and Lilith found herself craving the attention that connecting with guys and having sex gave her.

Thursday evening was a particularly slow night and within an hour of being home, Lilith had downloaded the apps back onto her phone. The moment her profile reappeared, she realised just how much she'd missed this. This part of her life felt so secretive and naughty, but it was her life. Her own little piece of heaven that no one else knew about – and that gave her a rush just thinking about it.

The first (suitable) match back on the apps was a tech entrepreneur. He was into vertical farming – a concept Lilith wasn't remotely familiar with, so she hit a quick search into Google and read enough so she'd be able to hold a conversation about it. This was just one of the things she loved about her exploration. It wasn't just about the sexual discovery; it was also about all the new things she was learning as a result: about herself, about others, and about the world. It kept her young, curious, and willing.

She hadn't always been conscious of it but twenty-five to thirty-five had become Lilith's default age bracket. Was it to explore a different group of people? A different mindset? A different set of values? Or perhaps she simply didn't want to compete with people her own age. Perhaps she also knew there was usually nothing else possible than just casual encounters and fun. It was simple. No endless questions about a potential future or even establishing a traditional relationship. She got to bypass that part and continue with her life on to the next and the next.

Sometimes she felt like she wanted to be a big sister figure for them or, dare she think it, a mum figure! She knew it sounded weird, especially in this context, but there was almost this desire to be a role model and to teach them the ways of the world. And to learn from them. Sometimes it was about wanting to enjoy some hot fun with younger bodies (although a lot of them were also inexperienced and therefore not so great at sex – cue teaching role). Sometimes she was looking for a youth elixir to relive the years where she was that age and already married. But what it all came down to really was loneliness and the desire for human connections. To connect with another soul on this planet in the same place and time that she was. To feel wanted just for a couple of hours.

It was hard to generalise but so far all the millennials Lilith had had the chance to meet in NYC, either virtually or in person, had some common traits for sure. Some good and some not so good – which meant she had quite a thorough selection process to help wade through the bad ones. She'd chat to them initially via the apps – you didn't want to give your direct contact details to any old (young) random person. Red flags included receiving a dick pic within a few minutes of the conversation (nothing left for the imagination and something she found plainly rude), and/or a Trump or Republican vote. Both were a big no-no. Even for casual encounters, she needed to have standards. Easy, but not that desperate.

Most of them had interesting careers and lifestyle choices. Several projects going on at the same time, not wanting a linear career anymore, not wanting to settle down and do the whole marriage and two point four children thing – 'So I'm an entrepreneur', 'I'm in the tech industry', 'I've set up my own charity', 'I'm also an actor', 'I host my own podcast, 'and by the way I never want to settle', 'it's the end of marriage as we know it', 'Open relationships are the way forward'...

These were the conversation starters that always intrigued Lilith. Maybe because they were more aligned with her own values and how she was now looking at life. Nothing had to be clear-cut. You could do whatever you wanted, no restraints. Society's model of what was 'acceptable' was slowly changing. At least for these guys anyway. The millennials.

It was 'normal' for them to hook up on dating apps, have one-night stands, and have several dates on the go at once. And it was also normal to connect virtually first to get a feel for someone before you met them. It gave you the chance to weed out the people you knew weren't a good fit, instead of having to excuse yourself from an in-person date by feigning a family emergency or, worse, climbing out of the bathroom window. You just blocked and deleted instead. Much more efficient.

Lilith wondered where she'd be now if she'd have been born ten or twenty years later. Still, just because she wasn't born at the same time didn't mean she couldn't immerse herself in the millennial life and embrace the mindset. One of the hardest things though was keeping up with the various slang words and trying to sound cool. If her daughters could hear some of the things she said, they'd be so embarrassed. 'Dope', 'yolo', 'word', using all sorts of different emojis and knowing how and when to use them, typing fast on WhatsApp/Snapchat so guys didn't think she was a dinosaur, the phrase 'Netflix and chill' and what that *really* meant… All of it was keeping her young and in the know – and attracting the 'dudes' she liked in the process, even if she did end up taking on the role of confidant/coach/therapist more often than not.

Mr Tech Entrepreneur was, of course, a millennial. And as a first for Lilith, they met at his place during the day. A penthouse in Brooklyn with extraordinary views of Manhattan. Clearly, vertical farming was treating him rather well and immediately Lilith wondered how he'd do horizontally. He was well built (obviously went to the gym) and held himself with an aura of confidence and sexiness, so much so she felt younger than him, as if he was in control.

The sex was great. To Lilith's standards anyway. Deep, penetrative, attentive, plenty of eye contact. Rolling around on crisp white sheets with NYC in the background. She left content, with the sun shining brightly outside. A regular friend with benefits maybe? Lilith pulled out her phone and messaged him (also a first) but he didn't respond for a few days. It was so frustrating – to not have control – but those were the unspoken rules. You can't expect reciprocity either in time or in intensity.

He finally responded by saying that he didn't want to meet again. He was too scared to fall in love and couldn't take the risk to derail his attention from his (very successful) business venture. Lilith was both flattered and deflated. She'd clearly had an effect on him. What next? Or rather, *who* next?

Twenty

Oh my God, I'm so excited (and relieved) to be here! I'm back in London. Sadly, not for long enough, but, still, I'm taking in every moment – literally down to the second. A little work trip here and then on to Paris. I even managed the flight without my trusty Xanax. The moment I stepped on the plane, I felt my breathing return to its natural state. My chest rising and falling effortlessly and calmly. I didn't even need to order myself an alcoholic drink – just fuelled myself with coffee and hot chocolate.

I had over six hours to kill, though, so I focused my attention on watching some light series on my iPad. Mainly *Friends* and *How I Met Your Mother*. Nothing too taxing. Having Wi-Fi on planes is genius. I felt connected with the rest of the world the whole journey, so there were zero panic attacks. I was also tempted to join the mile high club via self-pleasure but the plane's set-up was pretty constraining, so I decided to save that for another time – or with someone else perhaps!

Instead, I switched to Tinder, changing my location to London (not sure that the app would have picked up my location above the Atlantic), and let my mind wander. Imagine if there'd been someone on the plane who was a good match and could have fulfilled my mile high fantasy – even though I'd determined it wasn't much of a fantasy I was particularly fussed about given the logistics and constraints. Anyway, it was my first time exploring on the app with potential subjects of Her Majesty and I was excited to connect with someone British. Something new to add to my repertoire!

I connected with a British guy with a French surname (go figure) who looked extremely dashing, and before I knew it we were having a very heated exchange that I was struggling to deal with whilst sitting in my tiny window seat with very minimal legroom, without raising the suspicions of my fellow passengers. We shared nude pictures and explicit messages – my pics obviously taken from my extensive private photo album on my phone as opposed to rushing to the plane bathroom to strip off. I learnt a few months ago (from my many millennial encounters) that it's called sexting. I wasn't sure I was going to be able to wait much longer before fucking him IRL.

Luckily, I had some spare time when I landed as my friends weren't expecting me for hours – plus I wasn't starting work until the next day. It was Sunday, after all. He seemed to be on the same wavelength as me and sent me his address. Special home delivery all the way from New York City, straight off the plane. With each encounter, I seem to surpass myself. I honestly never know what I'm going to do next. That's part of the thrill.

I was so horny in the black cab on the way from the airport to Islington (where he lived). It was an area I knew well – not far from where I used to live. It felt nostalgic in the weirdest way. The last time I was here, I certainly wasn't doing this, with this man. *A different lifetime.* We kept chatting during the journey, longing for each other a little more with every message. I was glad the cab driver wasn't in the mood to chat as I wouldn't have been able to concentrate, and I hate coming across rude to people. London, much like New York, is always bustling with busy people. There's often no time to stop and say 'Hello'.

When I finally got to Islington Guy's house (really must take note of names more – especially when they looked like him), he was waiting for me at the front door... looking absolutely gorgeous with the most luminous smile. My God, even just thinking about him now gets me weak at the knees – *or, more accurately, wet in my pants.* He was even better-looking than in his photos, which rarely ever happens. Anyway, he offered for me to freshen up in his bathroom, which I graciously accepted after my long-haul flight – even though I had a feeling I was about to get even more sweaty. His bathroom was almost as gorgeous as he was and I wondered if he'd designed it himself or if this was the result of a woman's touch at some point. The walk-in shower with olive green tiles and gold fittings was like stepping into a boutique hotel. There were even some matching bottles of body wash and moisturiser ready for me to use. What a treat!

I walked into the bedroom from his shower, wrapped in the tiniest towel that barely covered my bum, and found him waiting naked on his bed with the body of a god. Honestly, he was so fit I wondered if he was actually real – I found myself standing still and gawping at him for longer than I'd have wanted him to see but managed to compose myself at the last second, slowly letting the towel drop from my body.

There was a massive wall mirror behind his bed and I could see his dick rising hard as he watched me approach him. I positioned myself strategically so he could see my ass, opened my mouth and moved towards his beautiful, erect penis. I wouldn't usually say that about penises but this one really left its mark. I've seen a few and I know a good one when I see one. It's rarely about the size – I'd say shape matters more. But that's just me.

I blew him up and down, licking him all the way from his balls to the tip, around and down again. He moaned and stroked my thighs but I didn't want him to come yet. I sat on him and let him penetrate me deep, riding him and touching my clit at the same time (my signature move), as he held my breasts and pinched my nipples with just the right amount of pressure. We moved in perfect unison and as I watched myself in the mirror, I felt invincible. Like a goddess. I felt powerful. Beautiful. But most of all, I felt like me. For the first time in a very long time. I felt less empty and less lonely. As if I just knew things were going to be okay eventually. That I was on the right path. (And clearly I was on the right person at this moment in time.)

We both came hard at the same time. Pretty magic. It felt so natural. And even though we didn't speak much, there was no need because the connection was there. He offered me a cup of tea with a cloud of milk (how very British!), which I happily took. Then I sat on the edge of the bed, swinging my feet, and admired my surroundings. A beautiful apartment in the heart of Islington with the coolest, sexiest guy, and an encounter to remember. We smiled, acknowledging this moment only strangers could share, and I made my way back to my hotel feeling like I was walking on water. Who needs wings?

Twenty-One

Lilith was back in NYC after her soul-cleansing trip to Europe, feeling utterly refreshed – and satisfied. She hadn't needed to match with any guys once she got to Paris as she was still riding the wave of her London encounter and enjoying the feeling of not feeling so lonely anymore. She'd spent time with friends and family, and even though she didn't share with them about her life as much as she wanted to, it was good to be back in a familiar setting with the people she loved.

Winter had finally ended, so it could only get better from here. There were no interim seasons in this part of the planet. Simply from snow to hot days, with no transition. Coming back to an actual office and colleagues in sunny NYC made such a difference – even if they weren't technically her colleagues just yet. Lorna had just texted that morning to tell her there'd be a job opening soon and she should apply. Perfect! How great would that be to properly belong and have a permanent desk?!

To celebrate, Lilith decided to go for a drink with one

of the guys she'd been chatting to for the last few days. He seemed super nice and respectful and luckily didn't send any dodgy dick pics, which was always a relief. She even managed to remember his name this time. *Kyle.*

They agreed to meet at a rooftop bar Lilith had been eyeing up now that the weather was good, and they'd take things from there. How civilised of them. Once she reached the top of the stairs, she started looking for him but couldn't find him in her immediate scan. Maybe he had decided not to show up? It wouldn't be the first time for something like this to happen in the world of dating and hooking up, but it would be the first time for Lilith.

Finally, after reluctantly sloping over to the bar to drink by herself, she spotted someone waving from their chair. It was him. Lilith found it a little odd that he wouldn't stand to greet her but as she walked towards him, she realised he was sitting in a wheelchair. What was the etiquette here? He was so cute, she was sure they could have fun – whatever he was comfortable with.

She decided to ignore the elephant in the room for now and instead bent down to greet him before asking him what he wanted to drink. It was nice to buy the drinks sometimes instead of the other way round.

'You're gorgeous,' he said as Lilith passed him a beer and settled into a chair next to him, slowly brushing her hand across his lap.

'You're not so bad yourself,' Lilith responded as they continued to flirt openly.

She loved his energy so they had a few more drinks together and discussed fantasies. He'd never been with an older woman before and that was one of his biggest ones.

Lilith told him that she found him very fuckable and would love to explore more. He agreed. With that, she booked a hotel room nearby on a Dayuse app, which didn't reveal the room type until you got there. An app she'd definitely be using more often – how convenient!

The hotel was showing as just a couple of blocks away, so they downed the rest of their drinks and made their way there – Lilith was impressed at how quickly he could get around in his chair with his arms. She was almost trotting to keep up.

All of a sudden, she became so much more conscious of everything given his situation and realised just how unfriendly NYC was for disabled people – or anyone remotely physically or emotionally vulnerable, for that matter. NYC was such a rough city, where gentleness didn't seem to have a place. You needed to be young, healthy, and wealthy to survive. On your toes, constantly prepared for your next move – always on the go. It'd either break you or make you and Lilith wasn't sure what camp she was sitting in at the moment. There was a song with lyrics she loved that described this feeling well, about living in NYC once and departing before it made you too hard. She pondered on it for a moment before realising they were standing outside the hotel.

'After you,' said Kyle as he ushered her to the front doors with a glint in his eyes.

'Why thank you.' Lilith giggled as she let herself into the foyer, holding the door wide open so he could navigate safely in himself.

Lilith checked them in quickly at the reception desk, finding that the receptionist didn't once meet her eyes. She handed her the key and pointed towards the lift. They were on the third floor. But as they opened the door of number 313, Lilith cursed the receptionist lustily. The room had two bunk beds.

She looked at Kyle and they started laughing out loud until they were howling. He clearly had a great sense of humour. She dialled reception from the room phone to be told that this was their only room left. The hotel was completely full. Whether that was true or not, Lilith wasn't sure, but she wasn't about to argue it. So what to do? One of them was already in a good position, so she decided they'd just adapt. He wheeled himself into the room and Lilith locked the door behind them, popping the 'Do not disturb' sign on the outside handle.

Out came the boom box (her most loyal companion) and her sexiest playlist. She'd been playing around with different songs lately to find ones that had good rhythm and turned her on. She started stripping slowly, in time with the music, and revealed some sexy pink underwear underneath her dress. Her room companion seemed to be enjoying the show and she got the answer to the question she hadn't dared ask.

She approached Kyle and unzipped his trousers before shimmying down to her knees. She was fully naked now and gave him a blow job to remember (her favourite phrase). Something to remember over the bunk beds at least. Then, she stood and turned around so she had her back towards him, squatting on his dick as he stayed in his chair, making sure not to put extra pressure on him or hurt him. It definitely required some core strength and a little extra workout for Lilith but the angle worked well.

She slid up and down whilst massaging her clit, before they both came quickly, continuing to laugh.

Lilith would never know what his disability was but he clearly didn't want the moment to be defined in that way and she felt it was important to honour that. What an experience. And what a top guy.

Twenty-Two

3 June 2018

I can't believe it's June already. And it's hot! For so many different reasons…

My first virtual sex guy, Victor, from Paris, has been messaging me on and off since we first virtually 'hooked up'. Yes, the guy from Christmas who made the holiday period far more enjoyable than it was planned to be. That one! In fact, we've had a few more virtual sex encounters since then – each one more steamier than the one before. The last time we spoke, I told him my fantasy of shaving each other and letting him come all over me. *It's a good one – definitely something I'll keep for future courting.* We ended that conversation agreeing to meet in person in Paris. The day before yesterday! It felt like we'd had a long-distance relationship even though we'd never met so I was equally excited and nervous to meet him.

Anyway! (I'm getting butterflies just writing this down.) I flew to Paris three days ago as I'm pairing a work trip with attending a friend's wedding a couple of days later. I flew a couple of days early so I could meet Victor. How could I not?!

The day before yesterday, I walked to the pizza place he'd booked. The weather was glorious, so I was able to wear a slinky day dress and my favourite sunnies. Honestly, I was already feeling on top of the world, so I knew the experience could only top it. He was already sitting outside at a table by the Seine, beaming at me. I hugged him tightly and sat down opposite him. We both love food, so shared a massive pizza – half meat, half veggie. He was carnivorous and I was dying to be devoured. We chatted about an array of topics as if we had a lifetime to catch up on. In a way, we did. It was fluid and felt so natural. Like meeting up with a kindred spirit.

We walked back to his place around the corner, arm in arm. It felt intimate. Right. He usually lives with his older brother, who wasn't there, thankfully. Not that I didn't want to meet him but just that I was so desperate to rip Victor's clothes off.

We kissed in his bedroom and he undressed me first. I was wearing my blue lacy underwear with a purposely placed hole at the back. He unzipped his trousers and whispered that he wanted to take me, and I must stay very still. Obviously I obliged.

He pushed me onto the bed firmly and penetrated me, slowly. I was already very wet and came fast. He followed quickly. The last six months combined into one as our bodies finally came together.

We showered with natural soap from Marseille, giggling as we lathered each other's bodies and playfully kissed each other. I broke one of my rules by sleeping in his bed overnight before flying out to Barcelona early the next day for a work conference. Oops. I'd do it all over again, though.

And we did. We agreed to meet again at my hotel in Paris last night. I couldn't get back quick enough and found myself daydreaming about him all day instead of focusing on work. Who could blame me? We fucked each other hard again and he stayed for the night. All my rules thrown out the window. Out of which the Eiffel Tower was scintillating, not that far away.

I'm now on my way to spend the day with my parents and as much as I want to see them, I can't help wishing I was spending some more time with Victor. Our connection is absolutely unique and he's the first guy I've met that I feel I can rely on. We're not in a relationship, let alone a conventional one, but I know we're going to stay connected for a long time. We've even planned to spend a weekend together at the end of summer in NYC. I feel much stronger than I ever have before. More human. More 'me'.

7 June 2018

I'm on the plane back to NYC after a whirlwind few days. Yesterday I was at one of my oldest friends', Sarah's, wedding. She'd met Laurent a few years before and fell madly in love. They engaged last year and planned an intimate ceremony just outside of my parents' place with close family and friends.

I found myself zoning out during the ceremony itself

despite the backdrop being so beautiful. We were sitting outside and there were flowers everywhere. It was like a scene from a movie. Only I didn't long to be those two people standing opposite each other, declaring their vows to be with one another 'till death do us part'. I was happy for them but I was also happy for myself. No strings attached. It's a totally different experience watching a wedding when you're no longer in love yourself and don't want that as your future. Still, I had a great time drinking and dancing with old friends and celebrating love. It's a beautiful thing and I don't want to become immune to it.

16 June 2018

This is turning out to be my favourite month so far. I applied for the job Lorna suggested, and I got it! I don't start until September but I'm over the fucking moon. Real-life colleagues at last. New beginnings! I've found I've not been on the apps as much either. No longer scrolling every minute of every day. I'm focusing more, although I do let myself get distracted sometimes…

I was invited to a networking event last night at a new friend's house. We first made contact at my co-working space – I've met some really cool people there so far. People from all walks of life, working on super exciting projects. Anyway, it was great to connect further over some drinks and nibbles, and meet even more people who I'm going to follow up with next week.

I got a new match on the apps earlier this week and, in my new sense of being, I only responded briefly. He seemed keen though and kept messaging me – something about that urgency appealed and I wondered if maybe he was someone like Victor. Based in NYC would be even better. So, in that spirit, I agreed to meet him for a drink late after the networking event.

It was already 11 p.m. when I walked into some small bar on the Lower East Side. He was there, waiting for me – his smile and dark eyes piercing through my strong armour. Fuck. I already knew it wasn't going to end well and had a feeling of dread. But I was hypnotised. I feel like I'm almost an addict to these connections. To these guys. I couldn't leave. My feet were rooted to the floor and I knew I wanted him. We had a quick drink before he invited me back to his place and I was a little peeved when we walked into a hotel. Did he live there permanently or was he some kind of super wealthy kid? Apparently, neither of those. He was on a work trip… with all of his colleagues staying in rooms next to his. (Little did they know they would be complaining to him the next morning about the noise level of a couple fucking and screaming from pleasure all night!)

He told me he lived in LA and was travelling to Istanbul the next day. So that explained the sense of urgency in his messages. I wondered if he did this all the time – if I was just another notch on the bedpost. Not that he wasn't the same for me – I just wondered about it. For some reason, it bothered me this time. He was already feeling like forbidden fruit.

The minute we entered his room until the minute I left the next morning, we kissed, fucked, and made love so many times, in so many different ways, it was electrifying.

It felt different to all the other times. I honestly don't know what's happening to me. I still feel breathless now. My whole body is on high alert, burning for his multiple touches. I'm completely under his spell and I refuse to accept that it was just a one-off encounter. I had to physically extract myself from his room to get to work. It literally pained me to close the door behind me in case I never see him again. I can't think of anything else other than sex with him, and, most alarmingly, of him. Who is he? This mystery guy? I've written down all the small clues he gave me during our night together. He's called Marcus and he's a management consultant. I'm trying to rationalise myself. He lives in LA and is going to be in Istanbul all summer. There's no way we'll stay in touch. He kept saying it was just a one-night stand. I'm scared this is quickly turning into an obsession and I'm going to get hurt. In fact, I already know that it's going to hurt because I can't stop thinking about him and it's not even been twenty-four hours yet. I can't seem to do or think of anything else. I can hardly focus at work – thank God I'm not in my new role yet. Although my first event is going to be in… LA. Unbelievable. I have an official excuse to meet him again but I'm not sure that's a good thing. I *know* it's not a good thing. But I don't want to lose contact.

28 June 2018

Somehow I've managed to keep in touch with Marcus, even if not exactly in the way I'd like. We've been sexting since he got to Istanbul. Always when he's in his hotel room, never anywhere else. I suspect he's lonely (or bored, or both) and that's his way of entertaining himself. The thought of a one-sided interaction where I'm the one always available and oversharing – messages, pictures – lurks in the back of my mind. I feel like I'm on a leash. All he needs to do is pull and I'm there. Is it lust or love? I don't know. But it's probably not healthy.

He's even downloaded a special software so we can keep messaging each other despite the restrictions in Istanbul. I've been sexting him at work. On trains. In the supermarket. On walks. On boats. On the beach. With friends. With my kids. In the car. In my room. On my sofa. At bars. In shops. When exercising. When sleeping at night (yes, it's possible). Everywhere. All the time.

I've noticed I've started to lose weight. I'm hardly eating anything because my mind is so focused elsewhere – in the wrong place. I don't even play on the app anymore because I'm so engrossed with him. This one encounter two weeks ago has seemingly flipped my life upside down. Once again. I was doing so well… Even Victor has told me to be careful and not burn myself out. Wise man. I've got these incandescent desires that nothing will stop.

30 June 2018

Marcus has gone offline as he's travelling for two weeks. He's been sending me the odd cryptic message to make sure I'm still hooked but otherwise it's been radio silence and I've just been left hanging, waiting for his return. I decided that if he's going to be offline for a couple of weeks playing hard to get, I'm going to have my own fun. Revenge, you could call it.

I'm on the plane back to NYC now but I was at a wedding in France yesterday. I felt like I was on the hunt to replicate the same level of intensity I've been feeling recently. Honestly, I was feeling pretty wild – verging on feral. (I know, hard to fathom.) I drank a lot more than I should have done. Alcohol is my best friend at the moment, although I'm not sure it's the healthiest of relationships. It's the only way I've found to numb the pain – and I'm not into drugs (the other kind). I decided I needed to be fucked by someone last night. A friend's wedding, I agree, was probably not my best location, but it was what I had to work with.

I spotted someone from the groom's side that would do the job. He was young, late twenties – matched my usual demographics. I also decided that if I closed my eyes, he might just have looked like Marcus. He definitely didn't but I was too drunk to care. Luckily for me, so was he.

We danced together on the dance floor, flirting, all eyes on us. I didn't give a damn even though I should have. It was the first time I was openly myself in front of people who knew me. That part felt good. But I'd probably have to deal with the consequences later.

It was a warm evening and the wedding was being held in the most gorgeous castle grounds. Luckily for me, that meant plenty of nooks and crannies and outdoor space to explore where no one else was around. We kissed behind a tree, away from the noise and from everyone else. He was an incredible kisser and he smelt amazing. I breathed in his smell and kissed him all the way up his neck before returning to his lips. I was feeling high and very horny. Everything else forgotten about just for that moment.

I ordered him to fuck me rough against the tree – enough with the preliminaries. He unzipped his trousers, got his hard dick out, pulled up my dress, and fucked me deep just how I'd asked. It felt good. And for a short while, I didn't think of anything else. My brain was finally off. Marcus, NYC, Istanbul, the guys I've fucked and the hundreds I've chatted with, the fear, the loneliness, the void, the risks, the madness of the last six months… all of it disappeared for a few minutes of total ecstasy.

Today, however, I'm feeling completely differently. This morning at breakfast, me and my fuck buddy didn't even say 'Hi' or acknowledge each other. My friends were looking at me quizzically. And I've not heard a peep from Marcus. I'm in agony.

Twenty-Three

Lilith was settling back into her life in NYC. The height of summer had well and truly hit and it was steamy, sticky, and hot… but not in the way Lilith would have liked. She was still feeling rather flat and there was no news from Marcus. Was he ghosting her? He clearly didn't need her anymore now that he'd left his Istanbul hotel room. He probably had multiple women on the go from all different countries, ages, and backgrounds. Expanding his horizons. Lilith felt used.

She didn't have a lot of self-esteem left but enough not to chase him. She knew better than that – even if it was excruciating. More than that, she wondered how exactly he'd taken a hold of her. What was it about him that had drawn her in more than the rest? Why couldn't she let him go? What makes some people more attractive to others? What creates infatuation? And, most importantly, how does one move on from it?

She decided to try to focus on the current cohort. Not a lot of connections going on at the moment but that was probably for the best. It was Saturday and she had the whole weekend to herself. Something she would have longed for six months ago, but something she dreaded now. None of her friends were available and the girls were with their dad. She had no choice but to revert to what she did best – her favourite hobby. Back to the scroll and swipe.

The next guy lived upstate and picked her up from the end of her road in his not so glamorous car. He seemed nice, though. Normal. Genuine. They got back to his place and simply hung out – chatting about the mundanities of everyday life and throwing in some flirty banter. He lived with his siblings by the Hudson and he took her there to show her. An idyllic life, some could say. Lilith stripped naked on the riverbank as they agreed to go skinny-dipping in the river. They jumped in and swam circles around each other, enjoying the refreshing water. Lilith could see how it could turn into erotic water games, but for some reason she couldn't go there. She knew he was a great guy but she felt like she was using him – and that didn't sit right with her.

She got out of the water, put her clothes back on, and asked him to drive her home. He seemed a little disappointed but was respectful of her decision, put his clothes back on, and drove her back with his hand on her lap. Lilith felt a tear start to fall down her cheek, so she quickly wiped it away, kissed him on the cheek goodbye and retreated back into her house. It was getting late now and the sun had set but Lilith couldn't bring herself to turn the lights on. She simply sat hunched up on the floor in front of the sofa, rocking herself back and forth, wondering what was wrong with her. Had she lost her mojo? She'd definitely lost her mind…

An hour later Lilith was still sitting in the same spot, although by now her bum was well and truly numb and it was time to at least crawl up to the sofa and get comfortable. She decided to team this with getting herself a glass of wine from the fridge and a handful of nuts from the cupboard. She hadn't eaten since breakfast time but she wasn't really hungry and it felt too late to eat a big meal now.

As she sat back down, her phone pinged with a message. Who would that be at this time?

It was Evan. Her first vice. Her heart didn't pang for him like it used to. That was a feeling now reserved for Marcus instead – even though it currently felt like it was wasted. She and Evan had been in touch sporadically after the French exit disaster and slowly started building their connection again, but zero action. No sexting. No flirty banter. It was actually really nice to hear from him. He almost felt like an old friend. Comfortable. Safe. Warm. Lilith felt a smile return to her face and her breathing started to return to a normal rhythm. He asked if she'd like to meet the next day to go to the museum and a meal afterwards. It felt rather like a date, but why not? Lilith replied saying she'd loved to, before downing the rest of her wine and taking herself to bed. She felt like she was going to sleep better than she'd imagined when she'd first got home, so that was something.

The next afternoon, Lilith was waiting outside of the museum, looking out for her handsome Latino guy she hadn't seen for over six months. The first man she'd properly connected with on the app. It felt nostalgic and wholesome. Things she hadn't really allowed herself to feel for a long time.

She spotted him from a mile off. You couldn't miss him. Those piercing blue eyes and charming smile. Her cheeks hurt from smiling back at him as he gave her a big wave and came running over, picking her up off the floor in a big hug.

'Long time no see, beautiful!'

'It's so good to see you,' Lilith found herself gushing as she gave him a big squeeze back.

All of the tension she'd been experiencing over the last few weeks started to evaporate and ease up being in his presence. He was like a big ray of light and she realised she needed this kind of energy in her life.

The evening went by almost too quickly. They chatted for hours – they had a lot to catch up on – and spent the whole time laughing and enjoying each other's company. It was full of warmth and love, but very platonic love. And Lilith liked that. She started to wonder if what she was actually looking for was companionship? The kind that made you feel safe and warm and fuzzy. Friendships were so much easier and valuable than those damn illusive hot guys. Especially the ones who lived in LA and travelled the world.

After Evan and Lilith parted ways at the foot of the Rockefeller Center, Lilith took herself the long route round the city to the train station, taking in the lights and the hustle and bustle. Even if it was just for this night, she felt content and whole again. Like the little pieces of her heart were being mended, even if they might fall apart again the next day. Right here, right now, all was well.

But she still had this nagging feeling as she walked around the city. She always wanted more. And she was starting to feel pretty horny.

As she reached the train station and waited for her train back to the suburbs, she opened up her apps and started messaging one of the guys (name forgotten) she'd been in touch with recently and told him she was about to take the train back home. He was one of those that constantly sent her filthy dick pics and videos of his erect penis, usually full of his come, which she tended to respond to in a very pragmatic and non-committal way. That or she'd just block and delete. (It was yawnable and boring. If there's no thrill of the chase and it's all served on a 'hot' plate, what was the actual point?) Anyway, he'd managed to stay active on her phone and she'd obviously kept him there for a reason.

'Want to have some fun?' Lilith messaged.

She hadn't shared any parts of her body with him yet but he dared her to video herself in the train's toilets. Lilith took the dare and joined him there. Virtually, of course. He, however, wasn't on a train but in the comfort of his own home, which looked a little like a train toilet if Lilith was honest, but that was by the by.

They both wanked in front of their phones, whispering expletives to each other, and losing themselves in the moment. Lilith came hard and he did too – at the same time; how novel. She didn't see his face and he couldn't see hers. The perfect encounter. She was interrupted, however, by someone knocking incessantly on the cubicle door.

'Shit!' Lilith exclaimed as she typed her goodbyes, pulled up her knickers, and emerged from the toilets with a little pinkness to her cheeks.

She kept her head down as she slunk back to her seat, giggling to herself at what she'd just done. She'd completely forgotten where she was for a while. She hadn't quite ticked off the mile high club, but the train toilets were pretty close, so she'd take it. Not that she was sure she'd repeat it in a hurry. She'd struggled to find room for herself in there, never mind if she'd brought anyone else in real life. Virtual encounters were great for 'getting off' but there was nothing like two bodies connecting in person. That was what she craved. Well, what she really craved was Marcus – but she was supposed to be forgetting about him.

Twenty-Four

Lilith was trying something new tonight. Something else to push her boundaries and to discover a different side of her she never thought she would. She'd spent the previous night scrolling on her phone to no avail. So she started a Google search instead. 'Sex Clubs New York'. She didn't know what she expected to find but probably not such fruitful results on the first page. She found herself drawn to a blog of the five best sex clubs in NYC and wrote down the name of the first one. *The Secret Door.* Apparently, the mecca of sex clubs in New York, solely reserved for couples and single women. It sounded classy. Interesting. Sexy.

She wanted to expand her horizons from the apps, and this was certainly one way of doing it. So here she was on a warm Friday evening, standing on the corner of East Twenty-Seventh Street, working her way up to attending her very first sex party – alone. She'd wondered whether she should ask someone on the apps if they were up for going with her but she figured this was something she should experience on her own at first. See if it was something she liked. Plus, if there were other single women there, she might make a new connection. A friend connection obviously – she wasn't into women.

Lilith took a swig of whisky from the hip flask she'd brought with her. One of the things she'd read in the blog was that most sex clubs were BYOB (bring your own booze) and she hoped that would be the case here. Even so, the hip flask was in disguise as a hairbrush just in case.

She opened the door of an apartment building that led to the secret door of… The Secret Door. Very clever. And discreet. Not that Lilith was bothered. She no longer cared who she saw or what people thought of her. 'Here goes,' Lilith whispered to herself as she pushed open the door and was met with a cashier on the other side, waiting to take payment of thirty dollars – which apparently included a hot buffet too. Well, at least she'd be getting food tonight if nothing else. Although she wasn't sure how that was going to work with a load of naked bodies around. She was handed over a locker key and number (lucky number seven) and spotted the locker room before a door that Lilith assumed would lead to the 'main lounge'.

Lilith was staying fully dressed – at least for now. She'd worn a bodycon black dress to hug her figure – maybe not the best choice if she did want to take it off at some point, but, for now, she felt sexy and safe. She put her jacket and phone in her locker (one of the rules the cashier had stipulated was no phones) and made her way into the lounge. A sign above the door proudly proclaimed 'The Secret Door' along with the words 'established in 1985' underneath. Yikes, you could tell given the retro decor.

The carpet was dark pink (strange choice of flooring) and the walls were adorned with *Kama Sutra* style images and mirrors. Black vinyl couches were dotted around and Lilith spotted her first couple engaging in sexual activity. They didn't look up as she walked past them, unable to stop herself from staring at their sweaty bodies as they rolled around together.

For a Friday night, it was pretty quiet – and not exactly the vibes Lilith had expected, although she didn't know what she'd expected really. People swinging round poles and hanging off BDSM-type contraptions maybe. There was a pole with a young woman attempting to pole dance for who Lilith assumed was her partner, although he looked older than her. Not that she could judge – if she'd brought anyone tonight it would have been a younger guy.

Lilith could smell the buffet from where she was standing even though it looked like it was behind the thick black curtain of the next room. How bizarre. It felt like she was at a sleazy underground BBQ. Hardly oozing sexy vibes. She poked her head through into the 'buffet room' to instantly be met with a sign that said 'Please cover below torsos when eating at the food bench'. Lilith didn't think she'd be having any food – in fact, she was pretty sure she wouldn't be having *anything* here. Her only option would have been to engage in something with a couple and she wasn't into women, so that was off the cards. She'd been beaten by curiosity, but, still, it was an interesting way to spend a Friday night. Slightly better than cradling a bottle or two of wine in the depressing house in the suburbs. *Slightly.*

Lilith decided to head back to her locker to grab her things and pick up a takeaway on her way home instead.

Not the best way she'd spent thirty dollars but also not the worst either. She checked her phone for any messages and headed back outside. Nothing. Still no word from Marcus.

***

The following weekend, Lilith decided to fly to Miami for a solo weekend break. The girls were away with their dad so it was good to get away from the city lights for a little bit and experience something new and refreshing. Plus, she even happened to meet a fun couple at a sunset bar on her first night. They were in an open relationship, her age, and seemed very much in love. Maybe that was the answer? Allowing your partner to explore other connections.

Miami was beautiful and hot – if not a little too humid. The beaches were vibrant and the parties were wild. Everything oozed with sensuality and promises of good times. Something that Lilith was craving more and more these days. Good times. Good experiences. Good feelings. She was chasing her tail constantly, looking for the next 'good' thing. As if not doing something or someone left her stuck. Lost. Alone.

A few cocktails in and the couple Lilith was drinking with (Elise and Brett) started discussing their sexual fantasies. They wanted to try new things and push their limits – definitely something Lilith could relate to.

'So, we wanna go to a swingers' club,' Elise said, giggling.

'Oh God, here we go,' Lilith thought to herself before responding, 'Funnily enough I went to my first one last week in NYC.'

'No way!' Elise exclaimed, leaning in further.

Lilith laughed. 'It wasn't exactly the experience I was expecting. There was a buffet…'

'A buffet?!' Brett chimed in, clearly drawn in by the talk of food.

Lilith laughed again. 'I didn't eat any of it.'

'So, what was it like?' Elise asked, almost sitting on the edge of her seat.

'Erm, quiet and retro – but not in a good way,' Lilith replied.

'Would you come with us? To try a swingers' club here in Miami?' Elise asked, clearly not deterred by Lilith's response.

Lilith wasn't thrilled by the idea but she liked her new friends and it would be good to try again to see if she'd have a different experience. Plus, she didn't exactly have a better offer for the evening.

'Sure, why not – do you know where we're heading?'

Elise almost squealed in excitement as she squeezed Brett's hand and flagged down a cab.

The club was located on the outskirts of the city, which already didn't bode well in Lilith's mind. She'd expected somewhere more central. 'Round two here I come,' she thought to herself. Although she knew she wouldn't be coming at all.

It looked like a warehouse from the outside. Another inconspicuous venue that you'd only know about if you were 'in the know'. As soon as they got inside, Lilith was weary of the crowd. It was a mix of older men and younger girls – not being judgemental but she wasn't even sure they were legit. A few other couples didn't look up for it at all and then there were just a few single women looking like deer in headlights – Lilith sympathised with them as this was probably what she looked like last week at The Secret Door. Where were all the men?! There wasn't a single person in that room that Lilith would do. Not even with her eyes closed. The whole thing was verging on sordid, and a quick look over to Elise and Brett confirmed that they felt the same.

They had a quick drink together and decided to take their little group elsewhere. Back to the warm night and the adventures that await. They ended up drinking until the early hours, finishing the night back at their apartment and dancing around the living room at 3 a.m. to classic house music. Definitely a cool little weekend break despite a second failed attempt at attending a swingers' club. Maybe that would stay off Lilith's list for a while.

As Lilith boarded the plane home to NYC, she reflected on her time in Miami and the couple she'd met and would definitely keep in touch with. She'd even managed not to think too much about Marcus or her dual life back in NYC. Could this be healing? She wasn't sure it was, but it was *something*.

Twenty-Five

I'm on the plane back to Paris from Amsterdam. What the hell have I done to myself?

I've come back to Europe for the summer holidays. I was supposed to be in Paris for a couple of days whilst waiting for the girls to come back from the first part of their holidays with their dad in France and then head south with them. Keeping myself to myself and getting away from it all. Only, when I landed in Paris, before I got off the plane, I saw that I had a message from an unknown number. Only, I was fooling myself. It wasn't an unknown number to me at all. I knew every single digit off by heart. My whole body was getting close to a meltdown and I knew I needed to hold it together so that I could carry my own luggage down the plane steps without falling over. It was Marcus.

'I'm in Amsterdam for a few days – wanna join me for the night?'

And so, as the strong, independent woman that I am, I gave myself at least five seconds of deep reflection before saying yes to jumping straight on another plane from the airport to Amsterdam.

My heart was beating at a dangerous speed (and it still hasn't resumed to a normal pace), my hands were sweaty, and I swore my vagina was pulsing. I was so ready for him. For his eyes. His hands. His smile. His tongue. His teeth. (I didn't know teeth were one of my things but his were so white and perfect.) His dick. I could feel myself ready to beg for anything he was ready to give me. Anything he wanted, I would have done. I thought I was going to explode on the flight taking me to him. It was the longest Paris to Amsterdam flight ever, which finally managed to land at Schiphol airport without me either passing out or having multiple orgasms next to the poor passengers next to me.

I ran the kilometres of corridors (the airport was bigger than I expected but once I'd started running, I couldn't stop), I jumped the taxi queue with a family emergency lie, and I blurred out the sixteen miles to the city centre (forty-five minutes, twenty-seven seconds, and three microseconds...).

He was staying at a design hotel near the river. 'In the trendy area,' he told me. I thought the whole of Amsterdam was just one big trendy area. There's my age showing again. I didn't even know that I was in Amsterdam. I could have been anywhere or nowhere – my brain simply wasn't computing, except for one thing, and one person.

I walked in and he was sitting at the bar, waiting with a drink. His smile illuminated his face – and the whole room. I smiled back. Completely throwing my weeks and weeks of angst and resolutions out of the window. I was time travelling, back to that hotel room in NYC, back to our first night together.

We made our way back to the room, running. He'd already checked in. A suite on the canal. Fuck. What was he doing to me? It was like it was all planned. I was the bait and I'd taken it straight away. No thinking. Just lured in, surrendering my whole self to him. The minute the door closed behind us, we jumped on each other. Literally. He was holding me, pushing me against the wall so that our bodies were so pressed against each other, I could barely breathe. The heat and intensity were huge; I felt like I was on another planet. We were twirling around the place, managing to break a few things in the process. (Glad it was his room, not mine.)

He took me against the wall in the living area. He took me on the bed, all night, in every way possible. He took me in the shower – multiple times. With water dripping along my back. I took him on the bed, all night, in every way possible. I took him in the shower – multiple times. With water dripping along his back. We were panting, breathless, unable to stop. We only paused for some room service.

I've never felt this level of chemistry in my life – it's almost unhealthy. In fact, it's definitely unhealthy. He's like an addiction I can't get enough of. I literally can't get enough of him. I can't be filled enough or feel full. I constantly want more. We kept coming and coming and coming. I was electrified to the nth degree. Body fluids, DNA, and footprints all over the room like a crime scene. The smell of passionate, insatiable, destructive sex. The kind of sex that doesn't just connect your souls but pushes you to the edge of the precipice.

I'm in that dark place called obsession. In that darker place called addiction. I know I'm falling for him lower and deeper every minute, every second I spend with him. I've been desperately trying to mistake sex for love yet pretending to be detached and playing the game. Pretending it's okay to be ghosted. That it's okay to only meet at night in hotel rooms. That it's okay to never talk about anything except sex.

In between having sex, we talked about sex all night – making lists on what we wanted to do to each other the next time we met. 'The next time'. And that's exactly what I'm holding on to. Those words – 'next time'. Even though he's refused to commit to when that next time might be because it's not cool to plan and 'coz we're nothing to each other'. Because he's refused any connection. But it's too late for me. I'm already there. And I also know better than telling him that I'm making plans in my head because I've completely fallen in lust for him and surrendered all my powers to this inaccessible hot guy.

Argh. I'm utterly shattered and wired. Flying back to Paris with zero sleep and this longing to just be with Marcus twenty-four hours a day. I feel dangerously high and dangerously low at the same time. I know I've hooked him and I'm going to use this as my only anchor to ensure I see him again.

Just. One. More. Time.

Twenty-Six

The landing back was hard. Every cell of Lilith's body wanted to be back in Amsterdam – in that room, under his weight, on top of him, in the shower, feeling him behind her, filling her as she dripped every single drop of fluid out of her body. She was completely and utterly besotted. He had her right where he wanted her and there was nowhere else she wanted to be. She craved his touch every minute and every second of the day. When her head hit the pillow at night, she imagined him lying next to her, over her, under her, all over her. She smelt of sex – his sex and hers. Her skin was still burning and so was she.

Lilith wasn't sure how she was going to get through the next few weeks but at least she felt like she had a plan. She knew she was going to be in LA for work in September and there was a slight chance she might see him again. And that slight chance was the hope she was holding on to right now – because she couldn't imagine any other scenario. She had to see him again. She had to top up the way he made her feel.

She was also aware she needed a break. Some time away from it all. A detox. Time to whisk herself and the girls to the South of France for some much-needed R & R. It worked perfectly because the girls had some friends over there, so they'd be amused throughout the day, so Lilith could just 'be'.

She'd rented an apartment right on the beachfront and it was just stunning. Light flooded every room from the floor-to-ceiling windows and there was a huge sweeping balcony from the bedroom to the kitchen area, overlooking the ocean. She'd picked a quieter area of the coastline so she could just about see the girls in the distance as they enjoyed a beach day with their friends, but the view in front of her remained simply the sand and the ocean, and the odd passerby walking to the other end of the beach.

She took a sip of coffee and settled into one of the chairs on the balcony, kicking off her shoes and sliding her sunglasses down onto her face. The French sun just hit differently. It was warmer in every sense of the word – and homely. And even though she couldn't imagine herself here full-time (she'd miss the buzz of the city too much), right now it was exactly what she needed. Light, quiet, and warmth.

But as she watched the waves slowly ripple closer inland below, Lilith found it impossible to focus on the present. Her mind and body constantly meandered back to Marcus – to their two nights together in NYC and Amsterdam, to the intensity of the chemistry between them, even though he denied her any deeper emotional connection. She wondered if he was afraid to fall in love. But she couldn't kid herself.

She'd promised herself that she'd delete the apps from her phone and not message any guys, old or new, and especially not Marcus. It wasn't good for her – she knew it. She knew she couldn't keep going the way she was. It was dangerous and would only end in hurt and emptiness. But still the addiction lingered. She'd deleted the apps and muted his number from her phone but she was desperate to message him.

And so, she gave in.

'Hey Marcus. I'm in France. The sun is hot, just like your body ;)… How's life treating ya?'

She tried to keep it cool but he messaged back with more intensity and frequency, and before she knew it they were sexting again. Direct, playful, and raw. She didn't leave the balcony all day – forgetting to put more sunscreen on, and finding herself literally red raw at the end of the day, in all but the one area she wanted to be, for different reasons.

She and the girls were meeting friends for dinner that night and they told her she looked fantastic. That she had a glow about her and looked genuinely happy. As the week went on, even strangers commented on how smiley she was. It was literally oozing out of her and she felt like she was in a constant orgasm mood, floating in a parallel universe, orbiting around a super attractive star – yet always verging near a black hole.

It definitely wasn't the detox she'd imagined but at least she wasn't downing bottles of wine whilst sitting on the floor of her living room, weeping in a state of depression.

The second week flew by even quicker than the first. Every day hotter than the last – both the heat of the sun, and the heat of Lilith's exchanges with Marcus. She definitely didn't feel lonely but she was also missing out on in-person connections. She'd had dinner and drinks a few times with her friends but she could barely remember their conversations. She hadn't really been listening – instead finding herself floating off to her parallel universe at every given opportunity. Imagining herself elsewhere, doing different things. Well, doing one person in particular.

The day before their flight back home to New York, Lilith's phone buzzed in quick succession and she almost dropped it out of her hand as she rushed to the bathroom to open the messages. She'd assumed it'd be Marcus with another filthy message for her to respond to. Only it wasn't him this time. It was Victor. Her wonderful, gorgeous soulmate, Victor.

She hadn't heard from him for a good few weeks – not since he'd told her to be careful. And she knew she'd ignored that solid advice almost as quickly as it was given. But it was so good to hear from him. Something about him just made her feel safe and secure and she knew he had her best interests at heart. Plus he just made her feel good – in a way that wasn't an unhealthy obsession.

He was having a great summer travelling around Europe but was heading to New York at the end of the month – and he wanted to see her. Lilith wondered if she'd be available – she wasn't quite sure about the practical arrangements as the girls would be preparing to go back to school and she would be preparing for her new job – but she was sure she'd love to see him again. He was so charming, driven, and reliable. And even though she didn't know him that well, her gut told her she could trust him.

She typed out her message, 'Yes, let's hang for sure!'

He immediately replied, 'Great, I've already booked my tickets.'

Lilith felt her lips curl up into a big beaming smile. He was planning to come to NYC no matter what, so she liked that it didn't plan around her. Well, perhaps a little bit, but not too much. It was easy and effortless and exactly what she needed right now. A healthy distraction. Maybe flying back to the city tomorrow wasn't so bad after all. She had something to look forward to. Something real and less focused on sex.

That night, back in the suburbs, as she closed her eyes, she saw Victor's face for just a few moments before Marcus's came creeping back in. 'Damn it,' she found herself saying out loud as she shook her head and giggled to herself. Still, at least her mind was able to see something else even if literally for a few seconds.

Who was she kidding? She loved thinking about Marcus and imagining him touching her all over, making her beg for more. It was her vice. And so she resigned herself to letting her thoughts go where they wanted to go, wrapping her naked body up in the bed sheets, and slowly drifting off into a deep sleep.

Twenty-Seven

Ifeel like shit again. It's been a whirlwind few days and I've had some amazing moments – but just like that, the moments have gone, and I'm back here in the house on my own, feeling lonely as fuck. Seeing Victor again was a total tonic. I wish I could teleport myself back to him arriving in the city again and just relive those days repeatedly.

I decided to rent a place in the city so we could enjoy each other's company away from the suburbs and I checked in early in the evening so I had plenty of time to prepare before his flight landed at eleven. The girls were staying with their dad this weekend – perfectly timed. I'd text Lorna to meet me for dinner and we'd caught up over a few glasses of wine and the most divine seabass dinner. I can't wait to spend more time with her when we're officially working together. I'm getting close to telling her everything. And when I say everything, I mean EVERYTHING. I feel like part of my loneliness stems from feeling like I'm living a double life that no one else knows about. That the side people see of me isn't my whole self and like I'm basically living a lie. Fifty per cent of a lie anyway. It's exhausting and draining and I can't do it any longer.

Anyway, back to seeing Victor. The moment he knocked on the door of the apartment, I knew everything was going to be okay. It's crazy because it was only the second time we'd met in person but it felt like we'd known each other so much longer. Much longer than one evening in Paris two months ago. Christ, was it that long ago, already? My life is literally flashing before my eyes.

I like Victor because he doesn't play any games. I know where I stand with him, and vice versa. He's straightforward, honest, and respectful. And yes, it also helps that he's damn hot too. But there's no hidden agenda. What you see is what you get, and we're incredibly open with each other. After months of anonymous encounters, it's super refreshing.

He's not afraid to create bonds and connections. He puts his entire self out there for the world to see. Yes, we met in an apartment, but he kissed me at the door in the open and he'd run down the street with me hand in hand, no cares in the world. He believes that love can take many forms. He's an ethical hedonist (just like me). And, boy, what a hedonistic weekend we had together... Fucking, drinking, dancing, rooftopping, tons of (disgusting American) food eating, as well as sightseeing, biking, walking, US Opening... talking non-stop, revealing all of our selves to each other.

It was perfect, in a totally non-conventional, imperfect way. And I think that's the way I want to live my life.

I was exhausted by the end of the weekend but not in a bad way – in an exhilarating, joyous way. My cup was so full, it was almost overflowing. We tried to define what we share and concluded that there were no 'avai-labels' for what we have. It is what it is. It's rich, simple, and full of good energy. I like him. We get on well. I smile whenever I think of him. He mentioned he wants to have children one day and that's not something I'll ever consider again (not that he asked or anything!) but that puts a boundary in our 'relationship' and keeps things where they should be.

When I dropped him off at the airport, I felt content. Not content for him leaving – but content that I wasn't desperate for him to stay. I know now it was only a temporary relief as I sit here on the end of my bed, staring out of the window into the darkness outside. I've felt a massive wave of anxiety rising within me all day and it's now coming to a head. Emptiness has filled my lungs and I feel like I can barely breathe again.

Driving back earlier tonight had me going over one of the longest bridges in New York above cold and murky waters. That's when the deep panic hit my chest with vengeance. I started crying and I knew I had to keep going. There was nowhere to stop on that bridge and I knew I just needed to get back home.

Yet now I'm here, I don't feel any better. I didn't feel a wave of relief pass over me as I put my key in the front door and locked it behind me. I just felt more and more anxiety. Breathe, Lilith, breathe. Everything is going to be alright – eventually. Everything shall pass.

But fuckkkk, I'm feeling SO lonely. Thank God LA is only a matter of days away. Surely that's the answer to all my problems?

Twenty-Eight

Lilith was feeling grateful for Lorna. She'd text her the night she was feeling incredibly low and Lorna had immediately suggested a team night out before Lilith officially started work – and before the LA trip. That way she'd get to know some of the team on a more personal level before working with them to make her transition into the company as smooth as possible (given she got on with people, of course).

So, here she was in her little black dress, putting on her nude lipstick and applying it carefully as if she was going on a date. The truth was she felt more nervous than if she was going on a date. She was so used to hooking up with guys left, right, and centre and barely catching their names that she could meet someone with her eyes shut. But this was different. These people would be her work colleagues. Potential friends. People she would see on a regular basis and have some kind of relationship with – hopefully good ones.

She was anxious. What if they didn't like her? What if

she had to hold herself back? What if they had nothing to talk about and she dreaded going into work each day? So many questions but it was best just to get herself on the train into the city and find out.

Lorna was waiting by the door of the bar as Lilith rounded the corner from the station. She smiled as Lorna started waving her arms around as if Lilith couldn't possibly see her, then threw herself at her as though long-lost friends were seeing each other for the first time in years. Lilith squeezed her tightly back and felt her insides soften. Her stomach had been tied up in knots all the way here.

'Come inside! I've ordered you a drink.' Lorna beckoned, and Lilith dutifully followed.

The bar was already full and people were huddled together in big groups, clinking glasses and roaring with laughter. Lorna smiled back at Lilith and handed her a large gin and tonic with an obnoxious yellow cocktail umbrella floating on top.

'Thank you.' Lilith smiled as she twirled the umbrella round in her drink and took a big sip. 'I needed that.'

'Let me introduce you to my favourite person in the office,' Lorna said as she slipped away and returned with a tall, handsome Jewish-American guy (his own words). 'This is Aaron.'

Aaron had already stretched out his hand to shake Lilith's, so she shook it firmly back, almost pulling his arm out of his socket.

'Bloody hell, you'll almost have my arm off.' Aaron laughed as he shook his arm around, pretending it had hurt him.

'Oops, sorry!' Lilith replied, giggling. 'I haven't done a corporate handshake for a while so I'm a little out of practice.'

'We'll get you up to speed,' Aaron replied before clinking her glass with his own. 'Cheers anyway, it's great to finally meet you. Lorna's told me so much about you and it sounds like you're going to be a real asset – and a great drinking buddy.'

Lilith looked to Lorna, who beamed back at her and gave her a friendly nudge.

'I'm just excited to be around real-life people again and have colleagues!' Lilith replied. 'I'll fill you in properly another time but it's been a bit of a lonely journey for me since I moved here a year ago. The gin is very much needed – and I'm really enjoying this cocktail umbrella.' Lilith looked at her drink thoughtfully and then giggled.

Aaron gave her a big burly squeeze around her shoulders before saying, 'We've got you, girl. The city hasn't seen nothing yet!'

Lilith spent the rest of the evening in such deep conversation with both Aaron and Lorna that she barely got to say hello to the rest of her new colleagues. Everybody stopped by to introduce themselves but Lilith was enjoying her meaningful chat, so found herself only briefly looking up to smile and say hello before immersing herself back with her friends.

Aaron was married and lived in the city not too far away from the office. Lilith instantly felt safe with him – their relationship would be purely platonic and he had such a calming and funny presence about him. No wonder Lorna got on so well with him. He wasn't going on the LA trip as he had some important client meetings in the city but Lilith knew they'd be spending plenty of time together in the office and on future work trips. Just like Lorna, he was easy to talk to – and genuinely passionate about the work they did.

Lilith got back on the train that night feeling a level of contentment she hadn't experienced for a long time. This was the feeling she'd been missing. True connections. Feeling like she meant something. Feeling like she belonged somewhere. Feeling like she was going somewhere.

***

The flight to LA soon came along and Lilith found herself almost skipping to the airport doors as she saw Lorna waiting for her with a big grin across her face. They grabbed breakfast together and barely took a break from chatting until the boarding gate. It always amazed her that you could fly six hours one way and still be in the same country.

As soon as they boarded the plane, they continued chatting – in fact, they chatted the whole way and Lilith opened up to her like she was her sister. She was kind, smart, caring, and funny – and Lilith felt totally relaxed in her presence. The type of person you could say anything to without fear of judgement – but with guarantee of support.

As soon as they landed, they headed straight to their conference. Lilith felt grateful to be there. She loved her job and, for a while, she even forgot about Marcus and her cunning plan.

In the evening, she went out with her new colleagues,

trying not to drink too much. (She'd realised she was drinking a lot these days and that was another unhealthy part of her life she should probably try to rein in.) She also tried to convince herself that she'd resist. That she'd get through this work trip by hanging out with her new colleagues, confiding in Lorna, and doing meaningful work.

She managed to stay clear of messages all evening and as she headed back to the hotel at 11 p.m, she couldn't believe that she'd actually done it. She'd resisted all temptation and had a 'normal' night out. Only, just as she was scanning her key on the door, there it was. A message from him. Marcus. Asking her if she was in town. He was working late but could meet her later.

Lilith's heart skipped a beat. She felt torn. A part of her was really pushing back, refusing to give in. She'd done so well all day and she didn't want to go back on the word to herself.

'I might be asleep by then, sorry,' she replied.

But he was persistent. 'I'll get there as soon as I can. I can't wait to see you.'

'What's your ETA?' Lilith responded, pretending to be cool and not exhausted.

He remained non-committal. The hell with this guy! Yet Lilith found herself giving him her hotel address.

It was 1.30 a.m. A knock on her door. She'd chosen to wear her PJs deliberately not to be sexy. She opened the door to find him smiling – grinning like a Cheshire cat.

'Fuck him,' Lilith thought to herself as she pulled him inside.

And that's exactly what she did. Fucked him. Many times over. Many orgasms later. Another sleepless night.

Another night stuck at a hotel. She was starting to feel cabin fever and she could tell that he could sense it, too.

She showered and got dressed for work – a sexy skirt, blouse, and heels. That clearly set him off again. He looked at her with pure lust in his eyes, begging for her to take him without saying a single word. Lilith wanted him so hard it hurt.

Before she knew it, he'd pushed her back onto the bed, lifted up her skirt, put on some lube, and fucked her up the ass. This was the first time they'd had anal sex and she came hard. And so did he. It was so hot to have a man penetrating her in that way – it felt almost loving, something she was totally surprised by.

Uh-oh, Lilith snapped herself quickly out of it. How could she go there that fast – from being fucked up the ass? Boy was she in trouble. She got dressed again – no shower this time, plus it was a big fantasy of hers to walk around with hot come dripping off her bum cheeks – and said goodbye.

Lilith's work day was surprisingly productive. She figured she was still high from her morning explorations and found herself making waves with her new colleagues and proving herself as a valuable member of the team. Marcus had messaged her throughout the day but she was determined not to respond this time and make plans instead with her colleagues. Only, when it came to the end of the day, everyone was tired and decided to retire early. Lilith decided to do the same and looked forward to an early night.

But as she walked to her hotel with her colleagues, she spotted Marcus waiting in the lobby. What on earth was he doing there? It was way too early for him and he seemed sober. She couldn't acknowledge him in front of her workmates and she wasn't going to take him to her room tonight. So, she continued upstairs, had a long shower and got changed. She planned on taking her time and seeing if he was still there when she went back down. He could wait.

And he did. He was gentler than usual. Who was this changed man? 'It must be the anal sex effect,' Lilith thought to herself. He said he wanted to take her to his favourite spot in the city. Wow, another turn for the books. Were they actually going to get out of the sex-cell and out into the big wide world? It appeared that way but Lilith was still on edge.

They jumped into a cab and got dropped off at the bottom of a hill. A favourite spot for the locals apparently – the top of it, not the bottom. They found a liquor store round the corner to stock up on supplies (booze, cigarettes, and some unhealthy snacks for dinner) before ascending in silence for a while. Lilith felt like a prisoner out of jail, walking next to her jailor. It was the first time they were next to each other in the open air outside of their international sex-cells, and she had no fucking idea how to do this. Still, she was sure she could improvise.

After what felt like a lifetime, they reached the top of the hill to be met by the most breathtaking views. Lilith stopped walking and took a second to take it all in. They were completely on their own and the whole city was scintillating in front of their eyes. They sat down on some rocks, made use of their supplies, and engaged in some meaningless small talk. Marcus was reluctant to share anything personal and Lilith was the type to overshare, so she took the cues and held off. As a result, she started drinking and smoking even more than she normally would to fill the silence. Her stomach was doing knots as she tried to reach for something to say that would fit the moment but she was drawing blanks.

After an hour or so, they headed back to the hotel, hovering in the lobby. Lilith was quite drunk and could feel her body swaying as she tried to stand still on the spot. She suddenly realised she was scared to spend the night alone so she asked him if he wanted to come up. He said he hadn't planned on staying overnight but that he'd go get his things and come back.

Lilith found a seat in the lobby and waited, looking around for a water cooler to try and settle her nerves and sober up. Before she found one, he came back and they took the lift up to her room, standing in silence as they made their way to the third floor.

Once into her hotel room, they cuddled. For the very first time. Things were starting to become quite intimate and Lilith was both relieved and afraid. They even worked next to each other through the night – with some sex interludes, of course. But something had shifted in balance. Marcus kept telling her that he was worried he'd done everything with her and he'd have nothing left to discover in his future relationships. Was this the reason he wasn't fully opening up to her? Whether he liked it or not, they were obviously deeply attracted to each other but maybe he was scared of what that all meant.

Lilith found herself diverting from her work and instead researching on that topic that night, finding an article that perfectly explained it on dopsychologytoday. com...

'A single mind-blowing encounter becomes your new (impossible) sexual benchmark. You had one unforgettable high chemistry sexual experience with a near stranger and you can't get it out of your head. Lovemaking in any serious relationship now falls short of this impossible-to-repeat standard so you keep breaking up with people who could be excellent mates but can't compete with your brightly lit sexual memory. Replaying the memory in high-def feeds and embellishes it. That peak experience needs to be relegated to distant storage so you can focus on discovering unique sexual pleasures within your full-featured relationship without unfair comparators.'

Fuck. That's where his head was at.

After a sleepless night, Lilith was the first one to 'peace out' to work in the morning, leaving him behind as he barely opened his eyes when she shut the door. She just couldn't face goodbyes. Not like this. Not with him. She never knew with Marcus – each time could be the last.

Twenty-Nine

13 September 2018

I'm back from LA and I'm back in the game! I decided to numb the pain of my recent Marcus encounters and ignore him. It's funny, I actually feel like I've gained more confidence since LA as I could sense he was becoming a little bit more vulnerable. Sharing his fears about getting closer to me – because that's what was happening. We were getting closer. So now, it's my turn to pull back. Take back control.

It's funny how dynamics work. 'Je t'aime, moi non plus' as they say in French. Every day that I don't respond to his messages is a little victory. For my bruised ego (or, indeed, my asshole!) I think I'm slowly starting to heal. I can do this. All I need to do is to keep ignoring his messages and my feelings will go away. Poof. Gone. Easy. Just like that. Oh and add a few more distractions into the mix.

And that's exactly what I've been doing.

I was on the train home from work last night and the weather was gorgeous. The sun was hitting my face through the window and I'd lost myself just staring outside and detaching myself from everything. Until I noticed I was sitting directly opposite a group of rather cute guys – talking about golf. Not really my preferred subject, so I wasn't exactly drawn in, but one of them tried to engage me in the conversation. I politely declined, responding that not only did I not know anything about golf but I had zero interest and that it seemed to me golf was for bored, middle-aged men. *I know, I didn't mince my words.*

Anyway, it turned out one of them was a professional golfer. He started laughing and so did I, especially when I clocked on how handsome he was. Now I was interested. We chatted a bit and his friends got off at the next stop, leaving the two of us to keep chatting alone. He told me he was staying at a hotel not too far from my house. His competition was the next day – he couldn't go out with his friends that night.

We ended up getting off at the same spot so he could 'retire to his room'. As we started walking, he joked that he hadn't had any fun for months and why didn't we sneak into his hotel room without his coach noticing as it's completely against the rules on competition night. Obviously, I was game. It sounded like fun and I was always up for a little recklessness.

He snuck me in through the service door of his hotel and into the service lift. Clearly, this wasn't his first rodeo, but it was mine and I liked it, so I didn't ask. We rushed through the corridor and into his room – which was FULL of golfing apparel everywhere. I found myself giggling to myself but I also found it quite sexy. I also discovered he had a particular kink (nothing golf related); he actually didn't want to fuck, just to jerk on my face and breasts. That suited me pretty well considering I wouldn't be able to scream as much as I'd like, given the set-up.

I took off my top and bra, got on my knees, and held his legs firmly with my hands, licking his balls whilst he started wanking and panting hard. He came within minutes and I realise it clearly must have been many months since he'd last relieved himself like this. A job well done even if I do say so myself.

He thanked me and I wished him well in his competition. In fact, I checked the results today whilst wanking in front of my computer, watching him play, and he did rather well. I dressed and escaped through the service door last night like the true artist that I am, and now I'm ready for my next encounter.

20 September 2018

I found another new match. This time online – back to my trusty apps. A little different to my usual matches but I like to play the field. And playing the field it appears I am, as he was a professional football player. Tall and athletic and all he seemed to talk about was football and health. I wasn't sure how it was going to play out as I'm partial to greasy food and slobbing out on the sofa with a bottle of wine. I didn't tell him that, though.

Anyway, we met for a drink at a healthy kale (and other tasteless but trendy veggie juices) café place. I know, who even am I?! I felt like I was playing out the role of a completely different person. He didn't drink, didn't smoke, didn't go out, his body was a temple, blah blah blah, organic food, blah, blah… fitness training, swimming, running, weights, calorie intake, super foods, blah, blah fucking blah… Honestly I was either going to fall asleep or run away fast, but something about him kept me there. He was superhot but everything else about him really didn't work for me. Too many rules. Too many constraints. Too many restrictions. The opposite of fun. I could just imagine how boring sex with this guy would be.

And then he said something that piqued my interest… His fantasy was to dress as a woman.

I don't know why but I found that quite intriguing. I've never met someone who's expressed this before and here was this guy – this big, bulky, sporty, heterosexual guy, who wanted to wear women's clothes. I sat forward in my seat, pushing my green juice to one side (definitely not for me), and we started discussing the topic further. He finally opened up and became much more personable. I'm glad I gave him a chance. There was something very touching about this fit guy with cross-dressing fantasies. And so, I asked him if he wanted to explore further.

He told me that no woman would ever want that, so I challenged him back. I would be ready to give it a go.

We arranged to meet a couple days later and went on a shopping trip together. He was super grateful. You could tell how liberated it was making him feel to not only look and touch these clothes, but to get to take them home with him.

We hired a hotel room – not to fuck (yet) but to help him dress up, put make-up on, and wear a wig and heels. Honestly, he was a fucking gorgeous woman. I don't fancy ladies but to see him beaming and letting go of his inhibitions was somehow arousing.

When he undressed and wiped the make-up from his face, he instantly morphed back into his other self. The very manly and muscular self who gave me an enduring sexual performance, resulting in multiple orgasms. It turns out I'm not completely against health freaks after all.

25 September 2018

Okay, so September is the month for sports, or rather sportsmen. Which is hilarious seeing as I'm one of the least sporty people I know, except for my occasional jogs to the Dog's Beach. My next target? The local tennis coach. I know, I'm not even joking. We initially met online – I'm back to scrolling my apps but getting a little more selective with who I choose to talk to. We met in person at the tennis club. First a juice bar, now a tennis club. I'm a changed woman.

Clearly, I wasn't a member of said club (and still aren't – sorry, Coral!). There's so many of these fucking clubs in Suburbia America where either you belong or you don't. I fall into the latter – and I like it that way.

He came over to greet me and it was fun to pretend that we were discussing tennis lessons. All of the local mums were there with their kids, watching me chat to the hot, young tennis coach. I could tell all eyes were on me and they were probably gossiping until the cows came home, but I couldn't give a damn. They didn't know me from anywhere anyway – it wasn't my 'local' local tennis club.

He definitely wasn't 'local' either. I found out he was from South America and had a super-cute Latino accent. I bought him a beer and watched him play until he finished work, steering clear of the gossiping mums and simply enjoying the view. When he'd finished, we hung out a little longer at the club and got to know each other. My main takeaways: he was fun, young, and free.

He drove me to his local bar and we parked at the back. No other people in sight. He didn't ask but I knew there and then what he wanted – and it was what I wanted, too. We kissed deeply. Fuck, he was a good kisser – I can still feel his lips on mine now. I remember being so wet that I was worried I'd leave a patch on the front seat of his car – that's how much he was turning me on. He fingered me deep and I came on the spot! (Literally!!) We still hadn't seen anyone else around, so I unzipped his trousers, took his hard dick out, and gave him a blow job to be thinking about for years to come. He came really hard and gripped onto my hair. To see the pleasure in his eyes was a pleasure to me, too. And we got off without being arrested – another bonus!

We laughed, joked, and chatted some more in the car before heading into the bar for a celebration shot. He told me that I wasn't like 'the other mums'. Oh, you mean the other mums don't blow you in the car in a deserted car park at the back of a dive bar. How weird are those women, seriously?!

Thirty

After a sporty-themed month, Lilith was feeling positive about October. She had no idea what was in store for her, but things seemed to be looking up. She was continuing to ignore Marcus's messages, although they had started to become few and far between now, so he must have been taking the hint – that, or he'd found a new forty-odd-year-old French woman to seduce.

New York looked mesmerising in the fall. On her lunch breaks, Lilith would sometimes take herself off to Central Park to witness the leaves falling from the trees so she could crunch around in them like she did as a child. She was making sure to take pleasure in the small things in life these days – it's what stopped her from falling into a pit of despair, cradling wine bottles and crying herself to sleep, in the house she couldn't wait to be rid of. That, and getting 'swipe happy' on Tinder or Bumble.

Her next match was an accountant. She really was branching out these days. He was cute. And boring. Well, he sounded boring but she didn't actually know if he really was boring or if it was just his job title. She didn't know him. But from first glance, he didn't sound very exciting – poor guy. As soon as they started talking, he chatted about his job straight away – all the gory numerical details that Lilith really couldn't care for. She wasn't sure but she remembered her previous encounter with the professional football player and reminded herself to give it a chance. Plus, he was super cute.

He asked to meet for a drink and to take her 'somewhere cool that he knows'. Well that was an intriguing offer she couldn't refuse. She wondered what or where that was going to be – her curiosity greater as always. She was obviously going to have to meet him now and find out.

They met for a drink in the city – at a bar Lilith had been to a few times before. She was sure the barmen knew who she was but she averted her gaze anyway. Mr Accountant Man, whose name had escaped Lilith yet again (she really must start writing down names on her hand before her dates), was actually quite a nice guy, if not a little shy. Lilith assumed she'd have to take the lead with this one.

Or maybe not… He grabbed her hand and said he was taking her to a shop around the corner. And not just any kind of shop – a BDSM one. Now that was a surprise. He wanted to show her his fantasies and Lilith began to wonder if there was a bit of a theme emerging here. Younger men wanting to explore their kinks with her because they know she'll be open to most things. *They weren't wrong.*

This was something she hadn't explored before but was interested to find out more. So, they started with the basics. A mouth gag (for him), fancy handcuffs (for him), some latex outfits (for both of them), and a whip (for her). Lilith suggested that they meet up again in a few days so she could do a little research. This definitely wasn't her area of expertise – yet!

When she got home that night, Lilith instantly opened up her laptop and started Googling away. Good job the girls were not in. She thought nothing could possibly shock her, but it turned out there were still a few things that raised her eyebrows and had her pulling all kinds of funny faces as she tilted her head to try to work out what some of the objects were in the images she was looking at. She figured she should take it down a notch and do a little bit of research into sub–dom relationships. This was more like it – she'd enjoy being in charge. And luckily for her, that was exactly what the cute and demure accountant wanted.

They met again – this time at a hotel room. He followed her into the room a little sheepishly and Lilith could tell he was feeling a bit shy. She'd soon get him out of his shell.

'What do you want?' Lilith asked confidently.

'I want to be dominated,' the accountant replied.

So that's exactly what she did – no questions asked. She found it quite empowering to have a man at her mercy… Being the one pulling all the strings and shaping the whole dynamic.

They stayed 'vanilla' (if you could call it that) but made use of all the supplies they purchased earlier in the week. He came hard as Lilith whipped his firm ass up in the air, whilst gagged and handcuffed to the bed. (It wasn't the easiest of tasks to locate a hotel with the appropriate kind of beds that allowed for handcuffs to be attached to them.)

Lilith looked at his face full of satisfaction and came

up with a genius idea. How about they swap? She usually preferred to be in control but she was ready to explore something different. And the funniest thing happened. As she lay there, handcuffed and gagged, fully exposed at his mercy, she witnessed him transforming into a very skilled master. He went down on her, expertly – every inch of her longing for his touch. She couldn't move, go anywhere, or touch herself, and that really turned her on. Within moments, she was desperate to come – but she hoped he wouldn't stop there. Thank God he had no intention to be cruel, but he carried on diligently. She squirted everywhere on the bed and on his face and she looked up to see him grinning. Maybe it wasn't just about him exploring his fantasies after all!

After showering together and towelling each other off, Lilith sent him on his merry way with a huge smile on her face. She decided to stay in the room a little longer to allow her heart rate to come back down and to take in the day's events before returning to her somewhat different (boring) life in the suburbs. She was truly enjoying herself but she still felt so disjointed as a person. It was like the moment she got back on the train, she transformed back into a shadow of the person she'd just been. And she knew she couldn't ever really be truly happy until she was living in an environment that best suited her needs.

'Soon, Lilith,' she said to herself in her head. 'Soon.'

***

Three days later, Lilith was enjoying her lunch break at work. Aaron and Lorna were away on a work trip, so she was keeping herself amused via other means – the apps.

She scooped a spoonful of pasta into her mouth as she spotted a new match. A rather hot match. His smile and dark brown eyes were mesmerising and Lilith could feel herself getting lost in them before she'd finished swallowing. Plus, his opening line was unusual and intriguing: 'A night with me if you guess what language I speak, first time'. She liked his style.

But now was the time to think hard. What was her gut saying? Definitely somewhere in the Middle East. Can't be Arabic – too obvious. Lebanese, perhaps? Hmm, she decided to go for Farsi. He didn't respond straight away. Shit, had she offended him? Or had she simply got it wrong and he'd only respond to those who guessed correctly?

Turns out, she was spot on. Time to claim her prize!

A series of back-and-forth logistical arrangements followed, which almost put Lilith off, but she'd won a night with him and decided she wouldn't let go so easily. Plus, she'd now wasted almost an entire afternoon making sure it happened instead of finishing her work to meet her deadline early, which she'd be paying for the next day, so she needed something to show for it.

Finally, a rendezvous point was agreed, so Lilith booked a cool place in the city. It was fun to book something other than a standard hotel room – plus you didn't have to check in with suspicious or judgemental receptionists either. The only problem with Airbnbs was the added cleaning fee, although, in this case, they'd probably need the fee, and then some, to clean up after them!

She planned to arrive a little bit before him so she could get ready and let him in, being fully aware of her surroundings. However, it didn't quite work out that way...

When she got to the flat to check in, it was completely impossible to unlock the door despite looking at the Airbnb instructions over and over again and following them step by step. She tried absolutely everything but nothing seemed to work, but she'd already paid so she had to get in there somehow. Especially given how long it took to secure a meeting point in the first place. But what to do next?

One of the next-door neighbours must have heard Lilith's not so quiet commotion and frustration outside because she came out to try to help too. Bless her, she was quite a bit older and clearly curious about what Lilith was doing here, but at least she was trying to help. Still, no success.

But just when they were about to give up hope, the Persian guy arrived like a knight in shining armour to rescue the, by now, very frustrated independent princess… Not how Lilith would have preferred to have met him, but by this point she was just glad to see him. They shyly said hello to each other, and the lovely, elderly neighbour looked at them both and said, 'Oh, aren't you guys cute! How long have you been together?'

Lilith wasn't sure what or how to respond. Somehow, she didn't think honesty would work quite as well on this occasion. 'Oh, him? Oh, he's just a random stranger I've matched with on a hookup app and we agreed to spend the night together…'

But before she could come up with anything remotely plausible, the Persian Prince, who had been playing with the door since he got there, did two things simultaneously. He responded to the lady with 'We fell in love at first sight a few years ago when I was even younger' and that he'd always been attracted to older women. And just as he said that, the door finally swung open. (As did all of Lilith's chakras during the night.)

He was a fabulous lover. Attentive to Lilith's needs and determined to look after her body in a way very few of the younger guys she'd met so far had. Maybe she should have knocked on the neighbour's door to loan him to her for the next night. She'd looked like she needed a bit of extra loving – and there was definitely enough of him to go around.

Thirty-One

31 October 2018

It's Halloween and I'm stuck in the suburbs. It's a big deal up here. Like massive. Massive like those giant inflatables popping up everywhere in the pristine white picket-fence gardens. Pumpkins on every doorstep. Themed drinks at every coffee shop (not that there's many here).

I am in no mood, however, to trick or treat. I want to be in the city tonight. So many parties, so many possibilities. Not stuck here with a bunch of hysterical neighbours playing by the book and letting loose once a year. Holy shit these people need more going on in their lives.

Elena is busy with her kids, whilst mine are out with their friends. So, there's nothing else for it… If I can't be in the city, I shall bring the city to me! I've been on my phone all evening, matching with various guys, but there's just no Halloween sparks there. I find myself endlessly scrolling and swiping these days, only to look at their profiles and realise they're not the match for me. I've met so many guys now, I've kind of honed down what I'm looking for – although I'm always up for surprises.

I think I've just found my match, though. He's French. Young. Into sex (really?!) and mischievous. Exactly the vibe I've been looking for all night. Our chat quickly takes a different turn. It flows. I feel connected. It's hard to describe but I just know that the chemistry is already at work, just with our words. Our minds click. We flirt like mad. He's very daring – in charge. Not controlling, but simply in charge. And it already feels good.

We've agreed to meet tomorrow night for a drink only – to start with. He's not in a rush and nor am I. I couldn't have left the house tonight anyway because I'm waiting for the girls to get back from their party before they head to their dad's tomorrow. They have a better social life than I do, it seems. Still, at least I'll go to sleep tonight dreaming of a more exciting tomorrow. What's in store for me this time?

2 November 2018

This one's a keeper!

Okay, so I got to the bar early last night to meet my new French lover. He's called Quinn. Turns out he got there early, too. Same minds! No waiting game. But a LOT of play. He kissed me straight away. (I don't even think we'd spoken any words or even said 'Hello'.) A slow, real French kiss. One after the next. He whispered in my ear so many dirty words in French, I felt my whole body responding as I ran my hands through his dark brown hair and caressed his clean shaved face.

We were standing with him right behind me against the wall and I was just in front of him, pressing against his body. It was so hot, I felt like we should be in a porn movie. The bar was packed full of people and I could feel how hard he already was. And then, he gently ordered me to go to the toilets, take my bra off, and bring it back to him. He wanted to wank all over it later that night. I followed his orders and headed to the loos, brushing against the hard area in his jeans as I walked away.

I like a man in charge and didn't think it would be possible for someone younger. Especially someone some fifteen years younger than me. He grabbed my bra, folded it in his pocket, and walked out of the bar, leaving me wanting so much more.

I found myself giggling to myself in the bar as the barman gave me a look, wondering what on earth I was up to. I pulled up a chair and ordered myself another drink and watched the rest of the city party as I daydreamed about Quinn and what he was going to ask me to do next.

A couple of hours later, once I'd got back home, he sent me a video of him wanking and coming all over my bra. It was so hot, I came multiple times just watching it on repeat. He told me he wanted to meet with me the following Friday and spend the night exploring. It's only Friday evening now, so it's going to be one hell of a long week!

6 November 2018

This is turning out to be one of the most thrilling weeks in my sex his(HER)story and we're only halfway through the week. I've been sexting Quinn non-stop since our bar meet and bra encounter. (I wonder if I'll get that back or he's keeping it in his memory box/wank box.) I can tell he's super playful – and very skilled, too. I'm in for a treat when we finally meet in person again. He's had multiple experiences already, including threesomes with a man and a woman. How exciting! But I keep reminding myself 'one step at a time'. We still have to spend the night together, discover each other's bodies, and give each other maximum pleasure.

Another cool thing is I haven't felt inclined to match with anyone else. I haven't been mindlessly scrolling on the apps or feeling unfulfilled. Right now, I feel quite content. Granted I'm still a little distracted from work and have found myself sneaking off to the toilets a few more times than I can count to send another naughty sext to Quinn, but it's not feeling like an obsession – yet.

10 November 2018

The night finally arrived – and what a night it was! I'm still on the comedown this afternoon. Literally.

We met at Grand Central Station under the clock and kissed instantly. Like something out of a movie – a more romantic one this time. He's got a cheeky smile that I just love. Full of joy, of life, of youth. And when I'm around him, I feel the same way. Giddy, excited, full of hope.

We headed downtown to a super-nice hotel I booked for us. Only the best for this guy. I always love the knowing smiles of the staff at the desk. No problems with check-in this time and as soon as I opened the door, I knew I'd picked well. The room just oozed sexiness. There was a massive bed, enough for about five people (not that I was ready for that yet!), a balcony (although it was freezing outside), and a bathroom with a bath and shower. What a treat.

Barely any words spoken, we jumped on each other in the shower and devoured every moment – every touch, every kiss. I have no other words for it other than delicious. His body is gorgeous. His dick is gorgeous (I had a preview earlier in the week). And his hands are knowledgeable. 'Marcus who?' is all I have to say…

I blew him as the hot water, and then come, dripped on my face. No sooner had I done that, he was hard again very quickly and began to take me from behind in the shower, against the cold marble. I'm pretty sure I made enough noise for the entire hotel to hear as I came hard.

After our steamy bathroom session, we dried ourselves off and ordered some room service – although admittedly mostly drinks. (Why the hell not?!) And from there, we continued our exploration. Honestly, it was a masterclass in all of the good stuff. He wanted to show me how to deep-throat like a pro. Not something I've been particularly keen on before (or sure of how to do correctly) but I was surprisingly excited to learn.

He positioned me lying on the bed, which was quite high up, with my head leaning slightly backwards in the air whilst he stood right there. It was the perfect angle for a deep blow job and I was surprised just how deep I really could go. It took a bit of training, though, and we had a good giggle. That's the beauty when you're so open to sex and all the things it can offer you – it gets to be fun, exploratory, safe, sexy, and even funny.

Anyway, from that position, I lay still on my back in the middle of the bed with Quinn's dick and balls on my face and in my mouth. This time though my legs were spread and he started fingering me, shushing me and speaking dirty to me as I gagged on this dick at the same time. No lady likes to be shushed but on this occasion I let him off – plus it turned me on so much, I had multiple orgasms as a result. Or maybe it was just one long ongoing one that came in waves – I've no idea but all I know is it felt fucking good.

After all that action, we took a break. For a drink and some much-needed food. (I needed the energy as he'd almost wiped it out of me!) We had a hot bath together and I just felt so relaxed. The most relaxed I've felt in a really long time. I told him about my adventures and he told me about his. I felt equal to him and there were no bad games – only the good types. He told me he loves women and men, as well as giving and receiving pleasure. He's an extremely generous lover and human being that embraces sexuality fully. He then told me that he's always been attracted by older women and had this fantasy of fucking his mum's friend who apparently looked a bit like me. We laughed. I was quite happy to live up to that fantasy for him.

When we finally emerged from the bath, we decided to get dressed and go for a drink and dance in the club at the top of the hotel – with 360-degree views of NYC. He told me I wasn't allowed to wear my bra underneath my white tee shirt so he could see my breasts as we danced together. I've never felt more beautiful or sexy. Completely in touch with my sexual self, with no shame and no taboo. Like I was supposed to be here in this space, on this night. I wish I could have frozen time and felt that way forever.

Anyway, once we were all danced out, we headed back to the room. I needed some sleep and so did he. It's rare that I sleep with my lovers but we ended up crashing on the massive bed and I felt like I could trust him completely. Not sure why, but I did – and I do. He woke me up early this morning with a massive hard-on brushing my mouth. I laughed. Does he ever stop?! Apparently not – but I've definitely found a good teacher. I told him I had to get back to the suburbs but before I could get out of bed, he moved me to lying flat on my stomach and lay very still on top of me. I could feel the weight of his body and dick on top of me as he slowly penetrated me, taking my ass in a very gentle and expert way whilst pinching my nipples and whispering dirty, magic words into my ear. I screamed with pleasure yet again (sorry, hotel guests!) and he came soon after me. I felt completely wasted – in a good way. Light and free, as if I was floating on air, having an out-of-body experience.

Before I left, he suggested that we become fuck buddies or, even better, friends with benefits. I said yes, of course. As much as I don't want to get attached to someone, I also don't want to detach from something that feels good for me either. Whatever we are, whatever label we put on it, I'm having some more!

Thirty-Two

Lilith was finally starting to approach life a little differently than she had before. Things were slowly shifting – and in the best way possible – even though there was still a long way to go. She looked back to what her life was like at the beginning of the year compared to now and couldn't believe how far she'd come – or how many times she'd come for that matter.

She finally had a secure job that felt like it fulfilled her passions and purpose, at least for now. She had colleagues she genuinely loved, and her sex life was in a really healthy place right now. She still thought about Marcus every now and then (what was it that guy had on her?!) but she also now had Quinn, and he made her feel good with his cheeky messages whilst she did the food shop, presented in meetings at work, or sat on the train home back to the suburbs. It was a good distraction from continuing to live out the first part of her dual life. And, most importantly, she had her friends.

Lilith decided to try to arrange a night out with Lorna, so she typed out a text message.

'Hey Lorna, fancy heading into the city tonight and painting the town red?'

'Lilith! I'd love to but Chris is away with work so I've got the kids. Fancy a girls' night in instead?'

Lilith was glad they were texting so she didn't have to hide her disappointment. She'd fancied putting on a pair of slinky jeans and a touch of lipstick, and having a peruse of any eligible bachelors as she took in the New York skyline. She could still go out and do that herself, of course, but she'd probably end up feeling lonely, even if she was surrounded by a sea of people. So, a night in it was.

'Sure! Let me know what time you want me.'

A trip to the West Side was always better than staying in Little Haven, so Lilith perked up and picked out a bottle of white wine that had been chilling for a few days. She looked round the fridge some more and grabbed another one. Always best to turn up with too much than not enough – plus, she was sure they'd get through them easily.

A few hours later and Lilith was standing on Lorna's porch, ringing the doorbell frantically to get out of the rain. That was the problem with this time of year – it rained heavily for days on end with no sign of stopping. Something she probably should have got used to from living in London but the rain just hit differently here. It was stronger – and more frantic.

Lorna came running to the door, shouting, 'I'm coming, I'm coming!' as she did so, making Lilith stifle a giggle. She just couldn't help her mind from wandering sometimes.

'Sorry, Lil, was just in the kitchen chilling some wine. I forgot to put it in the fridge earlier. I have ice cubes, though!'

Lilith pulled out her two freshly chilled bottles of wine (courtesy of her cool cooler) and popped them into Lorna's open arms.

'I've already got us covered!' she exclaimed as she scurried inside and hung up her coat. 'I'm also a fan of my apparent new nickname.' She smiled.

'Lil' had a ring to it. It made her sound younger. More millennial. It was perfect.

Lorna smiled back and beckoned her into the living room. Her house was beautiful. Very white and clean – and minimalistic. Just Lilith's style. There were huge big windows in each room, too, so the place would be flooded with light when it wasn't a shitshow of weather outside.

Lilith sensed, though, that this wasn't Lorna's dream home. You could just tell by her whole demeanour in the house. She had such a powerful and confident facade at work, and she was just… different here.

'Shall I pour us a glass now?' Lorna said as Lilith positioned herself on the sofa, unsure whether to get comfy and put her feet up or not. 'Make yourself at home!'

Lilith smiled and took her cue by curling her feet up and propping up some cushions behind her. 'I'd *kill* for a large glass right now.'

Lorna tootled off to the kitchen armed with the bottles of wine whilst Lilith continued to admire the home. There was a ginormous glass fire in front of her that spanned almost the entire width of the room and numerous spotlights on the ceiling that looked like they changed colour to suit whatever mood you were in.

Lorna returned just as quickly as she'd left, with what looked like half the bottle of wine in Lilith's glass and hers.

She giggled and they clinked their glasses together as Lorna sat down at the far end of the sofa.

'Your house is beautiful,' Lilith exclaimed, still scanning her eyes around the room.

'Thanks. It's Chris's pride and joy. I'd probably prefer something a little smaller and less flashy,' Lorna replied with a knowing look in her eyes.

'I can relate to that,' Lilith replied, taking a large sip from her glass before setting it back down on the coffee table in front of her. 'I *hate* my house.'

'Really?'

'Yep. Ended up in the suburbs when I first moved here from London. With my ex. My plan was more city life than Connecticut.'

Lilith picked her glass of wine back up and took another swig.

'I pictured a big, sweeping apartment in the heart of it all – city lights, New York cabs, midnight coffee shops, bars on the doorstep… Instead of this ridiculous blue house in the suburbs with a white picket fence and a humongous tree in the yard that creates a depressing shadow over the entire house. Not to mention that it's placed in this awful village full of pretentious housewives who are members of all these exclusive clubs I can't, and frankly don't want to, join. And that's not even the punchline. The worst part is this house has been up for sale for the last fucking year and no one bloody wants it. Not a soul. No one. Nada. Tumbleweed. So I'm stuck in it. Until someone crazy enough wants to buy it… Which, right now, is looking around a million to one.'

Lilith took yet another big gulp of wine before looking back at Lorna and raising her eyebrows.

Lorna shook her head and laughed. 'Wow. Okay, I see your problem.'

'Aren't you glad it's not your problem?!' Lilith giggled before clinking their glasses together again.

'I mean, I might be able to top it.'

It was Lorna's turn now to take some big swigs of wine before she continued.

'We've lived here now for ten years. It was a wreck when we got it but Chris saw the "potential", and to give him his due, he's completely transformed it. But I also haven't seen him for the last ten years. When he hasn't been working on the house, he's been at work. And when he hasn't been at work, he's been out with the guys from work. And when he hasn't been out with the guys from work, he's been out with clients and God knows who. The boys don't really know who their father is. I feel like a single mother and widow. I'm working my way up in my career for what? My money's my own but I've got nothing to spend it on except for the boys. We don't go on family vacations. We don't go out for nice dinners. We don't go out and try new experiences. We don't do anything. We might as well not exist.'

It was Lilith's turn now to exclaim ,'Wow'.

Lorna hurried out of the room and returned with the remainder of the first bottle of wine to top up their glasses.

'I'm afraid to say I might just be able to top it, though,' Lilith said as she took a deep breath and prepared to tell her friend what she hadn't been able to tell anyone else close to her yet.

'I'm all ears,' Lorna replied, sitting back and cradling her glass of wine in anticipation.

'So, I've been officially separated for more than a year now, even though I don't talk about it much,' Lilith started, watching Lorna's eyes meet hers as she listened intently.

'It was my decision. I wanted out. Like I had this urge to be on my own, to be free. It's not been the easiest, as you can imagine. Anyway, I've been seeing some… men. Multiple men, in fact. Tall men. Short men. Cute men. Sexy men. Young men. The odd older man… I've basically been fucking half of New York City.'

Lorna almost spat out her wine. 'And you're telling me this is a problem, why?!'

'I mean that part hasn't been too much of a problem, although there's definitely been some challenges along the way. But it's the living two different lives that's the problem. I have this life where I go to the city and meet all these different guys and I experience all these different things… and then it's… over. I get back on the train to the suburbs on my own. And I walk into my house and it just feels like it's not mine. Like it's not my life. Then when I have the girls, I obviously don't go and meet anyone. I do the school runs, I do the food shops, I watch movies with them in the evening, and then they go to bed and I sit on the floor with my bottles of wine, and I just feel… empty.'

Lorna was quiet now as she took in everything Lilith was saying. It was amazing how quickly you could open up to someone and just lay it all out there. Both women were relieved to be in each other's company, but equally scared to put out there in the world how they were truly feeling. Because the one thing they definitely had in common right now was loneliness.

'Jeez, Lil, sounds like we've both got it going on,' Lorna finally managed to say. 'I'm glad you came over tonight.'

'I'm glad I came over, too,' Lilith replied before allowing a tear to trickle down her cheek.

Lorna pulled her in for a big squeeze and both women allowed the tears to fall from their cheeks as they held each other tightly and felt thankful for this new friendship. At least for one night, they wouldn't have to feel so lonely.

As they broke away from the hug, Lorna patted Lilith on the thighs before pushing herself up to get the second bottle of wine from the fridge. As she came back in with wine glasses full to the brim, she beamed. 'Right, now tell me about these hunky men!!'

Thirty-Three

The next day, Lilith was feeling strangely refreshed despite her looming hangover. She and Lorna had stayed up talking – and laughing hysterically – until the early hours, consuming countless bottles of wine and, subsequently, numerous packets of crisps. They'd shared pretty much everything now and the overriding feeling from Lilith was simply relief. Relief to have let her true feelings and fears out with someone who just 'got it'. And relief to have somebody to laugh and cry with, no matter the time of day. It was a good feeling – and one she hoped was reciprocated.

Her phone buzzed and she looked down to see a message from Quinn.

'Fancy a sexy shopping trip this afternoon?'

Lilith smiled to herself before replying, 'What's in it for me?'

It was her last night of 'freedom' before she was back to suburban duties, so she hoped he had a little more in store for her.

'Why don't you come meet me and find out?'

Lilith had to stop herself from smiling too widely. She'd taken herself for a walk to the infamous dog beach and it was surprisingly busy today. Busy being three separate dog walkers with their designer pooches and diamond-encrusted collars. She picked up the pace and headed back to the house to freshen up and change for her spontaneous trip into the city.

A few hours later and there he was. Beaming seductively at the corner opposite Grand Central Station. Lilith couldn't get across the street quick enough but had to wait for the traffic to stop and for the endless floods of people around her to disperse. He pulled her in immediately for a long, sensual kiss, before grabbing her hand and taking her into a nearby lingerie shop. He was a man of few words, really, but Lilith liked it that way. And when he did speak to her, she hung onto every last word – not least because he was usually whispering sweet nothings into her ear (or more like dirty nothings).

Lilith spotted a sexy black set as soon as she walked in the door, which she picked up and admired before Quinn gave her a wink and took it off her to carry for her (presumably to take to the till later). Lilith smiled and continued to browse the goodies around them. Quinn pulled her over to the toy section and picked up a large strap-on before looking to Lilith for approval. Another thing Lilith had never tried before, but, as always, she was willing to give it a go.

'Let's do it,' she said as they headed over to the till to pay for their purchases.

This was about to shape up into a more interesting night than Lilith could have imagined.

Quinn had booked the accommodation this time – and he'd picked a good one. It was a cool, art deco hotel right in the heart of it all, with gold wallpaper and smart doormen, who nodded almost knowingly as they opened the main doors for them. Oh the things this place must have seen – and was about to see. Like giddy schoolchildren, Lilith and Quinn ran up the stairs to their room. It was only on the first floor, so they hadn't wanted to wait for the lift – plus they weren't sure if they'd be able to keep their hands off each other in there, and going one floor up wasn't enough time.

Quinn scanned the keycard as they stumbled into the room, embracing each other and pulling off each other's clothes. Within seconds they were both naked, rolling around on the floor at the foot of the bed whilst Quinn expertly fingered Lilith until she came. As she tried to compose herself, he then instructed her to put on the strap-on and fuck him in the ass. This was a total first for her but she was curious about how it would make her feel – and him!

Turns out, she was a pro and managed to penetrate him deeply (with a lot of lube, she learnt) as he positioned himself on all fours on the bed whilst Lilith stood up towards him. She felt strong and empowered and completely sexually free. Which is exactly how he felt as he came all over the bed sheets. They lay next to each other giggling and kissing before deciding to shower off and order room service. Why go out when you could have food and drinks delivered to your bed and then pick up from where you left off?

Again, they decided they'd both stay the night. Lilith didn't want to peel herself away to stay more nights at the house than she needed to and Quinn was just his usual easy-going self. And besides, the hotel was too good to leave early – the bed sheets were heaven!

They lay for a moment in silence – their bodies entwined, as Lilith smiled to herself. She felt most herself when she was with him, and that's how she wanted to be more and more. Her phone buzzed and she went to reach down for it as it had obviously fallen on the floor at some point during their sessions. She realised she hadn't looked at it once since meeting with Quinn earlier in the day and that made her feel good, too. She was being present and in the moment. A rare trait that she wanted to embrace more of.

She swiped up her screen to see that it was a message from Victor and she couldn't help but smile again. He was simply sharing his life plans and projects and asking her what she was up to. Quinn massaged Lilith's back and asked her if she was okay.

'Sorry,' Lilith replied, 'it's just an old friend of mine called Victor.'

'Old friend, hey?' Quinn queried, knowingly.

Lilith laughed. 'Well, if you must know, he was actually one of the very first people I matched with almost a year ago and we had a rather steamy virtual session on Christmas Eve.'

'Well, then.' Quinn smiled. 'Sounds like my kind of guy.'

Lilith laughed again. 'You'd like him, actually.'

Lilith proceeded to text Victor back to fill him in on her latest shenanigans – including her time with Quinn – before putting her phone back under her pillow. Between the two of them – Victor and Quinn – she felt like she had it covered. No need for now to find anyone else…

Was this the way forward? Was this what polyamory was all about? She wasn't in love with either of them but she did love them – in her own way. She cared for them but she wasn't jealous or over-attached. She wanted them to be happy. They mattered to her and she mattered to them. It was easy. Effortless. Fulfilling.

Her phone buzzed yet again – this time it was a message from Marcus. She decided to ignore him, swiped away from her screen, and kept her phone firmly under her pillow. He wasn't part of what she had going on right now and she needed to keep it that way.

At some point, Lilith fell asleep and was again awoken in the morning to Quinn's dick in her face, which she proceeded to put in her mouth to practise her deep throating. She still hadn't quite got the hang of it but she was better and he definitely seemed to enjoy it. He scooped her out of bed and into the shower, before fucking her from behind as the water gushed down onto their bodies. Lilith put her hands on the glass as she screamed in pleasure and they both sank to the floor as they came, slipping and sliding amongst their body fluids and the hot, steamy water.

As they dried themselves, Lilith checked the time and quickly threw on her clothes so she could make the next train home. She could easily spend the day with Quinn again but she knew she needed to get back – plus things felt good right now and she didn't want to ruin it by making it more than what it was. Good fucking between friends. *Great* fucking, in fact.

They said their goodbyes as Lilith two-stepped down the stairs, nodded to the doormen, and jogged to the train station to resume her role in suburbia.

'Until next time,' Lilith thought to herself. 'Next time.'

On the train home, Lilith felt her phone continually buzzing, expecting to see messages from Sophia or the girls to see where she was. She was only going to be around thirty minutes late but she knew everyone was a sucker for their 'schedule'. But it wasn't any of them. There was another message from Marcus and one from Aaron, her work colleague turned friend. God, she had so much to fill him in on – and she wanted to before they headed on their next work trip to LA in a week's time.

'Want to go for drinks after work tomorrow?'

'Yes, let's! SO much to catch up on,' Lilith replied to Aaron, before quickly texting Sophia to ask if she could sit in with the girls for a few hours the next evening.

Her notifications continued to flash as she realised she hadn't yet opened Marcus's messages from last night and this morning. He wanted to see her and get back to where they were. Each message more insistent than the last. If only he knew she'd be in LA soon – all it would take would be one quick message – but Lilith stopped herself. She knew she couldn't establish the same type of connection with him that she had with other people. And that was because he was scared or he simply didn't care. Or was it because she was scared and cared too much? Either way, it had no future – only heartbreak. And as much as she wanted to see his face again and touch his entire body, she had to show restraint.

Did she have to? Lilith wasn't sure, but she was determined to keep avoiding him for as long as it took.

Thirty-Four

1 December 2018

What an extraordinary November I've had – seriously. I don't use that word lightly but it's the most fitting word I can think of to describe how the last month has been for me. Meeting and exploring with Quinn has been a godsend. It's so cool to have someone in my life that's sexually and emotionally available. Friends with benefits is definitely the way forward. And just 'normal' friends, too.

Me and Aaron went out for drinks after work last night and I filled him in on everything – although I was pretty sure Lorna had given him some insight given that his facial expression didn't change nearly half as much as I thought it would when I told him about all my crazy encounters over the last year.

Anyway, there's something to be said about platonic male friendship. He's happily married and we have no attraction towards each other. Sure, he's a good-looking guy, but when I look at him, I don't see a hot piece of ass (like with many of my matches), I see a kind, adventurous, funny guy who I can laugh and cry with in equal measures. A true friend. And I'm so glad he's coming with me to LA later this week.

Marcus has been continuing to message me recently and I'm finding it harder to limit my replies to him. I keep wondering if maybe things will be different – maybe he's different. I can feel this longing from him to see me again and I don't know why that is. Is it just about sex or is it something more? I know I felt it, but I don't want to feel it. Not if it's not reciprocated. Arghhh, help me.

10 December 2018

I've fucked it. I've fucking fucked it. I'm on the flight home from LA, feeling the worst I've ever felt. And I'm looking at my previous entry wondering why I decided to do what I did – even though I know it was inevitable. All of this was totally inevitable…

On the flight over here, I couldn't stop thinking about Marcus and the last night we had together in LA. I was determined not to tell him I was going to be there but one of the benefits (and curses in my case) of a geolocalisation dating app is that they do exactly that: they geolocate you. And by some weird magic, once I'd landed and checked in to my hotel, I realised that Marcus and I were still a match on the app and he could see that my location had changed to LA.

He messaged me almost immediately. I'd barely even put my suitcase down or taken off my shoes. I don't know if I was in shock or just still in my stellar stubborn mode, but I managed to resist replying to him all day. I had a conference in the afternoon, so my phone remained in my jacket pocket, and I went out for dinner with Aaron in the early evening. We realised we hadn't really eaten much, so went all out, stuffing our faces and sharing a bottle of wine. Of course, that one bottle then turned into another one, and maybe a couple of shots (my memory's a little hazy), and before I knew it, I was gripping onto Aaron's arm as he guided me back to our hotel, giggling about how unprofessional we were on the first night of our work trip.

He dropped me off at my room – I could barely remember the room number – and I fumbled my way inside. Marcus was on my bed. Naked. Smiling at me. I thought I was hallucinating. I still have no idea how he got in there – he must have gotten a key somehow, and I'm guessing I messaged him or else how would he have known what hotel or room I was in? – but all I knew was that no matter how hard I tried, I just couldn't resist. It was a big mistake and I was walking straight into it. I knew it, he knew it, the whole fucking universe knew it, but yet there I was being drawn in by his sexy, naked body, and that piercing smile.

I stood in front of him and slowly removed my clothes. I say that, but it probably wasn't slow at all and I imagine I was probably wobbling all over the place as I tried to stay looking seductive. Still, it worked because moments later I was on top of him and I swear it felt like we were making love. It was the most tender, caring, deep session we've ever had – caressing, whispering, and even kissing each other. I felt like I was in a fairy tale or a dream. And still now, I wonder if I did actually dream it. If I was imagining a situation that simply wasn't there. But as I lay next to him after we'd managed to pull ourselves apart, I felt my hand reaching for his, and I told him that I loved him.

And in that moment, I meant it. All I wanted was to capture the essence of our connection and check that he felt the same. It was like every other thought and feeling had gone out of the window and I was completely spellbound, imagining this life with him – this future. Thinking that maybe I really had found 'the one'. That I didn't need to sleep around with different men, seeking all these different connections. Because *this* was the connection. This is what I'd been looking for.

No sooner had I uttered those words, though, I felt his hand jerk back from mine and I looked to see him staring at me in a completely detached and disgusted way. He jumped out of bed and started freaking out – telling me he always knew I was in love with him from the start and that I'd been hiding it, pretending to be cool and that it was just about sex when it was anything but. That I'd been trying to trick and lure him in. His face got redder and redder and his voice louder and louder as he started shouting at me that this had to stop. That it couldn't go on a second longer. That I was a liar. That I was a freak. That he'd never had feelings for me and never would. That I should disappear from his life and never come back…

I don't think I moved from the bed as I sat up in shock, listening to him shout at me. I just froze completely still, watching him as he threw his clothes back on and picked up his stuff that was strewn across the room. I didn't say anything – I couldn't find the words. And I didn't want to beg or respond. I was still naked and aghast. It was like it wasn't happening to me – like I was having an out-of-body experience. He slammed the door shut as he left the room and that was my cue to break down and start sobbing uncontrollably. I think I actually howled – it came from that deep within me. All the angst, all the pain, all the expectation, all the rejection. All the loneliness of the year piling back on me tenfold. I could feel the panic and anxiety rising in me and knew I couldn't stay in this room on my own. I could already feel the walls starting to close in on me.

I called Aaron, not realising it was three in the morning. I don't even know what I said to him because I was so out of breath from sobbing but I told him that I needed him and he just knew. He gave me his room number and told me to come straight away. To leave my stuff behind and that we'd pack together in the morning. He had twin beds, so it was a safe place to sleep, and he'd be right next to me if I needed anything. Who was this guardian angel in my life?

I ran to his room, somehow managing to fill him in on the night's events without pausing for breath, and then collapsed onto the spare bed and fell into what felt like a deep coma, feeling protected and guarded.

Somehow, a few hours later, I managed to drag myself up out of bed, head back to my room, pack my bags, get to the work venue, and get ready for my big presentation. I think I was running on autopilot or something because everything just happened so mechanically. But as I arrived at the venue, I felt my stomach drop. It was right near Marcus's offices. I knew this because I remember him mentioning it in passing at some point.

And then the most improbable thing happened. As I stepped on stage and started speaking, there he actually was. Marcus – walking past the window to the right of me. Suited and booted, walking big strong strides in what felt like slow motion. I felt my eyes fixate onto him, taking him in, before returning to my speech. Was I hallucinating again? Part of me wanted to run after him so badly but the other part of me (the one that's so bruised from last night's brutal parting, the part that knows this is the last time I'll ever see him in my life) allowed him to walk on by.

My presentation seemingly went without a hitch, and I looked around the room to take in everyone nodding and smiling and clapping. But today, the job that meant so much to me meant nothing at all. I shook some hands, had a cup of coffee, and found Aaron in the crowd of people so we could grab our bags and head to the airport. He'd changed his flight to be on the same one as me but had only managed to grab a seat a few rows behind. Still, I needed him to navigate me through the airport and be a calming presence as we waited at the gates.

Now, on what feels like the longest plane journey home, I just feel immensely sad. Whatever that was – some form of love, lust, or infatuation – it's pushed me right to the edge. And I need to make sure something like this never happens again.

Thirty-Five

15 December 2018

The last few days have been painstakingly difficult as I've tried to 'settle' back into my life at home. I've barely spoken to anyone since the LA trip and I haven't even opened my apps. I can't face it yet. I can't face the rejection or the thought of getting close to someone like that again. Marcus texted me in the early hours of this morning, trying to reconnect with me as if nothing had happened. He was probably out getting wasted and desperately trying to find a booty call – even if it was virtual. I saw the text with great satisfaction and although I'm still wounded, and will be for quite some time, I knew that this would be the last text of our six-month frenzy. I blocked and deleted his number, and somehow managed to fall back asleep.

Anyway, it's nearly Christmas… again. And this year, for Christmas, I'm having a… divorce! That's right! The final papers have just come through, right on time before heading to France! OMG. Finally. It feels like I've been waiting for them for a lifetime.

At last, I can tell all my family. My friends. The bloody world. I need out of this house and out of this double life. A couple came to view it the other day and they seemed keen. A step closer to someone finally being interested in the home I can't wait to get out of. Obviously I'll still have the girls every other week but I want to live in the city. The dream I've had all along. The bright lights, late nights, and total buzz of it all. To roll in after a night out instead of looking at the time on my phone to make the last train, or hailing a cab that'd cost me a day's wages. To walk out of my door to alllll of the amenities I could possibly need. To fling open the curtains to the view of countless apartment blocks so I can spy on my hot new neighbours (hehe, just kidding). That's what I want. To feel alive again. Full-time.

Holy shit, just thinking about getting out of here makes me emotional and giddy. (Hallelujah, I'm going to be free!) I don't want to get ahead of myself but I am beyond relieved, and terrified at the same time – an emotion I probably wasn't expecting. I've been crying for the past hour, thinking about what all of this actually means for me.

But most of all, it feels like my identity is once again in limbo. Right now, I don't know what life holds for me. I don't know where I'm going to be living or how much longer this house will take to sell. I'll officially be a part-time parent (even though I've been exactly that for the last year). I expected to experience joy, excitement, and freedom when the papers finally came through, but right now, it's more the opposite. I feel anxious. Nervous. Scared. Lonely. Even though I was the one who wanted out. I guess it takes time…

30 December 2018

What a Christmas! Definitely looked a lot different to last year – and for that, I have to feel thankful.

Marcus has sucked up my life energy for the past six months but I'm determined to move forward now. Strangely, even though I've been separated for more than a year, being officially single to the world doesn't make me any hornier. The total opposite, in fact. I haven't once opened my apps on this entire trip, nor really thought about any of my guy connections. Obviously, I want to keep exploring, and maybe even see some guys on a regular basis (how crazy of me!), but in a more qualitative way.

I'm starting to slowly feel a massive sense of freedom for the first time in my life along with an immense sense of relief. And I want to savour it. Amongst all of the craziness, it's these moments that shape a life. And I refuse to spend any more prolonged periods of time feeling depressed and lonely. I have full control over my life and I intend to exercise it.

Thirty-Six

Lilith had a jam-packed January ahead, which she was glad of. It had been a quiet New Year's in France as the girls were with their dad, and Lilith found herself on the beach, dipping her toes in the freezing cold water as she said goodbye to all the things that no longer served her and got ready to welcome in a life-changing new year. She wasn't usually a fan of the whole 'new year, new me' crap, but this time it had a different meaning. She was a 'new her' and she planned to fully embrace that.

First on the agenda was a personal trip to London and Paris to blow away the cobwebs and catch up with friends, followed by a work trip in Switzerland with Lorna. She only had one night in London, so she needed to make the most of it – and, no, she wasn't going to spend it with a guy this time. Instead, she put on her glad rags and arranged dinner and drinks with a group of her much-missed friends in Soho. Letting them know about the divorce felt like there was no coming back and was so liberating. They were super understanding and gave her so much love.

They cheered to her new life and she felt really supported and at home. She was going to work on moving back here eventually – but one step at a time. For now, though, just being there for one night, and being herself, was enough.

The next morning she headed back to St Pancras International to catch a Eurostar to Paris. It felt strange to be going back to France so quickly but there were friends and family she hadn't managed to catch up with during the Christmas break – plus she'd arranged to meet with Victor, so it was well worth the extra train ride whilst she was over here. For the friends and family who hadn't been closely in touch, Lilith's divorce came as a real shock. She had to excuse herself early from a family dinner party as she couldn't deal with the endless questions and comments from some of her cousins who had seen her moving to NYC as a married woman to be now sitting there, single and happy. God forbid they learn the details of the journey she'd been on during that time – they wouldn't be able to contain themselves!

For Lilith, though, her transition was done. Everyone and anyone now knew. She'd even updated her status on Facebook – which again had led to a flurry of comments and private messages from people she didn't care for, so they were promptly blocked and deleted. If she was going to embrace this whole 'new year, new me' lark, that extended to getting rid of things and people who no longer served a positive purpose in her life.

**

The following evening was her long-awaited dinner date with Victor and she couldn't wait. It would be so nice to be in the presence of someone who'd been there throughout her journey – someone safe and reliable. Someone who genuinely wanted to spend time with her and support her in her endeavours. Someone who wasn't going to look at her in shock, disbelief, or disgust (because she'd had all of those looks, and more, over the past few weeks).

They met at a local hotspot in Montmartre – a part of the city Lilith loved. It was for the artists and the creatives, and it oozed quirkiness and freedom. Victor was already waiting for her at a table by the window – and it looked like he'd taken the liberty of ordering her favourite bottle of wine. Lilith smiled and hurried herself inside out of the cold. She was wrapped up in a big woollen black scarf, hat, and gloves, and giggled as she tried to unravel herself to give Victor a big hug. He kissed her twice on either cheek and pulled out her chair to sit down.

'Why, thank you.' Lilith beamed as she took a seat and stared into his eyes. It was such a pleasure to see him again.

Dinner went by almost too quickly as they barely paused for breath filling each other in on their life events since they last saw each other in October. Victor told Lilith that he was seeing someone. They'd started dating just before Christmas and it was going well so far – she'd even inadvertently met his parents. Lilith was completely cool with it – happy for him, in fact – and she embraced the feelings of non-jealousy that she wasn't sure she'd feel. The only thing was that she was counting on having sex with him tonight, so that was a little inconvenient. She'd seen him as 'one of her regulars', so that had already thwarted those plans – and she wished she'd paid more attention to Tinder.

'Always have a backup plan,' Lilith thought to herself.

Luckily for her, the night was still young, and as she kissed Victor goodbye (on the cheek, of course), she sat herself back down and started frantically searching on her apps. She'd already booked a hotel room (for her and Victor), so she wasn't about to let that go to waste. Plus, she was in one of the most romantic locations in all of Paris (the Eiffel Tower was overrated).

Lilith continued swiping and found herself spoilt for choice. She'd forgotten how hot French men were... Exactly what she needed on this cold, cold night. Only, she must have gotten a little carried away as somehow she ended up double-booking two guys within forty minutes of each other. Whoops! She knew from experience that changing plans last minute didn't go down too well with her millennial friends and the second guy looked too hot to miss. She would have to conduct her French affairs very efficiently.

The first guy (no name number one) arrived at her hotel on time, so Lilith expertly snuck him into her room. He started with preliminaries but she told him that she'd prefer to jump straight to fucking if he didn't mind too much. *She didn't tell him that she'd double-booked, though, as that might be a bit rude.* He was a little taken aback, but not enough to put him off, so he undid his trousers and jumped onto the bed. Lilith wasn't sure what position he wanted her in so she sat seductively in the middle of the bed, kissing his neck. From there, he pushed her backwards onto the bed and took her missionary style. Interesting choice but Lilith didn't mind – it was probably easier and quicker this way. He closed his eyes, which suited her just fine as it gave her a chance to check her watch and fake an orgasm – as loud as she could possibly be (a usually rare occurrence, but this was an emergency). Fortunately for Lilith, she was in luck as it immediately made him come. He politely thanked her and then asked if she'd like to go for a drink. Lilith equally politely declined. Poor guy. She knew he wanted more but she was a busy lady tonight.

He reluctantly left as Lilith hurried him out of the door and jumped in the shower fast, steadying herself as she almost slipped. She only had just under fifteen minutes before she was officially late for her next rendezvous and she wasn't keen on being found by the hotel staff in a naked lump on the bathroom floor.

Just as quickly as she'd jumped in the shower, she jumped out and threw her clothes back on, ordering an Uber as she pulled her top over her head. She'd gotten rather good at multitasking these days. It was only a ten-minute ride, and before she knew it (after some mindless chatter with her cab driver), she'd made it to the second guy's front door (no name number two). It was a little bit after 11 p.m. (she was only a few minutes late) and he was waiting at the door. Super hot and completely Lilith's type. If she'd done one thing right tonight, it was getting the order of these guys right. She wouldn't have been quite as keen to hurry this guy along like she did to guy with no name number one.

He had dark skin, dark eyes, dark hair, and the most amazing smile – the perfect combination. And no sooner had he closed the front door behind her, he had put his fingers on her mouth to stop her from speaking. He was playful and Lilith was relaxed. She had nowhere to rush to, nowhere to be, other than right here. Still, they didn't waste any time with preliminaries.

Lilith could hear his flatmates laughing in the living room but she wasn't in the mood to socialise. He seemingly read her mind, silently took her hand, and walked her to his bathroom. As he gently closed the door, he covered her mouth with his hand, and with the other unzipped his trousers. Lilith was so wet now that she could feel herself dripping through her tights, which he swiftly pulled down to her ankles. She let out a small gasp as he bent her over the bathroom sink. The lighting of which was ideal; they could see themselves looking at each other in the mirror, smiling – longing. Lilith got the sense that this was going to be a magical one.

He whispered in her ear to stay quiet and with both his hands started fingering her, touching her in all the right places. Lilith squirted everywhere on the floor (a party trick she had really mastered now). She was desperate to feel his dick inside her and she could tell he was ready. He fucked her from behind – hard. She could see the intensity of the lust in his eyes in the bathroom mirror, which turned her on even more. They both came very hard at the same time – without a sound. He offered to shower together. It felt close and intimate, yet they hadn't exchanged a word.

Lilith dried herself and got dressed, blowing him a kiss as she left out of the front door – his flatmates still laughing in the living room, completely oblivious to the steam coming out of one of the bathrooms.

It was a cold, January night but the stars were shining brightly and the roads were well lit, so Lilith decided to walk back to the hotel instead of calling an Uber again.

Somewhere in the distance, she heard the clock strike midnight as she picked up the pace with a giant smile on her face, feeling like Cinderella. As soon as she made it to her hotel, she crashed on the bed before picking up her phone to message Aaron.

'Two guys, one night. Well, technically three guys, but I only fucked two of them. At different times – not together. I'm exhausted!'

Aaron immediately texted back, 'LOL. Oh to be in Paris!'

And with that, Lilith tucked herself into bed and immediately fell asleep.

***

The next day, Lilith woke up late. It was a good job she had a late checkout *and* her flight wasn't until the afternoon otherwise they would have been very expensive fucks. Still, it would have been worth it. She felt as though she was walking on cloud nine this morning, if not a little tender down there. A few days off would do her good. She was heading on a work trip with Lorna to Spitlenden – close to a popular ski resort in the Swiss Alps (not that she was sure she'd have much time for skiing but she'd definitely try).

Anyway, she was excited to see Lorna – although she wished they were sharing a flight so she could fill her in on all her escapades. Lorna would be coming from NYC whilst Lilith had an awkward journey via a flight to Geneva and then one to Zurich, before grabbing a hire car to Spitlenden. Still, she could do with the time to catch up on work after an epic break.

As she boarded her first flight, Lilith deleted the apps from her phone and committed to no texting, or indeed sexting, guys during this next trip. She'd had enough to keep her going and she was determined to make the most of the snow-capped mountains, spending time with her friend, and making some positive waves at work.

Once she landed from her second flight in Zurich, Lilith went to pick up the hire car. Lorna would be arriving around an hour afterwards, so she planned to fill in all the paperwork and be ready to go as soon as Lorna stepped out of the terminal. A girls' trip, essentially – although their work probably wouldn't class it as that!

Only, Lilith ended up stuck in a massive queue as she waited to get the car. It turned out everyone was hiring big monster truck-esque cars to get them through the snow and ice. Lorna came to meet her as she'd just got to the front of the queue, clearly delighted to see her despite her obvious jet lag. The women hugged each other tightly, chattering away before they were handed the keys to their ride.

They were met, however, with a little black Fiat with two doors that Lorna couldn't contain her giggles at. How this was going to trudge through inches of snow, Lilith had no idea, but it made her laugh that this was the choice someone in the office had gone for. She'd be having words with them once they got back – or firing out a quick email now with an attached photograph, showing their unimpressed faces in the foreground. She could tell that this trip was going to be a barrel of laughs already and she was glad that she'd volunteered herself to go.

The only thing that worried her was the time away

from 'home'. The girls were with their dad, as planned. She'd barely been back in Little Haven since before Christmas – since nothing had really changed, but everything had. She hadn't yet really lived out her 'new reality'. She hadn't taken the girls to school as an unmarried woman, hadn't done the food shop, hadn't bumped into one of her nosey neighbours, hadn't felt what it felt like to do all these things 'alone', even though she'd been doing all of these things and more for the last year.

Lorna gave her a little nudge as they sat in the car – Lilith's eyes glazed ahead.

'What's on your mind?' she asked gently.

'Oh God, sorry, Lorna, I was in a world of my own there,' Lilith replied apologetically. 'Let's get this car started and I'll fill you in on the goings-on of my wild and crazy mind.' She gave Lorna a quick wink and put the car into gear.

It was just under a two-hour drive to Spitlenden – slightly longer because of the road conditions and Lilith's wariness of being in a foreign country in a car that drove like her grandma's old banger – so they had plenty of time to catch up.

Lilith loved how Lorna's facial expressions didn't change much when she told her all the things that others would class as outrageous. She, of course, updated her on last night's encounters (plural!), as well as everything that happened during the holidays. The divorce papers. The formal announcement to her friends and family. The house finally having someone potentially interested in buying it. And the strange feeling of feeling more 'alone' even though nothing had drastically changed from her previous reality. Lilith found herself choking up as she uttered that word again. That was what she was most afraid of. After all this. Being… alone.

'You're not alone, Lil,' Lorna said to her kindly. 'But I get it. It's a big change – and now suddenly everything feels like it's been pushed forward whilst you were treading backwards for so long.'

Lilith nodded along with her friend. 'You've hit the nail on the head there,' she replied. 'I think I just need to… talk to someone. Like this. But more. I looked for a therapist ages ago but something within me just wouldn't let me do it. I'd even narrowed it down to three different people as if they were in the running for some kind of award, but I just couldn't make a decision.'

Lorna giggled knowingly. 'We've all been there. Trust me. I might be able to recommend someone for you, though – but it depends if it's your thing.'

Lilith raised her eyebrows slightly and briefly glanced over to Lorna suspiciously before averting her eyes back to the road. She was proud of how well she'd navigated them here and they weren't far away now.

'Don't look so scared.' Lorna laughed. 'So, she's a coach and hypnotherapist. She's helped me through quite a lot of things – especially some of my anxieties. I find myself able to deal with stuff so much more calmly and rationally these days.'

Rationality definitely wasn't one of Lilith's strong points, so she kept her mind open.

'Have a think about it anyway and I can always pass her details on to you if you're interested,' Lorna continued. 'We'll have some drinks tonight and then you can decide.' She chuckled.

'Okay, done!' Lilith laughed back.

With that, they pulled into the car park of the ginormous hotel they'd be staying at for the next few days for their work conference. It was going to be quite the tonic and a welcome distraction from all the thoughts currently whirring around in Lilith's mind.

And it really was. They worked hard and partied even harder with no Tinder or hot guy to chat up in sight. Well, there were a few hot guys, but none that Lilith was interested in. Instead, she enjoyed dancing until the early hours with her friend, and knocking on each other's doors in the morning to head down to breakfast so they could fuel up for the day ahead.

On the final night, Lilith decided she'd take the details of the mysterious coach/hypnotherapist that Lorna had mentioned in the car journey over here, so added her email address to her contacts and vowed to reach out to her once they landed in NYC. No more 'woe is me', no more distracting herself too heavily from her real feelings, no more wishing to be somewhere else. She was determined to make the most out of living in New York, even if she wasn't where she wanted to be just yet.

Thirty-Seven

2 February 2019

Okay, so I'm officially cured.

Just kidding. But the therapy session definitely went better than I expected... I think? I'm still surprised at myself that I actually got her details from Lorna, contacted her, and booked a session. Especially when she had a business name of 'Flow with Fleur'. It sounded a bit too whimsical but still something inside me told me I should stop being so sceptical and just give it a try. So that's exactly what I did.

For starters, she was based in the city – on the third floor of a cool apartment building. Her room was minimally decorated with a calm and peaceful urban feel. You couldn't hear the traffic noise outside but, for me, there was definitely something relaxing about knowing that the city was only down a few flights of stairs – especially when I'd envisioned scenes of driving for miles to another faraway town/village in the middle of nowhere that made me feel trapped and almost unable to breathe. So, that was a good start.

Meeting Fleur also went way better than expected. I'd seen a photograph of her online but she looked a little corporate to me – which was fine – but I just couldn't imagine opening up to her or feeling comfortable. Turns out she was the least corporate person imaginable (I should have guessed by the name). She was warm and open, and I could see a tattoo peeking out under the sleeve of her jumper.

She beckoned me in to sit down on one of the plush black sofas (okay, I could get used to this!) and offered me a glass of lemon water. The session was going to be two hours long, so I was glad I had somewhere comfortable to sit. In fact, there were even fluffy blankets and cushions, so I was sure, if nothing else, I could have a good snooze.

Fleur explained to me how the sessions would work (I think she could tell I was nervous/confused). We would talk openly for around forty-five minutes about anything and everything that came to mind. She would ask me questions and I would hopefully answer them honestly and truthfully. Then, I'd 'go under'. I know, I know, it's not as crazy as it sounds! I think this was the part I was most wary of – losing control and being under someone else's. But that's not how it was at all. Hypnosis was more like a guided meditation rather than someone putting you to sleep and making you say or do things without your control. That doesn't mean I didn't find it scary still – especially when we went deep into inner-child stuff and faced some things head on that I've basically been compartmentalising my whole life – but it was also very grounding. I felt in control – of what I was saying, feeling, and uncovering.

When I 'came round', Fleur was beaming at me as if I'd just done something amazing. She told me I have so much energy and that it just flies from the universe and back to my body, up and down. I didn't know what to say. It all sounded a bit whacky to me. But I could feel something. I've always felt like I've got this incredible energy bouncing around me, and I guess now it's just a case of channelling it to the right places (perhaps not only fucking many young guys). I know there's so much more for me to explore in these sessions – we only just scratched the surface – but I'm genuinely excited to go back for more. My next session isn't until the end of the month as I'm heading to San Francisco for some winter sunshine with my friends from London, so my healing journey will have to wait. Although, I have promised myself that I'll disconnect from the apps again to focus on other types of pleasures. That's something we discussed in the session today – enjoying the simple things in life, getting out into nature, grounding myself into my surroundings instead of being 'go, go, go' all the time and making rash decisions. It's going to be good for me – all of it.

4 February 2019

Another day, another milestone. There's been an offer on the house today! Oh my God, I cannot tell you the sense of relief I felt when the real estate agent rang me to let me know there was an offer on the table after all this time. I haven't been particularly impressed with the agent – they don't really give a shit about your house, they just want to take your money. Which is surprising given how little work they've put into actually trying to sell the thing.

Anyway, I just hope the sale goes through and the process isn't too stressful. I've been told it can take up to six months... which terrifies me. But then, what's another six months on top of all this time anyway?!

I keep thinking about the darkness of the house and that tree – and the reason no one has wanted to buy the house until now is because of it. It's become the absolute bane of my existence. I usually love trees, but I've never wanted to cut one down and chop it into tiny pieces more than I have since I moved here (and that's saying something for someone who works in climate change and will do anything to protect the environment). I'm also questioning why we bought a house in the first place. Why didn't we rent? It would have meant I could have gotten out of here way sooner, and with much less hassle. But lessons learned and I know what I'm doing this time round in my new era. My 'my life is my own and I'm not going to tie myself down to anything' era.

13 February 2019

I'm back from SF! Completely forgot to take my journal with me but probably just as well in case I lost it – or my mates found it and read it. Not that I'm not being completely open with them now but you've got to have some things for yourself. Plus there's definitely some shocking entries in here – to the 'normal layman'.

Anyway, SF was amazing. Such a fun trip. It still baffles me how long you can be on a plane and still not have left the country. But saying that, SF has a totally different vibe to NYC. Chilled. Open. Free.

I stuck to my word and didn't use my apps, didn't message any of my guys, and actually didn't even flirt with anyone in person either. Well, maybe a little, but nothing to write home about. And I stuck to my word about engaging in the simple pleasures too... Swimming in the ocean, gorging on delicious food, jogging on the hilltops, sipping crisp white wine at sunset, hanging out with my friends and staying up talking until three o'clock in the morning... It's definitely something I want to do more of now I'm back home. Granted I can't go swimming in the ocean seeing as that's out of bounds to residents like me who don't own a piece of the water (I'll never get over that), but there's still so much I *can* do.

I want to read a book again. Multiple books! I've got a stack of them on my bedside table that have been untouched since we moved here. I just haven't been able to focus and to enjoy reading unless it's a kinky message from my next victim – but that's pretty sad, really. I want to watch the sunrise and sunset on my own or with the people I love. I want to sit in coffee shops, taking in the smell of the coffee and watching the world go by outside. I want to breathe in the fresh air right into my lungs each time I step outside and be genuinely grateful for being alive. Because I really, truly am.

But listen, a girl still has needs. And as much as I'm going to do all these things and more – I'm still curious to continue my exploration of my sexual desires and fantasies.

And why shouldn't I be?! I still see Quinn on a regular basis, and our exploring brings me so much pleasure (in both senses of the word). I also get to hang with Evan number one often, and with Victor when I'm in Paris – our relationships have not only survived but thrived and morphed into beautiful friendships, which is so special. I always shiver when I think that without Tinder, I would have probably never met any of them. On paper, we had nothing in common. And yet we do. So much in fact, it makes me smile. Don't get me wrong. I love those guys and I feel blessed to have them in my life. And I hope I do for a long, long time. But I like 'newness' too. I've realised that it's a big part of who I am.

There's this guy I've been in touch with since I landed back in NYC from SF who has a specific kink and scenario in mind. He seems perfectly mentally sound – probably more than most people who aren't listening to their desires – and in my book, as long as they're respectful of others and harmless, I don't ever judge. Granted, I don't always feel like taking part, but I don't judge.

So, here's his thing... He wants me to come to his house in Harlem, knock at the door dressed in nothing else other than underwear, high heels, and a (warm) coat. Considering it is February it's actually weirdly mild, but, still, that's what he wants. He then wants me to let myself in as the door will be left ajar, go straight into his bedroom where he will be tied up to his bed, gagged, naked, erect, vulnerable, expecting some well-deserved punishment, on all fours.

I'm leaving the house in T-minus three hours so will report back tomorrow, or later tonight if I've got the energy...

I did indeed not have the energy to write back in my journal last night, so here I am, sharing the story on what just happens to be Valentine's Day, with possibly a less romantic story than some might be hoping (but definitely sexy!).

So before I got there last night, dressed to the nines (or should I say 'to the nude'), my Harlem guy had shared some very specific words via WhatsApp that he wanted me to shout at him whilst I had my wicked way with him. We also agreed on a safe hand sign as he was gagged and not able to voice a safe word. All of this was obviously completely new to me and part of me really did wonder what I was letting myself in for, but obviously, as I always do, I dove straight in. Literally.

I felt so naughty sitting in the cab on the way to his place (I definitely didn't want to risk a train journey) but it was also super liberating. The kind of stuff you see in movies but don't actually think you'll ever do. Anyway, when I got there, the door had been left slightly open as planned, so I let myself in, striding confidently in my Louboutin heels and slowly unbuttoning my coat as he revealed himself to me on the bed. A whip had been purposely left out, so I began slapping his ass and shouting the extremities he'd requested (gently at first and then getting harder and harder until he came – no other forms of touching). As I was administering the punishment that he thought he deserved, part of me wondered how he managed to tie himself up to the bed. Did he get some help? It made me giggle internally as I imagined that conversation…

Needless to say, it turned me on a lot more than I thought it would and I realised I could happily get used to this role.

I quickly remembered that once he came, I was to dress again and leave, without a single word – so that's exactly what I did. An extremely well-executed fantasy turned into reality. Everything went according to plan and I enjoyed every minute dominating him and watching him lose his inhibitions. There's just something very pleasurable and powerful about being in control of someone else's desires. Exploration TBC…

Thirty-Eight

Lilith ended the month with another eye-opening therapy session. This time when she booked in, she actually felt a jolt of excitement, which was much more preferable to the apprehension and anxiety she was used to. There was something about carving out that time for herself where the focus was purely on her, her emotions, her feelings, her life. Some people would probably hate that, but for Lilith, it was an opportunity to slow down and reflect. She was so used to keeping herself busy every hour of the day, even if that meant being glued to her phone and looking for her next match. Things were changing, though, now – for the better. She was finally starting to slow down. She was even noticing little things she hadn't noticed before around the village. The same elderly gentleman picking up his morning newspaper from the shop, humming to himself as he slowly but confidently put one foot in front of the other without the need for a walking aid. The smell of fresh coffee coming from the coffee shop that filled the streets surrounding it with this air of energy that Lilith hadn't felt before. The runners who ran on opposite sides of the sidewalk and waved to each other jollily as they silently congratulated each other on their mileage.

None of these things were enough to make Lilith want to stay (this was not her fortress) but they were enough for her to pause and feel grateful for where she was living, even if it wasn't the place she wanted to be. It was the reminder to stop and notice what was going on around her, instead of immersing herself in a frenzied state. And this was something she was keen to tell Fleur about – she was ready to hear some praise and feel like she was achieving something.

Fleur opened the door widely before Lilith reached the top step and beckoned her inside with a big, glowing smile. Lilith wondered if she was always like this or if it was just a facade (could someone really be that happy all the time?) but she quickly snapped herself out of it, realising that she was the one here to be analysed, not Fleur. She hung her coat up, took off her shoes, and plonked herself down, curling her feet up under her bum as if she'd just had a hard day at work and she was kicking her shoes off at home.

Fleur smiled again.

'So, how've you been?'

'Great!' Lilith replied enthusiastically. 'I've been noticing the "little things" a lot more – and I don't feel as badly about where I'm living. Well, especially not since the house officially went up for sale,' she continued.

Fleur nodded gently. 'And what about self-care?'

Lilith went to open her mouth to answer but found

that no words came out. She sat on it for a while before answering, 'Self-care – what exactly do you mean by that?'

'So, what do you do just for you? How do you love yourself? Do you love yourself? Do you want to take care of yourself?'

Lilith's breath quickened. These were good questions but, all at once, they were a lot. Did she love herself? And if she did, how did she show that love to herself? She really wasn't sure. She'd thought she'd been loving herself by feeling confident in her sexuality and sharing that with all these guys on Tinder and Bumble, but maybe that was just simply sexual confidence, as opposed to love for herself.

'Let me rephrase it for you as it looks like you're struggling with what I've asked,' Fleur said, purposely interrupting the flow of Lilith's thoughts. 'Do you carve out any time for yourself where you really tune into your body and emotions?'

'Erm, here?' Lilith responded.

Fleur smiled again. 'Yes, this is definitely a good start – and I'm so glad you booked another session. But I'd suggest that self-care and self-love is something you should be engaging in every day. And I say the word "should" with love because I don't like using that word unless it's absolutely necessary. But loving yourself, looking after yourself, and treating your body and mind with the care and respect they deserve should always be at the top of our priority lists.'

Lilith nodded as she took it all in. She wondered if she had been treating herself the way she wanted to. She'd definitely made some big changes over the last fourteen months (good and bad) but there was also all the time before that – those moments and years she'd pushed aside and brushed under the carpet, instead of allowing herself to heal from. Probably because she didn't know how to heal.

'It could be fairly small things like taking yourself out for a coffee or lunch date, going to the gym, reading a good book, lighting a candle and having a bubble bath, or simply just lying on the sofa, closing your eyes, and making time for your thoughts and feelings. It's just about being at one with yourself and doing things that make you feel good.' Fleur continued. 'What about hobbies – what do you do for fun?'

Lilith giggled as she replied, 'Sex. That's what I do for fun.'

'Okay,' Fleur replied, barely breaking eye contact, 'that's great. That's really great. A healthy sex life is a good start. But maybe not if that's all you do for fun...'

Lilith bit her lip and looked down as she contemplated the fact that the only other thing she could say was drinking – or maybe running, but she hadn't done that for a while and it definitely wasn't something she'd class as fun. Either way, she wasn't going to give either answer to Fleur.

'Well, I guess it sounds like I could do with adding a different flavour of fun into my life,' Lilith said thoughtfully.

Fleur nodded. 'It doesn't have to be anything too crazy or strenuous, but have a think about what would feel nice for you and your body. What would energise you and make you feel good? Something for you to think about when you go away from this session, anyway.'

Lilith's mind started drifting off to the things she

could do. She was sure Lorna went to a yoga class in the city before work and that sounded like it could have the benefits she was looking for. Some good old self-care and some flexibility to help aid her sexual endeavours. How efficient.

The rest of the session went well. Even better than the first. Lilith felt very comfortable in Fleur's presence and she could feel herself opening up further, especially when they went into the guided meditation and started doing inner-child work. It was a mind-fuck but totally necessary – and she knew hypnosis would help her access her subconscious mind to process things and heal.

On the way home, she texted Lorna to ask about her yoga class.

'Omg, are you coming with me? I've not had a yoga buddy for a while, since I lost the last one. They drop like flies, I tell you. Not you though Lil, you're going to LOVE it! I'll book you in for tomorrow morning before work and I'll meet you outside ten minutes before with a coffee. You in?'

Lilith chuckled out loud. 'I'm in,' she texted back.

***

The next morning Lilith got up bright and early and skipped her usual morning coffee before she left the house. She could have had both but she decided it probably wasn't good to be too jittery – nor would it be a good way to take care of herself or her body, and she was keen to go back to her next therapy session with a positive logbook. (Not that she had one of those – yet.) She packed her work clothes neatly into a duffle bag and left the house with a spring in her step.

The train was even busier than normal and Lilith realised that this meant that all the corporates in the city either exercised before they started work or they began their working day at this time. She hoped it was the former, otherwise that was pretty depressing. One thing she loved about her job was that she never felt the need to come in early, work over her lunch, or stay behind late. Sure, she worked hard and sometimes she did extra hours, but only when she wanted to. *And she intended to keep it that way.*

The yoga studio was literally round the corner on the next block from work, so Lilith spotted Lorna straight away, waving enthusiastically with two takeaway coffee cups in her hands. It was definitely still too early to be that energetic but Lilith appreciated the enthusiasm and was genuinely feeling excited to give the class a go. She had never been the most flexible of people, but it would be fun to see what she could do – and what she could take home with her.

'Feeling supple?' Lorna asked chirpily.

'Erm, I'm not sure I'd say that,' Lilith replied laughing, 'but I'm ready to give it a go.'

'Honestly, you're going to love this class!' Lorna replied, handing the coffee cup over and taking a big slurp from her own cup. 'Ooh, it's still really hot, be careful.'

Lilith caressed her own coffee cup in her hands before slowly sipping it so as not to burn her tongue as she assumed Lorna just had.

'Show off!' Lorna giggled.

Lilith nudged her friend playfully. 'Right, is there

anything I need to know about this class before we go inside? Any surprises I need to know about or do I just sit on a mat and follow what the instructor does?'

'Oh, you've really not been to a yoga class before, have you?' Lorna replied. 'So, there shouldn't be any surprises but at the end we usually go into savasana, which is basically a little snooze. Some people snore but it's just a chance to lie down, be still, and relax.'

'Okay, I can definitely deal with that,' Lilith said, before taking a big sip of coffee, which she quickly spat straight back into her coffee cup. 'Jesus! It's like these cups are made of metal.'

Lorna giggled. 'Come on, let's go inside and get a good spot.'

By 'good spot', she meant at the back of the room – where they could see what everyone else was doing but no one would see what they were doing. And fortunately, they were in luck. They were the first ones there.

A tall, slim, blonde lady had just finished lining up the mats and was picking out a soothing playlist. She looked up and greeted Lorna with a big hug.

'This is my friend and work colleague, Lil,' said Lorna, as she introduced Lilith to the yoga instructor.

'Ah, so good to meet you. Thanks for coming on down. My name's Marcia.'

Lilith went to extend her hand but was instead greeted with an equally big hug.

'Have you ever done yoga before?' Marcia continued as she released her grasp and smiled back at Lilith.

'No, not really,' Lilith replied. 'I'm hoping it'll help me ground myself more – and get a little more flexible.'

'Well, that's definitely something I can help you with.'

A handful of people – two women and a man – came through the door and flung their arms around Marcia. It was clearly a popular and tight-knit class.

Lorna tapped Lilith's shoulder and guided her to the mats at the back of the room. 'Let's grab a mat and get settled,' she said.

Over the next few minutes, another five people came into the room, enthusiastically greeting Marcia, before parking their bums on the mats in front of them. It was a full class.

The lights dimmed and Lilith noticed some lit candles in a semi-circle in front of Marcia, along with what looked like a buddha and some cards. It almost looked like a seance. Still, Lilith had given the therapy her full effort, so she was going to do the same with this class. Not least for the fact that Lorna obviously loved it and was excited to have a friend join her.

Lilith scanned the room to look at the people in front of her. This was the thing with New York City, EVERYONE was beautiful. Especially the guy sitting directly in front – she could barely make out his face but his body was stunning and she felt her mind drift off into what she'd like to do to him.

'He's gay,' Lorna leaned over and whispered to her, with a cheeky grin on her face.

Lilith snapped out of it quickly and shot her friend a look, pretending she hadn't been thinking about the things she had. Was she really that obvious? Her face must tell a thousand words. 'Focus, Lil,' she said to herself in her head. 'Focus.'

The class went without a hitch and Lilith was actually sad for it to be over. She'd learnt lots of new postures that she'd practise at home, and the savasana at the end was the icing on the cake. She'd never felt so relaxed. Marcia came over to check in with her once everyone had left and Lilith found herself giving her a huge hug.

'Thank you so much – I really needed that,' she said as she released herself from the embrace and felt a small tear in her eye.

'Anytime,' Marcia replied, beaming. 'I'm so glad it did what it needed to for you. I don't know if you're interested, but I also offer Ayurvedic massages on a one-to-one basis. It's excellent for freeing emotional burdens, releasing energy, and focusing on relaxation. Lorna's had a couple of sessions with me, haven't you?'

'Yes, and I need to book another one with you soon. I'm feeling the need for your healing powers!' Lorna replied. 'They're great, Lil, and could be just what you need.'

'Sign me up!' Lilith responded.

It sounded like the perfect self-care ritual, and something she wished she'd done sooner. Why hadn't she been doing nice things for herself? She pondered on it for a moment before thanking Marcia again and agreeing to email her to book in a massage session. She'd also be attending this yoga class at the same time next week.

'Thanks, Lorna,' she said to her friend as they closed the studio door and headed down the stairs. 'That was such a great class.'

'I knew you'd love it!' Lorna replied. 'And you're going to love the massage – you'll probably want to have one every day!'

Lilith laughed. 'I know, I think that'll be the problem!'

And with that, the two women glided into the New York winter sunshine, feeling more than ready to take on the day – whatever that was going to bring.

Thirty-Nine

11 March 2019

Okay, so no exotic trips planned this month but I am heading to New Jersey tomorrow for a quick work trip. I'm going there alone, so I won't have Lorna or Aaron for company, which is a shame, but it also means I might be able to engage in my favourite pastime... (It's been a while!)

I've actually been feeling pretty content lately despite the impending chaos around me. No sooner had the offer been made on the house last month than it had been withdrawn – and I cursed that fucking tree a thousand times. However, the real estate agent must have finally done her job in terms of marketing as there's suddenly been an influx of prospective buyers coming to view the house. Maybe it's this spring feeling and people are finally coming out of hibernation. Maybe they've been told something I don't know about or maybe they're just really desperate but, either way, I've found the viewings quite sickening in all honesty. All these young couple and young family types who are picturing 'the American dream', admiring the white picket fences, and talking about how lovely the neighbourhood is. One of them even talked about attaching a swing to the tree and planting flowers at the bottom of it. I should be really happy because all this interest means there's definitely going to be another buyer to take the house so I can run far, far away from here. But I also just feel like telling some of them it's the furthest past their dream they could ever imagine – but who am I to say that? Maybe their dreams are very different from mine.

Anyway, the last couple of weeks have been all about 'self-care'. I've been going to yoga classes with Lorna before work twice a week and I had my first Ayurvedic massage session with the yoga instructor, Marcia, yesterday evening. It was incredible and I've already booked another one for later this month. I don't know what it was but the whole thing just felt… healing. Like I was shedding the old and making way for the new. I could just kind of feel all the bad shit leaving my body as I breathed in the oils and felt at peace with myself. Oh and I cried a lot. Like a lot.

I'm also really enjoying taking proper time out just for me. No guys. No work. No family distractions. Just me, myself, and I. I'm learning to fall in love with myself all over again. I've realised I still have boundaries and that I've not completely lost who I am deep down. And I know that to be the person I want to be and live the life I want to lead, it all has to come from me. No one's going to save me. No guy is going to ride in on a white horse and make it happen for me (except if it's to open a pesky Airbnb door). It has to come from me. And I'm okay with that. I'm more than okay with that.

Just got back from my overnight trip to Jersey shores. What a place. What a night. Before yesterday, I hadn't yet crossed the Hudson, so as soon as I'd finished my meetings, I knew I had to go check out the local scene. I ended up in a bar (obviously) in Jersey City, with the most stunning views across Manhattan, on the other side of the river. I ordered a large glass of white wine and, once I'd taken in the view, I started scrolling on my apps.

I got a match almost immediately and we started chatting. It was a local guy. Worked local, lived local, fucked local? I was soon going to find out. Well, it turned out he drank local, too, and he was in the same bar as I was – no wonder we'd matched so quickly! He walked over to me – looking like the boy next door with pretty blue eyes. We said hi to each other before he pulled up the chair opposite me and awkwardly sat down. I always find it strange to match virtual and then meet in real life, especially that fast. I got him a beer to help ease his nerves but at least he was rather cute – a typical American guy.

We got chatting and he told me he'd never been to NYC, let alone travelled outside of New Jersey! I wasn't even sure he completely understood the concept of being French. Our conversation was pretty limited and it didn't seem like we had much in common – which is precisely the reason I usually don't do chit-chats and instead get on with business straight away. It was beyond tedious… verging on painful. If he'd never even left his hometown, he'd probably not experienced much in the bedroom either.

He offered to head back to his apartment and I was tempted to call it a day, but I also wanted to live the full immersive experience so I acquiesced reluctantly. I was half expecting his parents to come to the door when we headed up the stairs to his apartment, but, to my surprise, he actually lived alone. Even more surprisingly, the sexual chemistry was intense – despite the clear lack of other shared interests. I decided I was done with men just looking after their own pleasure, so I told him exactly what I wanted and he willingly delivered, giving me the most amazing orgasm after licking my clit and fingering me at the same time. He didn't even expect me to reciprocate, so I didn't. Not this time at least. I'm putting him in my little black book (not that I have one – I've been missing a trick!) and I might just call on him again. It felt so empowering to walk out of his apartment knowing I'd just been fully satisfied without having to give anything in return. I'm growing fond of Jersey shores after all.

6 April 2019

Ooh, it's been a while since I've written here. There hasn't been much to report – until now.

I'm currently in Miami with three of my girlfriends from London celebrating spring… because, why the hell not?! At least it's warm in Miami. It still snows in NYC in April – I don't think I'll ever get used to it. Anyway, we arrived yesterday evening at slightly different times, but all of my friends have been jet-lagged today. By early afternoon, they decided to go for a nap in the hotel room.

We managed to get the most gorgeous suite with two bedrooms and a separate living space, so my initial plan was to catch up on some reading as it was tropically stormy outside, so the beach didn't appeal. But as the girls headed off to bed and I curled up on the sofa, I realised I wasn't really in the mood for reading. I was wide awake and wanted to do something fun. Something energetic. I wonder what I decided to do with myself... hehe! You guessed it... I suddenly had *the* lightbulb moment. I'd been chatting to a guy for a few weeks who's based in Miami (how could I have forgotten?!). It hadn't even crossed my mind to contact him, which actually made me feel pretty good because normally I would likely be planning days, or even weeks, in advance. Progress, Lil! Anyway, I opened up Tinder and sent him a quick message. He responded near enough straight away. Then it dawned on me... He couldn't come to the hotel – I don't think my girlfriends would have been up for a mini orgy, although he'd probably beg to differ. I told him the same and he told me he still lived with his parents (despite him being in his early thirties) but that he'd book a hotel a little bit out of town. The first part put me off, but I liked his initiative, just as long as he wasn't going to take me to the swingers' club – been there, done that, got the tee shirt, thank you very much!

Luckily for me, the RV was actually a nice little motel. I hadn't needed to sneak out of the hotel as my girlfriends were sound asleep, and if they woke up, they'd just suspect that I'd gone for a little exploration – which wasn't half wrong.

I got there first, so took the liberty of taking off my

clothes to save time and to let him know I wasn't there for a chat. He arrived just as I was throwing my tee shirt onto the floor by the bed, looking quite shy behind his glasses. My immediate thought was that he didn't have sex very often. Well, my immediate thought was completely wrong! He turned out to be one of the most experienced guys I've ever met, focusing solely on my pleasure. There seems to be a theme going on at the moment and, I must say, I don't dislike it.

Anyway, he was super gentle and whispered to me to lie on the bed and start touching myself. I love being told what to do – being directed and dominated – especially when it involves my own pleasure. What's not to like? But then, he did something that no other guy has ever done (yet). He stayed fully dressed, kept his Clark Kent glasses on, and came closer to my pussy to observe me and my fingers. I found him watching me so hot and intense that I squirted on his face, which he proceeded to slowly lick off with his fingers before pulling me closer to him and slowly penetrating me with two of his fingers whilst telling me to continue brushing my clit. I was close to exploding already (and I feel like I'm close to exploding again now, too!). He ordered me to hold and kept fingering me until he reached what I suspected was my G-spot – a total first for me. The intensity of the orgasm slowly built up in my entire body until I reached a point where I screamed so fucking loud, I felt like I was going to pass out. I was paralysed and my whole body was in spasms. It was absolutely incredible. No words. I honestly felt reborn. Just pure pleasure to the highest of heights. I thanked him and he knew it was my first time. He kissed my clit, slowly moving up to my belly button, gently licked around my nipples, before planting the final kiss on my lips and flashing me a cheeky grin and wink as he left the room. I'd offered to give him something in return but he'd refused – and now he was gone – leaving me in this state of complete and utter euphoria. How very generous of him.

It took me a while to compose myself again (although I still don't know if I've fully recovered yet!). I slowly got dressed and decided to make myself a cup of tea – figured I might as well make use of the room facilities, plus it was my London friends' trip, so it made sense to pay homage to them.

And now here I am back in our hotel suite, curled up on the sofa as if I haven't left the room. My girlfriends are slowly waking up. I wonder what dreams they had… mine were rather hot!

10 April 2019

A date I'm going to remember… Hopefully, second time lucky! This morning I got a phone call from the realtor to say an asking price offer had been made on the house. I cannot tell you the relief I feel knowing that I'll be getting out of here soon. Knowing I no longer have to wake up somewhere that makes me feel dark and gloomy. Knowing I get to be in complete control of where I live and how long for. It's freedom. And even though I can't experience it fully just yet, it feels like I'm at least halfway there. Part of me worries they'll pull out again like the last buyers, but if I'm learning anything on my journey through life, it's to trust the process – and all that jazz. Corny, I know, but it doesn't make me feel good to dwell on negative outcomes, so staying positive seems a much better option.

The girls are obviously a bit sad – unlike me, they've actually enjoyed living here and all the space we have. Plus, now that we have buyers again for the house, I can go and look at a new place – or places. I'm thinking about renting a small house in this area that the girls can stay with me in, as well as a cool apartment in NYC. The dream I envisaged when I first moved here. Eeek, I'm getting excited just thinking about it! And nervous, and scared, and emotional… All of the feelings. Time to ground myself and take things one step at a time.

Forty

Fresh from the news of her house sale, Lilith was the first one to arrive at the yoga studio – even before Marcia. She'd been awake most of the night thinking about the selling process, the rental market, and the new life she'd soon be living – so she was completely wired. She blinked open her eyes and leant against the outside of the door, slowly sipping her cup of coffee and willing herself awake. Before she had time to think of anything else, she felt a strong pat on her shoulder. It was Marcia.

'Bad night?'

'Ah sorry, Marcia, I was in my own world there. Can you tell I'm trying to keep my eyes open?'

'Just a bit.' Marcia giggled lightly before kindly stroking Lilith's arm and opening the door to the yoga studio so they could go inside.

'The house is just about to get sold,' Lilith blurted out before she could stop herself. She'd planned to keep it to herself a bit longer in case anything went wrong, and until she'd got her head around it and started planning the next steps, but at this point she just wanted her support network around her to lean on.

'Oh wow,' Marcia replied. 'How are you feeling? Relieved? Anxious? Scared? Happy?'

Lilith let out a loud laugh. 'ALL of the above!'

Marcia looked at her sympathetically as a couple of other class members bounced through the doors, looking like they'd had considerably more sleep.

'Nah, I'm fine,' Lilith continued, 'just a little wired and trying to get myself in the right headspace so I can plan what I'm doing next – and where I'm living!'

'You'll get there,' Marcia replied as she went to put some music on and laid out the mats ready for class.

Lilith turned towards the door just in time to see Lorna tentatively opening it as if she was late and had missed the best spot at the back, and waved her friend over. The pair embraced before cramming in as much gossip as possible before they were instructed to their mats to start with a gentle sun salutation.

***

The remainder of the month flew by. Lilith was knee-deep in work (that she loved) and had started viewing some houses in the village now that the house sale was progressing. The first few she'd seen were a straight no before she'd even made it up the driveway, but it was useful to see what she definitely didn't like. Points of contention included a children's play area at the back of the house (over a much-loathed white picket fence that was only about three-foot tall), another huge motherfucker of a tree (what was it with this place?!), nosey neighbours who had peered from every single window in their house and ended up mowing their lawn directly opposite when Lilith had gone to view the outdoor space, and one with a really, really bad smell. She was beginning to lose hope, but on her way home from the last viewing, she'd spotted someone nailing in a rental sign on a cute little white house with no white picket fence and no big looming tree, which looked almost exactly what she was after – here, at least. She'd be looking for something just *slightly* different in the city. Before the guy had finished straightening up the sign, Lilith found herself marching over, arm outstretched to introduce herself and to ask to book for a viewing asap. She'd almost been tempted to put a deposit down there and then without even looking inside, but she reminded herself to pause before making any wild decisions. It was fun to be spontaneous and decisive, but there were times where it paid to, you know, look around the house you might be living in for the foreseeable future. So, she booked an appointment for the following day.

***

The next morning, she was outside the house ten minutes before the scheduled viewing. She'd wanted to check out the traffic (not that it ever got particularly busy round here) and the neighbours. She hadn't spotted anyone peeking out of their curtains and no one had yet approached her car or walked past nonchalantly with their dog, so that was a tick for now at least. A smart black Range Rover pulled up behind her with dazzling headlights that definitely weren't needed for this time of day, so Lilith figured this would be the rental agent. They were always the same – driving flashy cars, turning up just a minute or two late to look like they were super busy and rushed off their feet, and walking with an air of importance as if they were Kim Kardashian's bodyguard.

A tall, slim figure emerged elegantly from the car, dressed in a bright green two-piece suit and a pair of heels that wouldn't look out of place at the Met Gala. Lilith looked down at herself in the pair of jeans she'd religiously worn for the last twenty years and a lilac, branded hoodie that kept her snug even though the weather was finally starting to get much warmer. Still, she was certain she was much more comfortable than the blonde woman now approaching her car.

Lilith got out quickly and moved forward to shake said woman's hand.

'Hi, I'm Emerald,' the agent said as she avoided a slight dip in the sidewalk. 'Did you have a safe journey?'

Lilith was still processing her name and matching it to the suit she was wearing. America never failed to surprise her.

'I'm Lilith,' she managed to reply. 'I only live a few blocks away, so it was an easy trip.' She forced a smile.

'Great! Let's head inside.'

'I thought you'd never ask,' Lilith murmured to herself, just enough for Emerald to turn back around to see if she'd missed anything. Lilith smiled back at her, praying it would be as painless as possible once they got inside.

Luckily for Lilith, near enough as they got inside the front door, Emerald's phone rang for 'an important call', so Lilith was forced to look around by herself – exactly the way she'd prefer it. The house was part-furnished with a three-seater, white sofa and matching armchair in the front room, which Lilith soon realised connected to the kitchen, in an open-plan fashion. There was a guest bedroom on this floor and small shower room, with a staircase leading to three bedrooms upstairs – one with an en-suite, and the others sharing a decent-sized family bathroom. The master bedroom overlooked the backyard, which was pretty small but looked like an ideal suntrap. There were no big trees looming over the house, no pesky squirrels, and no neighbours looking directly in.

As Lilith headed back downstairs for one last look around, Emerald was just ending her phone call and about to jump into a huge sales pitch.

'I'll take it!' Lilith said before a word could be spoken.

'Oh!' Emerald looked taken aback but clearly very pleased. 'I'll contact the landlord straight away. It's available from July and it'll be two months' rent upfront.'

'Great. Call me with the fine print. Your office has my details.'

And with that, Lilith took one last look at her new home and got back into her car.

Forty-One

Another month, another work trip. This time, Lilith was heading to Austin, Texas (sadly, Brad didn't live there anymore, she did check) – and Aaron was joining her. The two of them had met early at the airport so they could grab lunch together and have a couple of drinks before boarding their flight. They weren't on the clock properly until the following day (not that that would usually stop them). Lilith had also taken the opportunity to run through the paperwork and contracts for her new place in Little Haven. She was sure she hadn't missed anything but she still thought it best to run it by someone, and as much as she hated to say it, there was always something technical that guys seemed to pick up on that she might not.

'Looks good to me,' Aaron said, handing the papers back to Lilith. 'Have you got a move-in date?'

'Well it's available from the first of July but I don't think I'll be moving in until later in the month, once the girls have finished school.'

'Just let me know when you have a date and I'll make sure I'm around to help you move in.'

'Thanks, my love! I actually don't have too much shit to move this time – plus it's part-furnished. But you know I can always do with a wine buddy to aid the unpacking.'

Aaron smiled as they clinked their current wine glasses together and finished their final slurps before boarding.

As these work trips often went, the person who'd booked the flights had decided it was cheaper to book separate seats, so Lilith went to sit around ten rows behind Aaron, pulling a sad face and waving goodbye as if they would never see each other again – to which Aaron laughed and pointed to the drinks menu on the back of the seats.

Lilith slumped herself reluctantly into her seat and perused the menu, before pulling her phone out from her pocket. It had been a while…

She wouldn't say it was love at first sight (I mean, for starters, she hadn't even seen him in person yet), but she was highly attracted to this Latino guy called Jose who she'd had a couple of on-off conversations with on 'The App'. She connected to the in-flight Wi-Fi and typed out a message. Within twenty minutes, he'd responded, and they wound up messaging the whole trip, as well as on the flight back, too. He seemed lovely, if not a little intense – but Lilith liked the intensity. It had been a while since she'd felt that wave of passion inside her – she'd been too busy focusing on self-care, work, and house stuff that meeting her sexual needs had fallen to the wayside.

Once Lilith had landed back in New York after a whirlwind two-night trip in Austin, she hugged Aaron goodbye and they got in their respective cabs home. Only Lilith directed hers to a local suburban bar instead.

Turns out Jose lived locally to her, well, around ten blocks away, so far enough away not to bump into each other often, but close enough to meet at a bar and not have far to stumble home. She had clearly relaxed all her rules. This time, however, Lilith decided she didn't want to drink much – she'd much prefer to be in control, plus she was a little jet-lagged and anything else to drink would probably push her into the sleep zone, and that's not what she had planned tonight. They had a couple of drinks at the bar but Jose had driven, so he couldn't drink anything else either. He led her back to his car outside and they kissed before he turned the engine on and drove them to a spot a little away from the road where no one could see them.

Within moments, the car windows were already steaming up as they'd continued to kiss each other passionately. Lilith wanted him badly so began unzipping his trousers as he pulled down her tights and started touching her. They continued kissing, finding themselves at the back of his car, not thinking about anything else other than fucking each other hard. Which they did. Lilith's head banging against the seats, the roof, the window... everywhere. She almost didn't care if someone found them and arrested them – she was having so much fun and she came, hard. It was forbidden and felt so exciting, plus it helped that he was so fucking sexy. They lay down, intertwined on the back seats giggling, before Lilith got dressed and called herself an Uber from the bar. Jose had offered to drive her home but that was a step too far. Instead, she arranged to meet him a few days later at a local hotel, blowing him a kiss as he drove away into the night.

Three days later, and they were lying on the hotel bed, legs intertwined again, giggling. They were clearly super compatible sexually, and this was beginning to turn into a little summer adventure.

A week later and they met in a bar again, moving to the toilets because they couldn't wait long enough to get a room. Lilith had purposely worn a dress with no tights and he was inside her almost before they'd closed the cubicle door behind them. Every inch of her body pined for him and every time he touched her, she felt goosebumps go all the way from the tips of her toes to the top of her head. He smiled at her and Lilith was worried they were both starting to fall in love. But almost as quickly as that thought had entered her mind, she realised that it was in fact just lust – in a good way. And after this third encounter, the routine hit and they decided to call it a day.

**

Lilith spent the rest of the month attending therapy, yoga classes, and work, as well as viewing apartments in the city (as close to the office as possible so she could walk there and grab a coffee on the way). She was definitely romanticising it – which was easier to do when the sun was beating down and New York never looked better – but this was also something she'd dreamt about for a very long time. Her own pad. Just hers. She hadn't found anything yet but the rental market was hot here – you had to be in the know to find something because they got snapped up as soon as they went on. She called on some of her contacts from her little black book as well as her friends in the city to keep an eye out, and, in the meantime, she simply trusted the process. *That's what Marcia had told her to do, anyway.*

At the beginning of June, with still no apartment making itself known, Lilith had a work trip planned in Paris. The perfect distraction. Her cousin, Frederick, was going to be there, so on the first night, she'd arranged to meet him to go clubbing with him and his friends – after a day of working hard, of course.

Frederick flung his arms out to her as he came outside to meet her, and Lilith immediately felt at home. She had always felt really close to him and they had gotten even more so over the past few years. She loved coming back to France – and the party scene in Paris was something else. Everyone always looked fabulous. And as she danced away on the dance floor, taking her thick wavy hair out of its ponytail and letting herself loose, a tall dark-haired guy walked over to her and asked if he could dance with her. He was clearly handsome and had some very sexy moves, so the invitation was a welcome one. Lilith looked over at her cousin dancing on the other side of the dance floor and waving at her to have fun. Not that she needed any male approval. She decided she wanted to dance with this guy. In fact, her whole body wanted to dance with him – and she wasn't even drunk. She'd only ordered one drink at the bar before deciding that it was too cumbersome to keep going back and wading through the crowd, whilst simultaneously trying not to spill anything as she flung her arms around to the music. She was feeling happier every day, slowly regaining her confidence, and, most importantly, her self-esteem. She didn't feel empty anymore. She felt full.

After dancing for what felt like hours until her feet hurt, her partner invited her back to his place and Lilith had to turn him down. Her periods had started again (after a long time hidden in the woodwork) and she'd only realised when she'd nipped to the loo ten minutes previous. She'd cursed out loud and had to double-check, but it was clear as blood. And call her a prude, but she wasn't too crazy about having sex during periods – it just wasn't something she wanted to try. Plus, she was already starting to get stomach cramps and just wanted to lie down. Still. With no one or object inside her. She could tell her sexy dance partner was clearly disappointed and slightly embarrassed when she told him (what was it that made men so uncomfortable with periods?). Still, he was very gentlemanly about it, ordering her an Uber and wishing her a good night.

Frederick was still partying the night away and Lilith hadn't wanted to disturb his epic dancing on the tables, so she'd snuck out quietly and would catch up with him for dinner the following night.

She hadn't expected to be alone in a cab at this time, but she actually felt okay about it. She'd still had an amazing night – and she hadn't needed alcohol or sex to make it feel that way. 'Progress, Lil, progress.'

She smiled to herself, got out of the cab, and headed into her hotel room, before making herself a cup of tea, pulling on her big knickers, and sliding into bed with the pillows propped up around her. Her phone pinged to a text from Frederick.

'Hey girl, where you at? You missed my splits!'

'Damn,' Lilith replied. 'And here was me thinking your high kicks on the table were impressive. Sorry cuz, got a case of the stomach cramps so I came back to the hotel... alone. Go figure! Catch up with you tomorrow night? x'

'I'll dance for the both of us! See you tomorrow! X'

Lilith smiled and put her phone on the bedside table. She was speaking at a conference the next morning, so was glad to be tucked up in bed this time, with no risk of hangover or lack of sleep from fucking all night. Oh how times had changed.

Forty-Two

1 July 2019

Aaron called me yesterday to tell me one of his best buddies was moving out of his NY apartment into a house in the suburbs with his pregnant girlfriend. It wasn't on the rental market yet, so he passed me his details and said I'd get first dibs if I wanted it. He's never rented the apartment out before and Aaron obviously told him what a great tenant I'd be, so I went to see it this morning! It's amazing. Like, exactly what I've been looking for, and exactly what I dreamed of when I imagined myself living in the city. It's two bedrooms – which is fine, because the girls are unlikely to stay with me there, but if they do they can either kip in together or one of them can sleep on the sofa bed. It also means I have space for friends to stay over too after any wild nights out – it's pretty much walkable from everywhere in the city, including work. The rest of it is open-plan and I even have a tiny balcony off my bedroom that leads to the fire escape – also very handy considering I'm going to be living on my own for the first time… ever. Yep, I called it 'my bedroom' already because I literally signed the papers before I left! I knew I wouldn't be able to find anything remotely like it in my budget with such a good landlord, so it was a no-brainer. One of those scenarios where it paid off for me to not overthink and just dive in and do it. It won't be fully available until the first of August, so I'll be moving into my little suburbs house first and getting the girls settled – as well as myself.

It feels so weird to even be writing this. Almost like it's not my life. It doesn't feel completely real. I keep crying and I'm not sure why. Well I am sure why, but it's just this strange mixture of emotions. Part of me is feeling this deep relief – this huge weight being lifted off my shoulders – that I can finally be my true, authentic self and live the life I've been wanting to lead, fully. Then the other part of me just feels this immense sadness, grief, and fear. I have no idea how to live by myself. I know I've kind of already been doing it but the girls have been at home (or never too far away, at their dad's), and Sophia's been around.

Shit. I need to not dwell on this too much. Wine night definitely needed.

12 July 2019

Phew, it's hot in the burbs. I've been sweating profusely all day as I pack up the final boxes in preparation for moving tomorrow. It's finally happening, I can't believe it. Tomorrow is the day I finally move away from the dark, depressing house I've lived in for the last two years.

I thought that maybe once I'd packed everything away that I'd feel something towards the house – that maybe it wouldn't feel so bad after all. But then the tree swayed ever so slightly in the breeze and a squirrel sat on one of the big loping branches, staring me out, and I just found myself mouthing 'Fuck you' out of the window as it continued to glare at me, completely unfazed by my presence. A fitting way to end my final day here, I think.

Anyway, I've realised I don't want to spend my last night in this house on my own. The girls went to their dad's early to give me time to sort myself out but I'm regretting that now. I wish they were here with me, wrapping each other in bubble wrap or doing something silly to make me laugh. Still, it's probably better that they're away from the chaos and my impending emotions.

Once we're all settled, I'll be switching between my little house here in the suburbs and my cool apartment in the city every week, for the next year. And then, I think I'm toying with the idea of moving back to London. I know. Big moves. But for now, I'm focusing on the here and now. And right now, I don't want to be on my own, so it's time to revert to my trusty apps.

13 July 2019

No sooner had I finished packing last night than I immediately matched with a local guy called Nicholas who was visiting his family before heading back to Europe where he lives. He had a twinkle in his eye on his profile picture (most of them do, to be honest), and he sounded open-minded and chilled. After a little bit of back and forth, we met up at a local bar and had a few drinks. He was just as chilled in person as he seemed over message. Even the way he leant casually over the bar to order our drinks before giving me a little wink. (I'm a sucker for a wink.)

We ended up playing darts, chatting about so many different things. It just flowed, and the best part was it felt like an actual date. It was fun. I genuinely enjoyed his company. He was smart and light at the same time. It made sense to invite him back to the house. He randomly had a guitar in his car, so he brought it with him and played for me on the deck. I've never been serenaded, ever, so I guess there's a first time for everything. And my first time happened to be when I was spending my last night at my family home with a strange, handsome guy before moving out the next day. Coincidentally, I also had some old Japanese whisky left out, unpacked, so I poured us both a glass on the rocks as we sat outside and enjoyed each other's company.

We ended up talking and drinking late into the night (moving it inside after midnight so as not to piss off my neighbours – although not sure why I was so bothered considering I was moving, but the problem with Connecticut is you see everyone, everywhere, so not worth the risk). I felt so relaxed in Nicholas's presence. He was just calming and I'd almost forgotten about the mammoth task ahead (which I should be dealing with right now but instead I'm writing in my journal for the final time in this house). Anyway, at some point past two in the morning, we decided to call it a night, and I told him he was welcome to stay – with no other agenda. Just having a positive presence in this house for my last few hours here before the movers arrive (in T-minus fifteen minutes) was all I needed.

He casually agreed to stay, telling me he was too tired to go back home, and we had a drunken attempt at sex. It was a complete fail but we both laughed it off and went into our respective rooms to sleep (good job I hadn't yet packed up the guest bedding). As soon as my head hit the pillow, I fell asleep and had one of the most peaceful nights I've ever had in this house. A parting gift, I guess you could call it. And whilst me and the house definitely won't be staying in touch, I have a feeling me and Nicholas will.

31 July 2019

The last couple of weeks have been strange… I don't know what I expected, but I guess not this. Moving day actually went without a hitch – the removals guys arrived on time and managed to move all my stuff without breaking anything or damaging either house, so that was a positive. Sitting in the new house once they'd gone was a bit odd but got much better as soon as the girls arrived. They had decided they'd come and stay with me that first night so I wouldn't be on my own.

When they did come round, their first reactions were how small the house was and how they preferred the old house – and their dad's current one. So, that was a fun conversation. But mostly, it's just been strange knowing that this is my home now even though it doesn't feel like it. And I don't think it ever will.

I had friends stay over the week the girls were with their dad and then tomorrow is the day I move into my NY apartment! I think I thought I'd feel more excited but I'm actually pretty nervous. This is what I always wanted – my own place in the heart of the city – but now it's here, in these circumstances, it feels different. I'm scared to spend the weekend alone there. Everyone is away, so I've not got anyone to stay over, and I don't want to turn to my apps this time. I guess it's just all overwhelming and maybe I'd built this image up in my head of how amazing it would feel to leave the old house and start my new chapter, but I hadn't factored in any other feelings or emotions into that at all.

Don't get me wrong, I'm proud of myself for doing this – for taking control of my life and following my true desires – but that doesn't make it easy. I'm learning that, no matter how cliche it sounds, it really is about the journey and not the end destination. And that the journey won't always be linear – it might be messy, uneasy, uncomfortable, and challenging. But maybe that's the point. Maybe it's just about constantly re-learning. Re-tuning into what you want. Checking in with yourself constantly to make sure you're still going where you want to go and still being who you want to be. Ah, I don't know. It's getting late and it's time for move number two tomorrow, so I should probably try and get some sleep (even though I know I'm going to stew on this all night...).

Night night!

Forty-Three

Lilith opened the door to her new apartment, pushing it open with her shoulder as she carried in the first set of boxes from the hallway. She hadn't brought much with her because the place was already part-furnished – plus she preferred minimal design – but she'd brought some cushions and throws, as well as some sentimental titbits to make it feel as homely as possible.

It was midday and the sun was streaming in through the large windows – something Lilith swore she'd never take for granted ever again. She could laugh now at the big, old, looming tree that was the cause of so much angst and upset in the old house – and those pesky squirrels. A memory that now seemed so distant, she was sure she might forget it someday soon.

Once the boxes were unpacked, Lilith decided it was about time she went out to explore her new neighbourhood – even though she actually knew it fairly well considering the office was only a twenty-minute walk away. Central Park was a little further – a brisk thirty-minute stroll – but that's where she decided she'd like to hang out for the day, stopping off at New York Central Library on the way. She figured seeing as she had no plans for the weekend, she'd pick up some books and settle in for the evenings with a glass of wine and a good book or two. A pastime she'd been unable to engage herself in for a very long time. The wine, yes, but books, not so much.

Central Park was bustling with locals and tourists alike – and numerous dogs. Thankfully none were shitting in close proximity to where Lilith had decided to set up camp for the afternoon, and she giggled to herself thinking of the infamous dog beach back in the suburbs. It was a million miles away to the lifestyle she was going to lead here – and that was a good thing. She was surrounded by people here – activity and aliveness. The city that never sleeps – or so they say. But somehow, as she sat on the grass and watched the people around her having picnics with their families, or gossiping away in small groups, she felt a pang of loneliness hit right into the centre of her stomach and a small tear fell down the left side of her cheek. No matter how much she tried to sugarcoat it, change was hard. It wasn't all rainbows and fairies and butterflies. It was hard-hitting, tear-jerking, and real. But there was still no place she would rather be. And she knew that's exactly what she needed right now. Spending time with the only person who would be in her life forever: herself. She just didn't know how.

That evening, as she poured herself a large glass of white wine from the fridge and curled her feet underneath herself on the sofa, the tears started to fall again. This first day and night alone in her NYC flat was brutal, and Lilith realised she was going to have to start facing her fears of being on her own. She picked up her phone and messaged Fleur to book an emergency therapy session for Monday.

***

'So, how have you found your first weekend in the city?' Fleur asked as Lilith started pondering her response.

'Different, I guess?'

'Good different or bad different?'

'I'm not really sure. Just… different. Different to what I'd expected.'

'And what had you expected?'

'I guess maybe I thought that it would all feel different. That I'd walk into my flat and feel like a new woman. That I'd finally be living my dream. That I'd be bouncing off the walls and dancing around each room, almost.'

Lilith looked thoughtfully into the distance as she clasped her hands around her cup of coffee and sunk back into the cushions on the sofa.

'Okay. So what did you feel instead?'

'Sad. Overwhelmed. Lonely… Definitely lonely. It's obviously my place, just for me, and I suppose I hadn't really thought about what that entailed. My little house in the suburbs is for me and the girls, but this place in the city is just for me.'

'Mhmm.'

'Part of me wanted to fill the place with a man so that it didn't feel so lonely but for once I didn't turn to my trusty dating apps. I just turned to a bottle in the fridge instead, which I'm not sure is any better…'

Fleur smiled kindly at Lilith.

'Well, I definitely wouldn't advise overdoing it or using it as a crutch for the loneliness, or anything else for that matter. But what I will say is it's completely "normal" to feel the way you've been feeling. It's a big change. You've never truly had your own place. One that belongs just to you – or two places, in this case. It's an adjustment. It's about getting comfortable with being with yourself. Creating a routine that works for you, without having to think of anyone else's schedule. Feeling content with your own company. Feeling safe and secure with yourself.'

'Yeah, I definitely feel like I'm on a journey with that. It's almost this realisation that I don't *need* a man. Sure, if one came along at an opportune time and it felt right, then I'd revisit that, but it's like you say, feeling content with my own company and knowing that I'm my own hero. No one else is going to save me. Only I can do that – and that's pretty powerful.'

Lilith smiled and let out a big, long sigh. A happy sigh. Fleur's eyes started to well up slightly as she watched Lilith starting to figure things out for herself – a therapist's dream.

'I don't know. I guess when I messaged you asking for a session, I was in a state of panic. I felt like I needed you. And I did – I needed this session to talk things through, to get out of my own head, and to remind myself of who I am, as well as giving myself grace. It's just happened. It's a big change. And I made it through my first weekend in NYC! I'm on a journey, and there's always going to be ups and downs – it's just how I choose to react in each moment. I'm sure I'm going to still have times when I feel lonely, but it's just knowing in that moment that it's okay, that it will pass, and that I've got my own back.'

'And you know it's okay to need people too,' Fleur interjected. 'It's okay to call up your friends, your therapist, or your next booty call, to ask for some company.'

Lilith let out a loud giggle. 'I know.' She continued chuckling. 'And on that note…'

'Oh, am I interrupting a date tonight?'

'No, I was just kidding. August is my month off.'

***

She might not have been dating or 'canoodling' with anyone this month, but that didn't mean she wasn't enjoying some nice offline messages. Nicholas was back in the suburbs again for a few weeks, so they'd agreed to meet the following afternoon for a coffee in the sunshine.

As Lilith arrived at Grand Central Station to make her journey back to her little suburban home that evening, she was almost in a trance as she rushed to board her carriage before the train pulled away from the station. Just before she went to put her foot on the steps, someone grabbed her by the arm, pulled her towards them, kissed her on the cheek, and murmured in her ear that she was the hottest girl in town. By the time she'd whirled around and clocked who it was, he was already gone. Off to catch another train. Jose. Her Latino lover. She sat down on the nearest seat by the window as the train pulled out of the station, and felt her phone buzz in her pocket.

'Good to see you looking so radiant. Hope life continues to treat you kindly. Goodbye gorgeous.'

Lilith put her phone back in her pocket after responding, 'Likewise. Take care of yourself, wonderful man.'

She smiled all the way home and went to bed that night feeling truly content. A feeling she wasn't sure she was capable of feeling. And for the first time in a long time, she slept all through the night.

The following day treated her even better. Seeing Nicholas again was like seeing an old friend. He greeted her with a big bear hug, before pulling out a chair for her to sit down on – in perfect placement for the sun. She was a little late as she'd lost her keys, so she'd had to borrow the set she'd given to her new neighbours in case of an emergency, as both the girls were out for the day. She hadn't quite intended to call on them so soon but she was glad she'd at least thought to do that. 'Who needs a man?' She'd chuckled to herself as she'd picked up the spare set of keys and jogged her way to the coffee shop.

Nicholas had already ordered her a coffee, which was served almost immediately as she'd sat down, and she instantly felt a wave of gratitude.

'How've you been?' she gushed.

'Great.' He grinned. 'I've been travelling all over the place for work, so it's nice to come back home for a bit and slow down.'

'I bet,' Lilith replied, sipping her coffee and wishing they'd ordered something a little cooler.

'It's a bit too hot for coffee, right?' Nicholas said, reading her mind.

'Is it too early to look at the cocktail list?'

'Never.'

And with that, they spent the whole afternoon, into the early evening, sipping cocktails, exchanging tales, and enjoying each other's company, safe in the knowledge that this was simply two people who liked being in the other's presence, no strings or expectations attached.

As Lilith went home alone that night, she realised something. She would never feel the fear of being alone again – at least not so deeply. Because, honestly, she never truly was. Even when she was on her own in her New York flat, she was always surrounded by love and friendship and passion. And she'd created all of that.

Forty-Four

16 September 2019

I'm in Asia for a month, for work. Kuala Lumpur to be exact, with a few mini exploration trips in between. I couldn't come all this way and not explore more of what Malaysia and the surrounding islands have to offer! Anyway, I'm beyond grateful to be here. Although I only landed last night, so I'm still suffering a little from jet lag. The girls are staying with their dad whilst I'm out here, which made things a hell of a lot easier. They're super independent now and like doing their own thing, so he'll probably barely see them – but at least I know they'll be safe.

The journey here was longgg. An airport layover in London before heading from there to KL. But, of course, I ended up sitting next to a super-attractive guy, a little older than me, on the second leg of the flight. Before the plane had even taken off, we got to chatting – and ended up chatting the entire way – and that's a LONG-ass flight. Eleven hours or so maybe. I don't know, I actually lost complete track of time, which was probably a good thing – although I definitely missed out on a good nap that I could do with now. Anyway, we had such an intense emotional and intellectual connection, I couldn't believe it. What is happening to me? Normally, I would have been plotting a way to the toilets or finding my way underneath a blanket, but I was content with the few kisses, as well as the pleasure from sharing stories with each other and feeling close and connected to a stranger. He even brought me back a glass of water from the back of the plane! Sounds stupid, I know, but I'm so used to doing everything for myself, it was just… nice. Really nice.

I had to put my pen down for a moment because even just thinking about that moment again brought tears to my eyes. Get a grip, woman!

We didn't promise to stay in touch, didn't exchange numbers, none of that stuff. We just enjoyed the magic of the moment – no other expectations than just the present. And it got me thinking, if that's what we all did, just appreciated the moment for what it was, we'd probably all be a lot happier – and definitely a lot more at peace, free from the noise of internal dialogue.

1 October 2019

I am LOVING being in KL. It's so cool to be here – deep in my work, but also deep in appreciation for being on the other side of the world. I love the heat and the sense of freedom that comes from immersing myself in a new culture. It's just *chef's kiss*. And you know what else is *chef's kiss*? Matching with a new guy. Sadly, he's based in LA (no, his name is not Marcus) as opposed to me having an exotic South East Asia romance but I'm really enjoying chatting to him. The first photo he sent to me was of him in hospital following a motorbike accident. *I know, not the usual naked selfies…* Anyway, I just automatically felt for him even though I'd never met him. We've been in constant communication about anything and everything. He's witty, smart, and very present – and we're both rather emotionally intense, which I'm not sure is a good thing but I'm embracing it.

We've covered all topics, all areas – no subject out of bounds. No taboos. Possibly not enough boundaries, too. I've told him all about my life, my loves, my heartbreaks, my stories, my feelings. And he's told me about his. Literally no holding back. The funny thing is, we've not even had virtual sex or discussed having sex in person – it's completely platonic. I told him that I was missing some of the comforts of home (my face moisturiser, for example, that I ran out of two weeks into being here) and a few days later I received some more in the post from him. In return, I sent him some KL delicacies along with a quirky postcard.

It's nice. Easy. Heartwarming. So much so we've even planned for him to come to NYC for a long weekend and stay over. He bought his tickets yesterday. I'm super nervous to meet him IRL. I'm worried that it's just supposed to have been about this trip, this time, and we're never meant to really meet. But then the other half of me is desperate to embrace him, touch him, and see his smile in person. I've only got a week left here until I head home and we've arranged for him to come the week after. For now, though, I'm going to enjoy our continued chats as I sit outside in the blazing heat, listening to the loud hum of traffic in the city that seems to sleep less than NYC.

10 October 2019

I'm back in New York – well, the suburbs to be precise – and it's already getting cold (probably not helped by having been in Asia for the last month). My in-person meet with my LA Love has been cancelled. The night before my flight home, we were chatting about all sorts as per usual, and I told him I was nervous to meet him. Cue him telling me that he was even more nervous, before freaking out to the point where he said he wanted to stop because he was scared we were developing feelings for each other without even having met. He wasn't wrong, so I couldn't argue with him. We agreed for him to cancel his trip and to let each other go.

Now that I'm back home, I'm feeling a little sad because I enjoyed the (virtual) intimacy. It was nice to have someone to chat to when I was struggling to fall asleep, and to share my daily adventures with. I wonder if you can actually fall in love with someone virtually... Is that going to be the future of dating? Developing deep connections before you even meet?... Hmm, another thought to ponder. Anyway, we've agreed to stay in touch – albeit not messaging each other to the same extent – so I'm feeling content with how we've left things. I guess you really can make connections anywhere – and everywhere

– no matter where you are or what you're doing. And that's pretty special.

31 October 2019

It's Halloween and I'm celebrating in the city by heading out with Lorna, Marcia, and some of their friends – in fancy dress, of course. It's such a different vibe to the suburbs, and I LOVE it. Everywhere is decorated – and I mean everywhere. No matter if you live in a sprawling apartment or a tiny studio, people decorate their steps, windows, communal hallways, fire exits... Carved pumpkins everywhere. It's brilliant. Plus, we're heading to the NYC village parade tonight before we hit the bars – apparently if you're dressed up, you can join it, so that could be a good giggle.

It's funny but I feel like I'm in my early twenties again. It's like I'm reliving my youth. Every day I feel like I'm getting younger instead of older – which can only be a good thing, right? I've always been young at heart, but living this lifestyle now, I feel younger than ever, despite any creaking bones... Life. Is. Good.

2 November 2019

Halloween was a BLAST. I think I'm still recovering from it now. I've never seen so many people out all at once in the city – literally thousands and thousands of people lined the streets for the parade, which, of course, we joined! I dressed up as a cat, which wasn't particularly inventive, but I don't have much in the way of fancy dress clothes (well, I have plenty that are suitable for the bedroom, but definitely not to wear out in public at family times!). Anyway, it was just a totally fun evening that went way into the night – and I was definitely glad to be rolling home in the early hours instead of trying to find transport.

I had a bit of a flirt with a guy dressed up as a Dalmatian, who hooked me in with a cheesy one-liner about cats and dogs, but we shared nothing more than a cheeky kiss before I was dragged to the next bar by the girls. We talked, we laughed, we danced on tables until our feet hurt, and we sang at the top of our lungs until we could barely speak. The sign of a truly good night when you've lost your voice the next day. I'm just genuinely in love with my life right now. It's not what I imagined but it's perfectly imperfect and I'm here for the ride.

12 November 2019

It's fucking freezing. *Literally*. I forgot how much I hate the cold but New York has a habit of reminding you, particularly when your landlord refuses to put the heating up (I'm having words with Aaron!). Still, times like this get me resourceful, and I figured I would find other means of warming up…

I connected with this cute guy who lives only a few blocks away and, for once, I changed my opening line: 'I want some cuddles and heat, are you up for it?' He was and so we met for a hot choc – in full daylight and not an alcoholic drink. OMG, what's happening to me?! We spent the whole afternoon getting to know each other, snuggling up on the café seating with a blanket pulled over us – warming up, just like I said. It was lovely, so I invited him for the night at my apartment – something I hadn't done yet.

He accepted and cooked me dinner! I mean, what next? We'll be watching some Netflix and he'll be moving in if I'm not careful, hehe.

The thing is, I just felt really comfortable with him around. I didn't need sex but if it was an option, it certainly wouldn't be something I'd have refused. Luckily for me, he stayed the night and we had some super-cool morning fun the next day – I woke him up with a long blow job and he came hard before going down on me.

I had a warm feeling but I didn't feel the panic rising as he got dressed and said goodbye. I simply thanked him for a cool time and smiled as he left my hallway and trotted down the stairs of my apartment building, feeling grateful for all the special moments in my life – with guys, with friends, and with myself.

Forty-Five

It was snowing again and Lilith was watching the thick snow drops pouring down outside the window of her New York apartment, landing crisply on the ground below. It was early on Saturday morning and she was feeling really happy and at peace with herself as she cradled a cup of tea and tucked herself tightly under her duvet.

What a vibrant year it had been for her. As she sat mesmerised by the snowfall, she found herself flashing back throughout the year – thinking about that first weekend in her flat on her own, knowing that she'd never fear being alone again. It hadn't always been easy at times but she felt reborn. She was being who she wanted to be and doing the things (and people) she wanted to do.

Lilith was in a cheerful mood, as she often was these days, and got a match with some cool-looking dude called Tom who lived on an artist farm with a group of other artists near the Hudson. He invited her to hang out for the day, and with a full weekend ahead of her with zero plans, Lilith answered 'yeah, why the hell not?!'

Giggling to herself about her spontaneity, she got dressed, packed a bag full of overnight things, and raced downstairs to her car. As she started driving, she realised what a beautiful, crisp, blue-sky day it was, with snow everywhere on the trees and ground even though it was no longer snowing. She arrived at the farm a little while later and there he was, waiting at the wooden gates to welcome her. She pulled up her car onto the gravel and hopped out into the embrace of his arms. She wasn't sure what she'd been expecting but he smelt good and he had the most beautiful smile – a prerequisite she'd found during the years of her encounters.

A cute bum also helped and this guy definitely ticked the box for that – Lilith was desperately trying to focus on the farm tour, but she was clearly distracted. She made a mental note to herself that she should keep saying 'yes' to spontaneous adventures such as these, which also reminded her to text Aaron to let him know the address of where she was staying. Spontaneity was great, but safety was even more important.

As Lilith looked around the farm, she spotted quite a few artists working on their books (or whatever artists do these days) and smiled at how peaceful everyone seemed. The farm was huge and they walked through the grounds away from the other artists, stopping down by a small frozen lake where Tom cupped her face in his and kissed her. She looked up at him and smiled, before they continued to explore and chat, wandering through the snowy woods as if they were in Narnia or some faraway land.

The sun was shining but it was freezing cold, so Lilith was glad he'd told her to wear boots and a heavy coat. She was snuggly and warm and felt cute all wrapped up as if she was in a Hallmark movie or something. Tom showed her the barn and another old building, which he said was haunted. Surprisingly, Lilith wasn't scared – in fact, she was quite fascinated. Was there a presence she could feel brushing past her? Or was it Tom's hard dick brushing up behind her? Lilith suppressed a giggle as he led her to the vegetable garden where they picked up their late lunch/ early dinner. 'How cool to not be so far away from home but to be living a totally different life just for the weekend,' Lilith thought to herself.

They made their way back to the main house and Tom prepared them a delicious vegan meal. Lilith was impressed with how well he had cooked – effortlessly and lovingly – and they'd eaten it whilst sitting on a pile of colourful cushions on the living room floor, in front of an open fire. In that moment, Lilith realised it truly was about the simple things in life. Good food, good company, good atmosphere. You didn't need all the bells and whistles, you just needed comfort and care and love – and in that moment, Lilith felt it all.

After dinner, Tom pulled out a book about their astrological profiles and started discussing how compatible they might be sexually. Lilith suggested they find out. Theory was important, of course, but practice even more! Tom beamed at her, got up quietly, and locked the door.

'Just a precaution,' he said as he locked eyes with Lilith. 'No one will be walking in on us as they've all gone out for a meal in the next town.'

'Perfect,' Lilith purred as she watched him walk

towards her, slowly undressing himself. They had plenty of time to explore each other's bodies.

Turns out, his astrology book was right – they were indeed highly compatible! The fire was roaring next to them, as their bodies collided in perfect unison and the heat poured out of them. He made her come several times, in incredible ways, and Lilith made sure she did the same. The night was drawing in and she felt completely relaxed, safe, and very satisfied, so much so, they fell asleep by the fire, intertwined with each other.

Lilith woke up in the early hours whilst it was still dark outside, but felt as though she'd had the most glorious sleep. Tom's eyes fluttered open as she sat up and looked around for her clothes.

'Good sleep?' He grinned.

'The best.'

Lilith pulled on her clothes as he gently kissed her neck, and they said goodbye at the living room door, thanking each other for a wonderful encounter. They parted with a quick kiss on the lips and a cheeky wink, and as Lilith got back in her car to make her way home, she knew that it was just about this day, with this guy, somewhere on this amazing planet. And that was enough. She was enough. She was *more* than enough. And she couldn't wait for even more moments like this that would make up this beautiful thing called life.

Acknowledgements

I want to thank:

Amy – for believing from the get-go, for becoming my storyteller and for discovering your own amazing self in the process. www.killercopy.co.uk

François – for the direction artistique, conception graphique et design éditorial and for creating the most beautiful sexy cover illustration for the book. www.flamidon.com

All the dudes (yes, all of you!!) – for the mind-blowing experiences, connections, and pleasure – especially E, V, and Q – I ain't naming any of you but you know who you are.

My NYC crew, particularly L, A, L, M, and F – for giving me hope, accepting me as I am, and helping me heal.

My top London girlfriends, Z, S, C, K, and L, my brother and my sister-in-law, my cousin, my chosen family – for being there for me through my highest ups, my very downs and my lowest lows.

B, my hot BF – for being the coolest human, for never taking things for granted and for sharing your love of life with me.

And to anyone reading this book – I hope it empowers you to believe, explore, and transform.

Go raibh maith agat!